Shadows

of the

Past

A Novel

O. L. Brown

A Sequel to *Northern Lights*

Unless otherwise noted, all scripture quotations are taken from the King James Version (KJV) of the Bible

The Hymn: *Amazing Grace*
By John Newton, 1779
Copyright© by G. I. A. Publications, Inc.

This book is a work of fiction. Names, characters, places, and incidents are either products of the author's imagination or used fictitiously, and any similarity to people, living or dead, is purely coincidental.

Cover Design by Balboa Press

Stock imagery © Getty Images

ISBN-9781719566421
ISBN-10:1719566429

This book is published by the Author and Kindle Direct Publishing.
Revised—09/28/2022

Books by O. L. Brown

Northern Lights

Sappa Creek Road

The Prairie Wind

Shadows of the Past

The Man from Wyoming

Superstition Mountain Dreams

The Letter

The Cabin

The Tall Stranger

Dedication

This book is dedicated to the memory of my mother, Marie Chilson Brown. Some of my earliest recollections are of my mother reading to me, especially when I was ill with a cold, or a childhood sickness. She is responsible for my love of books.

Acknowledgements

A special thanks to my daughter, Trisha Schwerer, for taking time from her busy schedule to review this book and suggest revisions and improvements. And thanks to my wife, and friends, who have encouraged me during the writing of this book.

For thou, Lord, art good, and ready to forgive; and plenteous in mercy unto all them that call upon thee.

Psalms 86:5

Shadows

of the

Past

CHAPTER 1

Return to Blackberry

The dilapidated old car rattled along the street, past several small business establishments, and came to a smoky halt at the entrance to a small garage and filling station. The bearded old man, who sat at the wheel of the car, looked at his passenger. "Well, were here! Ya said ya needed a lift to Blackberry. I'm right happy I could be of some help to ya!"

The passenger, a man whom the driver judged to be in his early forties, turned, reached into the back seat, retrieved a battered suitcase, opened the car door, and stepped from the ancient vehicle. He eased the door shut, taking care to make sure it was securely latched, as he didn't trust the old rattletrap. He stooped and looked in through the open window. "Thanks for the lift. I'm much obliged."

"Yer welcome; I'm right glad I could be of some help to ya." The whiskered old man dropped the car back into gear, as he looked through the window at his departing passenger. "Ya have a good day. I live a few miles on down the road from here. Perhaps I'll see ya again!" He eased out the clutch and pressed his foot down on the gas pedal. The old car belched out a cloud of black smoke, rattled off down the street, rounded the corner, and was gone.

The passenger stood at the edge of the street and watched the antiquated car until it was out of sight. He gave a sigh of some relief;

9

he was surprised the old jalopy had held together long enough to get him to his destination. He had been standing beside the road, about fifty miles east, thumbing for a ride, when the man had brought the ancient car to a shuddering halt and offered him a lift. "Blackberry!" the old man had exclaimed through stained whiskers. "Yeah, I can take ya there as it's on my way. We should be there in about an hour or so. It all depends on how hard I push my car!"

Randell Cordell, recently discharged from the United States Army, stepped to the sidewalk at the edge of the service station and set his suitcase down. He stood for several minutes looking both ways along the street, as memories welled up from the backroads of his mind, and an involuntary shudder coursed through his slender body. It had been many years since he had fled this small town, under less than exemplary circumstances. He could see a few changes; the street was now paved, and a brick sidewalk had been constructed along both sides of the street. Except for these improvements the town didn't appear to have changed much.

His eyes left the street, and he looked up at the sky. It was a typical northern Minnesota spring day, with a deep blue sky and a few high clouds drifting along on a gentle breeze. Heavily forested hills of pine, aspen, and spruce trees made an encircling backdrop to the little hamlet. He took a deep breath. The air was clean and crisp and felt good to a tired and worn ex-convict and war veteran.

His gaze returned to the street, and he watched the few pedestrians as they made their way along the short thoroughfare, his heart full of memories, and some considerable pain. If asked, he would have been hard pressed to give a coherent explanation for why he had returned to this town. It seemed as if he had been drawn, even compelled, to return to this little community. It had been twenty years since he had left this hamlet in considerable haste, with a woman who wasn't his wife.

He stooped to pick up his suitcase and then paused and stood, looking along the street again. From the street he lifted his gaze over the buildings and toward the tree-covered hills. Why *had* he returned to this little hamlet? Was it an attempt, a deep-felt need, a compulsion, to right the terrible wrong of heartache, pain, and death, he had caused a young woman; a woman who had been his wife? Could he ever make things right again? Would returning here, to the place where it had all begun, make any difference?

An old friend had come to visit him while he was serving out a prison term and had told him of the death of his wife shortly after he had abandoned her. "From the reports that have come to me it appears your wife died, all alone, in a little cabin in Blackberry, Minnesota." His friend had looked at him with pain filled eyes. "Randell, did you know your wife was very ill when you left her?"

He had hung his head. "Yes, I . . . I knew she was very sick."

His friend had shaken his head. "You shouldn't have done that Randell. That was wrong!" His friend had never returned to the prison to visit him again.

He continued to stand in silence; his eyes roaming the tree-covered hills. No, he couldn't make things right again. He couldn't undo the past, but he hoped to make a new beginning, here where it had all happened, and rebuild his life on a firmer, and better, foundation. This would be his penance for deserting his wife when she was dying.

But could he really do this; make a fresh start here where his life had started to unravel? He had his doubts. It was a small community where everyone knew everybody. Would the people accept him after what he had done twenty years ago? The challenges would be great. He would stay for a few days, look things over, and then decide.

He shook the memories from his troubled mind, stooped again, picked up his small suitcase, walked slowly south along the street until he came to the first intersection, and then turned to his right. He would need a place to sleep. If his memory was correct there used to be a rooming house, which let rooms by the day, two blocks over from the main street. He wondered if it was still open, and if the same woman still operated the little establishment. He thought her name was Nettie Herriot, and he remembered her as a high-strung woman, given to strong opinions. If she still owned the rooming house, she'd be about seventy years old. He knew he had changed over the past twenty years, so he doubted if she would recognize him. He hoped she wouldn't, as he didn't want to be recognized, or remembered; at least not now. If he decided to stay in Blackberry, he would eventually tell people who he really was. But until his decision was firm, he'd use a false name.

The years, since he had left this town had not been kind, and he looked older than his forty-one years. He was six feet tall but walked with a stoop to his shoulders, and a slight limp. The stoop came from years of hard labor breaking rocks, and hand grading roads, during a long stretch in the Wisconsin state prison, and the limp came from a German artillery shell that had landed too close during the Battle of the Bulge in the forests of Belgium. His hair was still dark black but had begun to thin along his forehead. He had been a rather handsome young man, but the hard years had taken a heavy toll. He doubted if anyone would call him handsome today.

He had been released from prison for good behavior, and because he had volunteered for front-line grunt duty as a United States soldier. He had gone through basic training and had been shipped to Europe in time to take part in the Battle of the Bulge. The war had been over for several months, and he had just recently been discharged. He was thankful he had survived both the harsh prison conditions, and the death and destruction of the war.

During those hard years of breaking rock, and even while hunkered down in a cold and snow-filled fox hole, his troubled thoughts, and dreams, had always seemed to drift back, over the years, to Blackberry, Minnesota. He often thought of the woman who had been his wife, who had died a tragic death in a lonely cabin. There seemed to be something tremendous, intangible, even terrible, that he could not forget, or erase from his troubled mind. It was an abysmal

12

black spot on his past, and it filled his heart with an indescribable longing to do something, anything, that would atone for those terrible past mistakes.

Within a few weeks of his discharge from the army he had made the decision to return to where it had all started. Some unseen force was drawing him back to this little community where he had once owned a cabinet shop and lived with Louise, his young and beautiful bride. He had committed a terrible wrong when he had walked away from her for another woman. It had been a terrible mistake, which had led to prison, stooped shoulders, much heartache, and a bum leg.

He knew the community cemetery was located on the north edge of town and Louise was probably buried there. He intended to find her grave and at least look upon her resting place. He couldn't undo the pain and heartache he had caused her, but he could, at least, stand at her grave with his hat off, and his head bowed in contrition, and ask for her forgiveness. She was most likely in heaven, and perhaps she would hear his heart-felt plea.

He looked up from his reflections on the past to find that he was nearing the rooming house. He could see it had changed very little over the past twenty years. However, it badly needed a coat of paint, and the trees and shrubs could stand a good trimming. The passing years had turned it into a rather shabby and run-down rooming house. He mounted the porch, sat down his suitcase, and rapped smartly on the door. Within moments the door opened, and he was looking into the face of an elderly woman. Her face was devoid of a smile, as she spoke in a flat voice. "Are ya lookin' fer a room?"

He was pretty sure she was the same woman who had operated the boarding house twenty years ago. She was thicker about her waistline. Her hair was thinner, and grayer, than he remembered, and her face seemed to carry a sad and worn look. "Yes . . . yes, I need a room. Not sure for how long."

She looked at him for a long moment, as if accessing his suitability to stay in her rooming house. "Yeah, I got a room. Come in and I'll let ya take a look."

She led him through the living room, up a flight of stairs to the second floor, and along a short hallway. She stopped, opened a door, and motioned for him to enter. She spoke from behind him. "It's not fancy, but the beds firm and there's a small closet for yer clothes. The baths at the end of the hall, and I change the sheets on the bed once a week."

She stood beside him now. "If yer not sure how long ya will be here I'd like a week's rent in advance. Rents a dollar a day."

He glanced about the room. Not fancy, but it did have an outside window and was clean. He'd lived in worse. He turned to her. "I'll take it."

She turned toward the door and then paused. "Leave yer bag here and we'll go down ta the living room. You can pay for the room and I'll give ya a receipt." The living room was of medium size and nicely appointed with old, but serviceable furniture. She took a seat at a small desk near the corner of the room. She paused and looked up at him. "If ya would like to take two meals a day, morning and evening, the extra cost is fifty cents a day, payable in advance. And what's yer name? I need it for the receipt."

He hesitated for a moment. It would relieve him from worrying about taking his meals, except for one meal a day. "Yes, I think I'll take the two meals a day." He shifted his eyes about the room for a moment. "My names Jimmy Smith."

She wrote out a receipt for the room, and the meals, and handed it to him. He retrieved his wallet from his pocket and counted out the money. He wasn't broke, but he would need to find a paying job before long. His thoughts went to his old cabinet shop. He wondered if it was still in operation.

As she laid the receipt book on the corner of the desk she looked up and studied him with wondering, and questioning eyes. "Mr. Smith, ya sure look some familiar ta me. It seems like I've seen ya somewhere before, some years back. Have ya ever been here ta Blackberry before?"

He swallowed hard and fought to keep a straight face. "No ma'am," he lied. "I've never been here in your town before!"

"Interesting! I hardly ever forget a face, and ya sure remind me of somebody I once knew, but I can't rightly place just when, or where. Perhaps it'll come back ta me!" She turned back to her desk. "I'll let ya get unpacked and I hope yer stay here in our town is enjoyable." She looked up at him. "Suppers at six. I've only got one other boarder, so it'll just be the two of ya!"

His suitcase was emptied within a few minutes and his few pieces of clothing were hanging in the small closet. He went to the bath and washed his hands and face and then returned to his room. He stood at the window for a moment, looking at the tree-lined street as he took out his pocket watch. It was a few minutes past noon and he realized he was hungry. He left the rooming house and walked back to the main street. He had seen a café as the old man had driven along the street, before dropping him off.

He didn't remember the café. Perhaps it had opened during the years he had been away. He pushed open the door and entered. Several tables were neatly placed about a small room and he selected one near a window, took a chair and looked around. The café was empty except for an older couple who were eating at a table across the room from him. He relaxed and leaned back in the chair. He wasn't sure just why, but it felt good to be back here in this small town. He was surprised, as this was where his trouble, and pain, had all began.

He looked up to see a pretty woman looking down at him. Her face held a pleasant smile as she said. "Hi there, can I get you something to drink?"

She was an attractive woman who appeared to be near his age. "Yes, have you got a bottle of Dr. Pepper?"

She laid a small printed menu on the table. "You look over our menu while I get your drink. I'll be back in a jiffy!"

He watched her as she walked away. Nice personality! He glanced through the menu. His eyes fell on the meat loaf. That sounded good to his hungry stomach.

She was back in a moment and placed a bottle of cold Dr. Pepper on the table. She smiled again. "See anything in the menu that catches your fancy?"

"I think I'll try the meatloaf."

"Good selection," she said. "Mrs. Oxford, our cook, makes the best meatloaf in the county! You just relax and enjoy your soda, and I'll be back with your lunch in a few minutes."

Ten minutes later she sat a hot plate of meatloaf, potatoes, gravy, and green beans on the table. "Here you are," she exclaimed. "Hope you enjoy your lunch!"

He looked up at her. "I'm sure I will. It sure looks good to a hungry man!"

She looked down at him. "I believe you're a stranger hereabouts. Thanks for stopping in at our cafe. You gonna be here long?"

He quickly swallowed his first bite of food. "Not sure," he said. "I used to live here many years ago and just decided to stop by and check out my old stomping grounds." He stopped speaking. He hadn't meant to say so much; especially the part about living here some years past. It had just slipped out.

"I hope your stay here is pleasant and that you come back and visit our café. I'll bring your check in a few minutes." She turned and was gone to attend to the couple across the room.

16

The food was good, and he dawdled over it as he looked out the window at the people moving along the street. It was a very small town and few people were about. His thoughts drifted to his deceased wife, Louise. They had lived in a small, two room, cabin, which they had rented from a Mr. Southerland. The cabin was located about two miles south of town. He wondered if it was still there or had been torn down.

He finished his meal, paid for it, and stepped out onto the sidewalk. He looked at his watch. It was a little after one-thirty. He remembered the cabin again. It was a pleasant day and it would be a nice walk to the cabin. He was anxious to see if it was still there. He pulled his cap down against the afternoon sun and began to walk. It wouldn't take long to reach the old cabin.

CHAPTER 2

The Cabin

The walk to the cabin was pleasant and he didn't hurry. He drank in the bucolic countryside; cows grazing in green pastures, tidy farm buildings, and fields of corn and oats. It was spring, and the corn was only about two feet high. He enjoyed looking along the straight, green, rows. The fields of oats were a pleasant light green against a deep blue sky, set off with billowing white clouds.

Was the cabin still standing among the pines? Many years had gone by and it may have fallen into disrepair or torn down and removed. If the cabin were still there, the desk was probably there as well. It was not a movable desk, as he had built it into the wall of the cabin. It had been their first home, and, as things had turned out, their only home.

When he left the gravel county road and turned down the narrow lane, that led to the cabin, he was pleasantly surprised to see the cabin standing in the clearing, surrounded by a forest of pine, spruce, and birch trees. His heart quickened as he drew near. To his pleasant surprise he could see that it was in good condition. In fact, it looked as if had been painted within the last few years. In addition, the yard was well cared for, with a colorful flower bed along the front porch. The old hand pumped well was still there near the front of the cabin and he could see an early spring garden along the side of the cabin. A small, two-door, car stood in the driveway near the cabin.

He walked to the three steps that led up onto the porch, and hesitated. The porch was in good condition, no broken boards or railings. Whoever lived in the cabin was taking good care of the property. He paused, looking up at the door of the cabin, and his heart began to beat faster, and he was unsure of himself. Standing at the door of the cabin suddenly filled his heart with conflicting and painful memories. Should he step up onto the porch, and knock on the door, or just turn and leave? He had a strong feeling that seeing the inside of the cabin was going to be very difficult, and painful, for him!

IIe had taken the first step up onto the porch when the inner door opened, and a lady looked out at him through a screen door. She remained silent for a moment as she studied him, as if she expected him to identify himself. He stood, one foot on the first step, his heart gripped with uncertainty and trepidation. The memories of the cabin and the sudden appearance of the woman left him tongue tied and unsure of himself. The woman unlatched the screen door and stepped out onto the porch. She appeared to be in her late thirties, was neatly dressed, and was as pretty as the flowers that had been planted along the front of the porch. She broke the silence, as she smiled down at him. "Can I help you?"

He suddenly realized he should have given some thought to what he would say to the occupant when he came to the cabin, but he had not, and now, in his confusion he blurted out. "Well ma'am, I . . . I used to live here in this cabin many years ago and I stopped by to see if it were still here. I . . . I walked out from town." He paused as he looked about the porch. "It looks as if you've kept the cabin in good shape. It sure looks nice!"

Her smile was pleasant as she stepped forward and extended her hand to him. "Why thank you for the compliment on the cabin. I keep up the flower beds and the garden, but the cabin's not mine. I just rent it. I'm Helen Bedford and I'm pleased you stopped by. May I ask your name?"

He had gathered his wits about him as he quickly replied. "My names Jimmy Smith, and I'm pleased to meet you Miss Bedford." He paused as he looked at her. "I'm sorry, is it Miss or Mrs. Bedford."

Her smile seemed to wane a bit, as she replied. Well, it's actually Mrs., but my husband is deceased."

"I'm right sorry ma'am . . . about your husband. So, you . . . you live here all alone?"

"Yes, it's a nice little cabin and I enjoy the peace and quiet here in the country, near the fields and woods." She motioned towards the door. "I'm sorry; let's don't just stand here on the porch. Won't you come in? I'm sure you'd like to see the inside of the cabin. Perhaps it'll bring back some pleasant memories!"

They entered the cabin and she led him through its two rooms: a small kitchen and adjacent living room, and a bedroom. "It's small, but cozy, and I love it," she exclaimed. "I rent it from Mr. and Mrs. Adams, who live about a mile west on their dairy farm." She paused, as she watched his eyes roam about the cabin, and then she said, "I'm a schoolteacher at the little school in Blackberry."

He glanced at her, but his mind was on the cabin. "That's nice; that you're a schoolteacher."

They stood near the middle of the living room and his eyes roamed, back and forth, about the cabin. The two rooms were in excellent condition and appeared to have been recently wallpapered, and the trim painted. His eyes settled on the wall of the living room. The desk he had built for Louise was still there. It was clean and neat, and the natural oak finish gleamed with polish. A vase filled with colorful flowers sat near the corner of the desk and a typewriter stood near the center of the desk. A sharp pain went through his heart. He remembered Louise's typewriter setting on this desk.

She noticed his gaze resting on the desk and she spoke with cheerfulness in her voice. "I love the desk! Whoever built it was an excellent carpenter!"

"Yes . . . yes, it is a nice desk." It would be best not to tell her that he had built the desk.

Her eyes shifted from the desk and back to the man. She thought he looked a little haggard and tired. She could see a stoop to his shoulders and she had also noticed that he had walked with a slight limp. She surmised there was a story here, and she suspected the past years had been difficult for him. She found her voice. "When did you live here?"

He continued to stand in silence, as if contemplating his answer, and then he stammered. "It was quite a long time ago; about twenty years. Its . . . its, been a long time!" He wished she wouldn't ask questions as he didn't want to tell her too much.

She discerned that something was making him uncomfortable and she felt it best not to ask more questions. She wondered; where had he been during those many years, and why had he returned now to the little cabin? Was he a single man or did he have a wife? If he had a wife, why wasn't she here with him? Was he here in Blackberry just to see his old home, or was there another reason? She wanted to ask him a lot of questions, but something about his conduct restrained her, and she remained silent.

The silence continued as he looked at the desk and about the living room. It appeared to her that his face was filled with sadness, even pain. With a sudden movement he walked across the living room and back into the bedroom. She watched him as he stood just inside the doorway, looking all about the little room, and then his gaze seemed to settle on the bed. This was a little unnerving to her. Why was he interested in the bedroom, and especially the bed?

The bedroom flooded his mind with memories of Louise, and the past. This was where she had died, probably here in this very room! He stood transfixed, as pain and contrition welled up in his

21

heart. Involuntarily his hand went to his forehead, and eyes, as if trying to wipe away the pain and hurt. He stood, just inside the bedroom for what seemed a long time, his head bowed.

She watched him from the living room and wondered at his actions. They were all very strange!

Slowly he turned and walked back into the living room. He remained silent for a long moment, looking at her with anguish filled eyes. And then he blurted out. "I . . . I must be going! Thank . . . thank you so much for showing me the cabin."

Within a moment he was out the cabin door, down the porch steps, and walking rapidly along the little lane toward the county road. His mind was a cauldron of pain and hurt as he stumbled back toward town. He shouldn't have gone to the cabin! It had been too painful. Louise had died there. She had died, all alone, with no one to care for her!

Helen Bedford stood on the porch, and watched, as the man walked rapidly away. She noticed again that he walked with a slight limp and that his shoulders were stooped. Most men his age didn't limp or walk with hunched shoulders. Where had this man been over the past twenty years, since he had lived in the cabin. Why had he returned to Blackberry? Was it to just visit the cabin or were their other reasons? He had suddenly been overcome with very strong emotions. She was sure she had detected a look of extreme sadness, pain, and sorrow in his face. Was it the desk, the bedroom, or something that had happened here in the cabin long ago, that had unnerved him? People didn't usually act that way when they returned to visit a previous home. Very strange, indeed! Slowly she turned and walked back into the cabin. She wondered if she would ever see him again.

Helen stood in the small living room and looked out the window. The stranger was now walking along the county road and would soon be out of sight. The man's visit, and his conduct, had stirred her interest and left her vaguely troubled. She wanted to know more about this cabin. Who had lived here twenty years ago? Perhaps her landlord, Beth Adams, would know some of the history of this cabin. On an impulse she took up her shawl from the back of a chair and went to her car. She would go and speak to Beth Adams about this man, and the cabin.

She didn't know a great deal about Beth and Charles Adams. She knew they owned the little cabin and rented it to her, and they owned the large dairy farm a mile west of the cabin. She believed they had once lived in the cabin and had inherited the dairy farm when the previous owner had died, but this was all vague in her mind. She needed to know more about the cabin and who had lived in it twenty years ago!

Beth Adams greeted her knock on the door. "Why Helen, it's good to see you. Do come in." She directed her to the kitchen and motioned for her to take a chair at the table. "I'll get us each a cup of tea and we can visit."

Helen looked about the kitchen. She had been here before and she always found the Adams home to be comfortable and filled with a happy family of a loving husband and wife, and four sparkling children. The children ranged in age from the twins, who were about six years of age, a girl of about eight, and a boy of ten. The children were very well behaved and always polite. Beth was a happy, upbeat woman, of nearly thirty-five, who went out of her way to be kind and helpful to others. She was pretty, but not beautiful, but she was always pleasant to be around. Helen always felt refreshed after a visit with Beth.

Beth sat two saucers on the table and then two cups of hot tea in the saucers. She sat down across from Helen. "It's good to see you Helen. How are things going at the school? Summer is nearly here, and the school year will soon be at an end."

"Oh Beth, everything is great at the school and I do enjoy teaching there." Beth could see a cloud come into Helen's eyes as she continued. "Beth I've come here to ask you some questions about the cabin and who lived there about twenty years ago." She paused as she discerned a startled look cross Beth face. "Beth, a man just stopped by the cabin. He looked to me to be in his early forties. Nothing significant about his appearance, except his shoulders were a little stooped and I noticed that he walked with a slight limp. It was the way he acted that caught my attention! Beth, there was something strange about the way he acted. Not dangerous, but just strange, if you know what I mean. He . . . he said he had lived in the cabin about twenty years ago and had stopped by to see if the cabin were still there. I invited him into the cabin, but once he was inside, and I showed him through the two rooms, he just seemed to lose his composure. Beth, I thought he was going to break down into tears. He seemed particularly fascinated with the desk, and, of all things, with the bedroom; it was a little unnerving! You remember the desk; it's a very nice hardwood desk, built of oak; sort of out of place in the little cabin. But why would a man be so emotional over a desk, and especially the bedroom. Beth, this man seemed terribly troubled once he was inside the cabin!"

Helen looked across the table at Beth and she was surprised to see that her face was gripped with astonishment. "What is it Beth? Didn't you and Charles live in the cabin a few years back? What . . . what do you know about who lived in the cabin twenty years ago?"

Beth sat in stunned silence, as she looked across the table at Helen and her voice was almost a whisper, as she said, "Did . . . did the man give you his name?"

"Yes, he said his name was Jimmy Smith, but he didn't tell me anything else about himself, except that he had lived in the cabin about twenty years ago. Do you know if a Jimmy Smith lived there twenty years ago?"

Beth's hands were tightly clasped together, and her face continued to carry a look of astonishment, and then she gushed. "Helen, something awful happened in that cabin twenty years ago. A young woman died there under terrible circumstances. I believe she died in your bedroom! She had been abandoned by her husband, who had run off with another woman!"

Helen leaned across the table and all thought of the tea was gone. "What . . . what was the name of the woman?"

"Her name was Louise Cordell, and her husband's name was Randell."

"Beth, this man, who came to the cabin, a short while ago, said his name was Jimmy Smith, but . . . but I wonder? Perhaps he's really Randell Cordell! Do you suppose he's come back to Blackberry; and if so, why?"

Beth stood up. "Stay seated Helen and enjoy your tea. I'll be back in a minute. I have something I want to show you." Beth left the kitchen and went into the living room.

Within a couple of minutes, she returned to the kitchen and laid a small padded book on the table. Helen thought it looked like one of those old diaries, with a clasp which came around from the back of the book and snapped shut at the front. Beth sat down and picked up the diary, but she didn't open it. She looked across the table at Helen. "I'm going to tell you about Louise Cordell and how she died, and a few things about her husband, Randell. It's all here in this diary. It's a very sad story!"

Beth paused, as she ran her fingers along the diary, and then she said. "But I must begin when Charles and I, and our kids, moved into the cabin. It was five years ago, and we had left Colorado Springs, Colorado and moved here to Blackberry with Charles' large family. It was the tail end of the Great Depression and good jobs were hard to find. Charles' father, Carlisle, had secured a job with a mining company, as a mechanic, at good wages for those bad years. We moved here with them, hoping that Charles could also get a good job. Well, the good job never materialized, and when Charles did find work it only paid a dollar a day, so we had no money to pay rent. We moved into the little cabin, which had been abandoned for many years. Mr.

Southerland, who owned the cabin, agreed to let us live there, rent free, in exchange for Charles repairing his farming machinery."

Beth paused again as she stared out the kitchen window for a long minute, as if she were gathering her thoughts. And then she looked across the table at Helen. "But Helen, a funny thing happened. By the next spring we were still as poor as ever, but we had survived the winter and our kids were healthy and happy and . . . and crazy as it sounds, we had fallen in love with the little cabin; it had become our home; a warm and cozy home for our family!" She fell silent again for a few moments, as memories caressed her mind, and then she continued her story. "Ralph and Bertie Steinhart, an elderly, childless couple, lived here on this farm where we live now. In desperation I had gone to them, when we first moved into the cabin, and asked for milk for my children and they were so kind as to give us whole milk, for free, all through that long winter. Well, to make a long story short, we assisted Ralph and Bertie by helping them with their farm--milking, getting in the crops of hay and corn, canning fruit, and whatever else needed to be done-and when Bertie died she left this dairy farm to us. She was a loving woman and it was a wonderful gesture. We had many wonderful memories of the cabin and decided we wanted to keep it, so we purchased it from Mr. Southerland. We fixed it up some and have rented it out ever since."

Beth looked across the table at Helen. "Bertie told me, when I first met her, about the tragic death of Louise Cordell there in the cabin." She paused and laid her hand on the diary for a moment. "There is a secret compartment in the back of the right front drawer of the desk, and by chance I found the diary one day when I was cleaning the cabin. She glanced at the diary. "Louise Cordell's story is all here in this diary, written in her own hand during the last two years of her life." Beth's face took on a look of pain as she continued. "Louise and Randell were from the Chicago area and when they married they moved here to Blackberry, where she taught school and he opened a woodworking and cabinetry shop. But within a year Randell took up with another woman and Louise had become ill. The doctor told her she was suffering from advanced tuberculosis, and it was doubtful if she would live very long. Randell had sold his shop and ran off with this other woman, and Louise died, all alone, there in the cabin. Her body was discovered a few days after her death. She is buried in the cemetery on the north side of town. I believe that some of the people in the church paid for her funeral and put up a headstone."

The two women sat in hushed silence for a long moment, and Helen could see that Beth's eyes were brimmed with tears. Helen spoke first. "What a tragic and sad story! Do you suppose this man, who says he's Jimmy Smith, is really Randall Cordell?"

Beth looked across the table at Helen. "Perhaps this man is Randell Cordell, and he has returned to where his wife died!" She paused, as she looked out the kitchen window, and her voice was soft as she said. "But I wonder why?"

Beth looked across the table at Helen. "In addition to this diary, I also have the typewriter that belonged to Louise. We found it in the attic of the cabin." Beth paused and then continued. "As you probably know, I write short stories for the *Saturday Evening Post,* and some other publications. I wrote my first short story on the old typewriter which had belonged to Louise Cordell. I still have the typewriter. It sets on a cabinet in the living room."

Helen stood up from the table. "Thanks for the tea Beth. It's always a pleasure to visit with you." She smiled across the table at her host. "I wonder if we'll ever see this 'Mr. Smith' again?"

Beth fell silent for a moment. "I have a feeling that we will! I suspect we'll learn more about this Mr. Smith in the next few days!"

* * * *

Within an hour Randell was in his room at the boarding house. He took off his shoes and lay down on the bed. He needed to think and clear his mind. The evening meal would be served in about an hour in the dining room. He fluffed up the pillow and reclined back on the bed.

The visit to the cabin had been hard, painful, and had left him badly shaken. The cabin and the oak desk had brought back memories, but they were, in fact, good memories. It had been the bedroom that had shaken him, for he knew Louise had died there, all alone in that little room. To stand in the room where she had died had nearly overwhelmed him. And the thought that his actions had contributed to her lonely death, had left him badly shaken. He knew he had not handled himself very well in front of Mrs. Bedford. He wondered if she knew anything about his wife's death twenty years ago, and if she suspected that he wasn't Jimmy Smith, but was, in fact, the unfaithful husband of Louise Cordell.

The play of events twenty years ago crowded his mind. If he could only live them over again! A vision of Louise filled his mind. A vision of a vivacious and happy bride, and wife, who had always treated him with love, affection, and kindness. Why had he abandoned that lovely woman for the illicit affections of a loose woman, and then followed her along a downward spiraling pathway of crime, pain, and sorrow?

He had loved Louise, and they had been happy when they had moved into the little cabin. It was their first home. Louise had aspired to be a writer but had taken a teaching job at the school in Blackberry. He had opened a small woodworking and cabinet shop and had secured many clients, mostly from the more well-to-do in Grand Rapids, located six miles north. In his spare time, he had built the oak desk into the wall of the little cabin. Louise had loved it and had placed her new typewriter, which her girlfriends had given her as a wedding present, on the desk. She had spent many evenings at the desk typing short stories, which she had sent off to the popular magazines.

Shortly before she had taken ill she had said to him, as they were eating their evening meal. "I've got an idea for a short story. It's about a young couple who fall in love as they watch the Aurora Borealis, the northern lights of Minnesota. I hope to write it as a warm and touching love story!"

28

But about a year into their marriage, he had met Stella quite by accident. However, in hindsight he questioned if the meeting had been as spontaneous as he had assumed. He liked a drink now and then, especially at the end of a hard day at the shop. Before returning to the cabin, he had stopped at the local saloon. Just a drink or two and he would be on his way home. Strong drink had clouded his mind and had pushed him along a treacherous path of sorrow and heartbreak.

Stella had slipped up beside him and seated herself on the adjoining stool. Her voice had been husky and soft, and she had leaned close and told him that he was a handsome and attractive man. He had ordered more drinks for the two of them, and then the darkness of night had come, and they had left the saloon and went to her room. She had been delicious, and habit forming, and within a few weeks he had abandoned Louise and had spent his time away from the shop with Stella. What a fool he had been!

Stella had told him she worked at the little hardware store in Blackberry, but she wasn't what she appeared to be. It had all been a set-up, a trap set for him. They had gone off together to Milwaukee, Wisconsin, where she introduced him to "old friends." Stella and these old friends were bank robbers, and, in his foolishness, and infatuation for Stella, he had joined them in their scheme to tunnel into a bank vault and make off with a lot of money. His skills as a carpenter were useful to them in the tunneling and shoring operation, and they had promised him a handsome cut of the money. They had tunneled into the bank vault and made their way out with several bags of money, but the bank security personnel had discovered their partially finished excavations and were waiting for them when they exited the tunnel. He had been sentenced to twenty years in prison for his part in the bank robbery.

When he had left Blackberry, he had put his cabinet shop up for sale with a local agent, giving him a power of attorney to sell the little shop. It had sold quickly. He didn't remember the name of the buyer. He had spent the money on Stella, buying her jewelry and babbles. What a fool he had been: all for the elicit favors of a fallen woman.

While he had been in prison he had been given a Bible by a pastor who regularly visited the men who were incarcerated there. Randell was not a religious man, but reading material had been at a premium, and while resting in his bunk, following a day of back breaking labor, he had occasionally spent some time just reading random passages from throughout the Bible. He had come across several verses in the book of Proverbs, which had both startled and sobered him, and had finally brought him to his senses.

For the lips of an adulteress drip honey, and her speech is smoother than oil; but in the end she is bitter as gall, sharp as a double-edged sword. Her feet go down to death; her steps lead straight to the grave.

Sadly, and tragically, both for himself and for Louise, he had succumbed to the lips of an adulteress woman, and both he, and Louise, had paid a heavy price for his folly.

And to make matters even worse he had known, before he had run off with Stella, of the tuberculous which had struck Louise. But in his infatuation for Stella, he had ignored his wife's illness and abandoned her. She had died all alone, without the comfort and love of a husband. What he had done haunted him nearly every day.

Tomorrow he would visit his old shop and see if it were still in operation. He was unsure just why he wanted to visit the old cabinet shop. But in his soul, he felt that somehow it was the key to his recovery from the terrible hurt and depression which gripped him. Yes, he would go to the cabinet shop tomorrow.

He hoped the next few days would be better, but he doubted if such would be the case. What painful memories would the cabinet shop bring back? He also planned to visit the cemetery, on the north edge of town, and find her grave. He was sure it would be very hard. He wondered if there was a headstone, or was her grave marked with only a simple marker provided by the cemetery? He would go to the cemetery within a day or two. He was anxious, but reluctant to go. He was afraid of what would happen to him when he stood, looking down on her grave.

CHAPTER 3

The Cabinet Shop

The breakfast of ham, eggs, and hot cakes was tasty and Randell dawdled over his food; some because the food was good, and partly because he was nervous and unsure. In some respects, he would confront the same demons he had found at the cabin yesterday. Would he flee as he had fled the cabin yesterday?

He finished his breakfast, left the boarding house, and walked in the direction of his old shop. The town was small, and it would take only a few minutes to arrive at the shop. Three blocks north, along main street, then one block west, and he would be there.

It was another beautiful northern Minnesota spring morning. The sky was a deep blue and the air was fresh and crisp. He breathed deep and the cool spring air filled his lungs. A squirrel scampered away, and up a tree, as Randell's approach interrupted its hunt for acorns, and a robin strutted along a grassy area hunting for worms. Two young boys were playing with a ball in their front yard and across the street two girls were setting on a porch playing with their dolls. A smile came to his face as he walked along the quiet street; it was a pleasant town and a lovely place to live. What had ever possessed him to succumb to the lure of a loose woman, abandon his wife, and leave this enjoyable little community? It had been a tragic and foolish mistake!

When he turned the second corner he could see the building, which housed the shop. At least the building was still there! As he drew near he saw a large sign above the entry door and spread across the front of the building. In bold letters the sign bore the inscription: *BLACKBERRY CABINET SHOP*. The shop was still in operation!

He came to a halt near the front of the shop and surveyed the building and sign. The building looked pretty much the same as he remembered, although it appeared that a small extension had been added onto the east side. The building had been about five years old when he had purchased it, and he could see it had been painted within the last few years. It pleased him that the shop was in good condition and still in operation.

He stood, looking at the building, for several minutes, as old memories drifted through his mind. The cabinet shop was different from the cabin. His wife had died in the cabin, leaving it tainted and haunted. But nothing bad had happened here in the cabinet shop. It was clean and free of the stain and blemishes of his sordid past.

With a slightly renewed confidence he walked forward, slowly pushed the front door open, and stepped into the shop. He paused just inside the door and looked about the large workroom. It was a typical cabinet and woodworking shop. He could see two table saws, a lathe, and plainer. A large quantity of lumber, of various lengths, widths, and variety; oak, pine, mahogany, teak, was stacked along a side wall. A variety of small woodworking tools lay on shelves built along the side wall. Several hardwood work benches sat about the room. He could see that most of the equipment was powered by electricity. When he had opened the shop twenty years ago, almost all the wood working had been done by hand. He had had few electric tools. Times had changed.

He continued to stand near the entrance as his eyes took in the shop floor and pleasant memories engulfed his mind. He had always had a natural talent for woodworking. He had enjoyed building fine cabinets, and furniture, and remodeling kitchens. The smell of sawdust, paint, and varnish, which filled the room, was comforting, and put him at ease.

He looked up from his surveillance of the shop as an elderly man, who appeared to be in his middle sixty's, stepped through a doorway on the right side of the room, and advanced across the shop floor toward him. He was a short, slightly balding man with a round face and heavy eyebrows, which gave him a bit of a shaggy look. He was dressed in khaki work clothing, which showed evidence of wood stain, varnish, and paint. "Hello," he called out over the hum of the table saw, where a young man stood, ripping several oak boards. He motioned to Randell and shouted. "Come into my office where it's quieter."

Randell followed the man across the shop floor, through the door, and into the adjacent room. The room was small and held a desk, a couple of chairs, and several wooden file cabinets. The man turned and shut the door behind him. "There, that's better! That saw makes a lot of noise!" He paused and held out his hand. "I'm Harold Stewart. What can I do for you today? Do you need some cabinets built?" A smile filled his round face as he continued. "If so, you'll need to get in line as were pretty busy right now!" He motioned toward a chair. "Have a seat." Randell seated himself as Stewart said, "I'm sorry, I didn't catch your name!"

This was a kindly and friendly man, and in that moment, Randell Cordell decided he should come clean; he would not lie to this man. "Mr. Stewart, I'm Randell Cordell. I used to own this shop nearly twenty years ago and I believe you're probably the man who purchased it from me when I sold it."

The elderly man sat silent for a moment and then his eyes brightened. "Why yes, I did purchase this shop about twenty years ago. I'd forgotten the name of the man I bought it from. In fact, I never met the man, as I purchased it through an agent who had a power of attorney from the seller. But come to think of it, I believe the paperwork indicated the seller's name was Cordell." He stood up again and reached across the desk and extended his hand to Randell. "Well, it's especially nice to meet you! What brings you back here to Blackberry." He paused for a moment as his eyes roamed over Cordell. 'You must have been a pretty young man twenty years ago!"

Cordell was pleasantly surprised that he remained comfortable and relaxed as he shook Mr. Stewarts hand again. He liked this friendly man. "Yes, I was a young when I sold this shop to you, but it seems like a long time ago. I . . . I just got into Blackberry yesterday and I thought I would come by my old shop and see if it were still here. I'm pleased to see that it's still in operation." He paused again, as he looked across the desk at the old man. "I enjoyed building cabinets and remodeling kitchens. I . . . I've always remembered this shop with good memories!"

Stewart's swivel chair protested with a loud squeak as he leaned back and looked across the desk at Randell. He fell silent for a long moment and his voice seemed to take on a note of seriousness as he said. "You just passing through, or do you plan on staying here in Blackberry?"

What were his plans? Truth was, he had no firm plans; he was just seeking, looking for something that would take-away the ache in his heart and soul. The cabinet shop did hold an allure for him! It was a bridge to a part of his life which had been good, not sordid and stained, like so much of his past. "I'm not sure, Mr. Stewart. You see I'm kind of foot-loose right now. I just got out of the army a few weeks ago, and I'm a bit unsettled as to my future."

The old man leaned forward and the chair squeaked again. He held Randell in his gaze for a long moment. "Young man, would you be interested in buying your shop back? I need to sell this shop and I'll . . . I'll try and make you a deal you can't refuse!"

35

Cordell was stunned, and at a loss for words. "Well . . . well," he stammered. "I haven't much money, so I . . . I don't know, but perhaps . . .."

The old man settled back into his chair and made a little steeple with his hands, as he looked across the desk at Randell. "It's right interesting that you should show up here just now." He paused for a moment, as if unsure of what he would say next, and then he leaned forward, and the chair let out another loud groan. "Mr. Cordell, I've sprung this proposal on you sudden like, without any explanation. I don't mean to scare you, but I'm in a bit of a pickle. My wife's grown right tired of the cold, and long, winters here in northern Minnesota and she went off down to Florida when winter came on last fall, and she's been after me right hard to get shut of this shop and come on down there and join her. We have a daughter, who lives there, and they are both pushing me to sell this shop and come down to the sunshine state, as they call it! We're both getting along some in years, and the truth is, I need to sell this shop and go to Florida and be with my wife!"

Stewart glanced about the office for a moment and then continued at a fast pace. "Young man, you know how to run a cabinet shop so it's a perfect fit. Why don't you take your old shop back? There's a good backlog of work and you'll do fine! What do you say?"

Cordell's heart was beating at a fast pace and he struggled to catch his breath. "Well, I . . . I think I would like that, but like I said, I don't have much money. About a thousand dollars I saved while I was in the army."

Stewart sat in silence, and contemplation, for a long moment, as he appeared to be studying Cordell, and then he smiled. "You look like a good solid man that I can do business with; someone I can trust!" He chuckled, "I did it once so why not a second time!" He gave a hearty laugh. "Tell you what: if you can come up with five hundred dollars as a down payment, then the shop is yours. And you can pay the balance of twenty-five hundred dollars off over the next three years at five percent interest." He stood abruptly to his feet and the chair let out another squeak. Stewart came around the desk and put his hand on Randell's shoulder. "Mr. Cordell, why don't you sleep on my offer overnight and then come back in the morning. We can seal the deal then. How about it?"

Randell stood quickly to his feet, but his head was light, and seemed to be spinning. "Yes . . . yes I'd like to think on your offer. I'll come back in the morning."

CHAPTER 4

At the Grave

Cordell walked a block from the cabinet shop, turned the corner at the intersection, and then stopped. He stood quietly, looking along the tree lined street, his mind a vortex of emotions. He needed to think. He lifted his gaze from the street up to the low mountain, which rose up beyond the town, and then higher, toward the blue sky. Slowly the realization came to him that the driving force behind his return to Blackberry had been a vague notion, buried deep in the back roads of his mind, of getting the shop back and making a fresh start to his troubled life. That notion had now exploded to the forefront, with the events of the past few minutes.

The incongruity of reacquiring the cabinet shop from Stewart hit him like a blow to his gut. If he purchased the shop everyone in the community would know, within a few days, that the man who had run off with a loose woman, and abandoned his wife to die all alone, had returned. He harbored no illusions: some of the people of Blackberry would look upon him with loathing, even hatred, and would never accept him. Why try and buck such animosity? There were other towns and other cabinet shops where he could find work, or even purchase a shop. The best course of action would be for him to visit the resting place of Louise at the cemetery, a few blocks to the north, and then

38

quietly leave town; move on to some other place that didn't present these challenges. That would be the prudent, and easiest, course of action.

Slowly his eyes shifted from staring up at the cobalt blue sky and back to the street and the homes which lay along the little thoroughfare. A gentle breeze rustled the spring leaves of the shade trees, and he watched a lady, kneeling in her flower garden, digging with a little trowel and planting small bunches of flowers. On the other side of the street a man pushed a lawn mower as he cut his grass. Nearby, two young girls knelt on a porch, built along the front of a house, playing jacks. Further along the street, he could see two boys playing catch with a ball.

He stood silently, his eyes drifting along the street, taking in the everyday activities of some of the people of this small town. Watching these routine activities stirred something buried deep within his soul. Something that had lain dormant, and long forgotten, for over twenty years. He had turned away from these humble and common events when he had abandoned his wife and left town with an enticing woman twenty years ago. The intervening years had been spent in prison and killing men in the vicious war. He was no longer in prison, and the war was over. What were his plans from this day forward; for the years to come.? Did he have any real plans?

As he continued to look along the street he was gripped with a longing, a deep-rooted desire. He wanted someone to love, hold close, and cherish. He wanted to be loved again! He was all alone in this world and he was a lonely man! He wanted a home, like the homes along this street, with a white picket fence, and his own children playing catch in the front yard and jacks on the front porch. Was such a dream possible, or was it beyond his reach? Was it too late, after the tragic, and foolish, mistakes of his past, and the passing of so many years? Was it something he had thrown away twenty years ago, and could never be recovered?

He resumed his way along the street. He walked aimlessly, his head cast down, his heart troubled and full of uncertainty. But desire, and hope, lingered in his anxious heart, and he clung to a dream of a new, and better future. His injured leg bothered him a little, and he stumbled a bit as he walked. Blackberry had been his home once: could he make it his home a second time, despite the obstacle of his tarnished reputation? Several minutes past, as he trudged on along the street. An arch caught his eye and he looked up. In bold letters he read: *BLACKBERRY CEMETERY*. His aimless walking had carried him to the resting place of his deceased wife!

He had intended to visit the cemetery tomorrow, but he was here by happenstance. Slowly he turned, walked through the archway, and in among the headstones. The cemetery was green with freshly mowed spring grass. Vases of flowers sat near the headstones of many of the graves. It was a serene and peaceful place, and it left him with mixed feelings of calm and apprehension. Deliberately he walked back and forth, along the rows of graves, noting the names on the headstones. Was there even a headstone marking her resting place? If so, who had paid for it? And then he saw the dark-brown, granite headstone.

LOUISE M. CORDELL
January 12, 1905 -- June 23, 1926

His heartbeat jumped, and his knees were weak, as he slowly made his way to the headstone. He stopped at the edge of the grave and looked down at her grass covered resting place. Slowly he ran his hand along the top of the stone marker, an instinctive, caring, and loving action. This was the grave of his wife! In his heart he felt as if it were hallowed ground. He stood in silence, his face grim and pale, as sunlight filtered through the nearby trees, casting soft shadows across the grave and stone marker. A shaft of golden, brilliant, sunlight paused briefly on the headstone, and was gone. A solitary rabbit hopped past him and disappeared behind a headstone. The cemetery was held in a hushed silence and he was conscious of faint sounds: the distant whistle of a train, the honk of a car horn.

Instinctively he removed his hat. She had been resting here in this quiet spot for twenty years. The shadows cast by nearby trees continued to cavort across the grave and headstone, and he could hear a mockingbird call in the stillness of this hallowed moment. His heart felt heavy and there seemed to be a great strain in his chest, as if long strangled passions were escaping from his breast. His breathing came in short bursts, and his head hung low.

And then the tears came. They came in a rush and he made no attempt to hold them back. His legs became weak and he slowly sank to his knees and buried his head in his hands, as violent shudders coursed through his body. Across the cemetery a caretaker noted the lone man kneeling by the grave. *"It's tough to lose a loved one."* He mused to himself.

Gradually the pain and trembling lifted from his heart and he wiped the tears from his face with the sleeve of his shirt. He slowly rose to his feet and stared along the rows of graves for a long moment, as his breathing returned to normal. He turned back to her grave and his feelings became expressions as he spoke in a faint voice. "Forgive me Louise! Forgive me for being unfaithful to you, and . . . and for abandoning you! I . . . I wish I could make it up to you, but I don't know how!"

He stood at the grave for several minutes and then he turned. He would go and purchase a vase, and a clutch of flowers, to place near the headstone. It wasn't much, only a gesture, but he knew it would help to ease his pain and heartache. And then, as he turned to leave, he saw the container of flowers. He was surprised he hadn't noticed the flowers when he had first found the grave. Perhaps it was because there was a small bush near the headstone, which had distracted him from noticing the flowers. The flowers sat just to the side of the headstone. It was a large vase of flowers and they were fresh, not more than a few days old. Someone had brought these flowers and placed them at his wife's grave within the past few days! Who would do this after all these years? And who had paid for and put up the headstone? He must find out and thank them.

His gaze once again found the small mountain that formed the backdrop to this hamlet and his mind and heart were clear now, and in that august moment he vowed that he would not continue to try and hide his identity. Whatever more he did here in Blackberry would be done in the open, as Randell Cordell. He would build on the foundation of this hour, here at the hallowed grave of his wife, Louise Cordell. He was determined to leave this consecrated ground a changed man.

He stood a little straighter, the stoop almost gone, and his step was sure and firm, as he walked from the grave. He noted a workman across the cemetery and quickly approached the man. "Sir, I have just visited the grave of a Louise Cordell. She has been buried here for many years, but someone is placing flowers on her grave. Would . . . would you have any idea who is placing the flowers on her grave?"

The man looked up at him and there was a smile on his face as he spoke. "Why yes, I know who the lady is that brings the flowers. Her name's Beth Adams. She comes every few weeks with flowers to place on Cordell's grave. She sometimes stops and visits with me for a few minutes. She's a right nice lady. Sometimes she brings her kids along with her. She's got four young ones."

He was startled! Beth Adams? Hadn't the lady, who rented the cabin, Helen Bedford, said that she rented from people named Adams? He was dumbfounded: why would Mrs. Adams place flowers on his wife's grave?

Randell stepped forward and shook the man's hand. "Thank you. Thank you very much."

His mind was full of wonder, and questions, as he walked back to the rooming house. He must go and visit this Mrs. Adams. What would she know about his deceased wife? And more important, what would she know about Randell Cordell?

42

CHAPTER 5

A Fresh Start

T he supper of roast beef, mashed potatoes, gravy, and vegetables, his landlady had prepared, satisfied his evening hunger. He was surprisingly relaxed following his visits to his old shop and the cemetery. He spent about an hour chatting with another boarder, a Mr. Kincaid, and then took a short walk about the town.

He retired to his room and sat in the chair gazing through the window and out across the lawn. The setting sun turned the western sky into a dazzling red and gold backdrop to the village. By the time the colors had faded into darkness he had made up his mind. He had saved most of his army pay and had accumulated a little over a thousand dollars. He would accept Stewarts' offer to sell him the cabinet shop. He was determined to make a fresh start to his troubled life, and it might as well be here in Blackberry, with his old cabinet shop, and near his wife's grave. Purpose and fortitude welled up into his heart. He would face the demons of his past head on, here in the town where his downfall had begun! Buying the shop and staying here in Blackberry implied that he must win the confidence of the people of this little community. He knew it wouldn't be easy. He was determined to show them that he was not the same man they had known those many years before.

During his walk he had passed a small white church. He didn't remember the church. It had probably been built during his absence. He had stood in front of the place of worship for several minutes and had made another decision. He would begin regular church attendance. It was time to begin a walk along a new pathway, which included a relationship with the Lord.

At the stroke of nine the next morning he walked into the cabinet shop, and by three that afternoon he owned the shop, the woodworking equipment, and inventory, including a used, but serviceable, pickup truck. The vehicle was a bonus, as he needed a means of transportation.

When they had walked back into the shop, after signing the papers in the lawyer's office, Stewart had clapped his hand down on Randell's shoulder. "I'm a happy man, Mr. Cordell," he exclaimed. "I'll be off to Florida right soon!" And then he turned to Randell. "Well, I'll stay on for a few days to ease ya into the business and then I'll take my leave." He took Randell's arm. "Let's go into *your* office and we'll begin by going over the accounts, and work orders."

Randell was delighted with the large backlog of work orders. "Business has been good, and I think ya will keep right busy for a good spell," the old man had ejaculated. "I only got the one employee; the young man ya see workin' in the shop and ya may even need to consider puttin' on another man to help ya along! I'll introduce you to him shortly." As they reviewed the individual contracts Randell was surprised to see that he was committed to remodel the kitchen of a Charles and Beth Adams. Very interesting! He would pay them a visit very soon. He had more than the remodeling job to review with them.

When they finished looking over the accounts and work orders, Stewart led Randell out onto the shop floor. A young man was working at the table saw and Stewart motioned for him to shut down the machine. When the shop was quiet Stewart said to him. "Robert, I've sold the shop to Mr. Cordell and he's your new boss. I hope you'll work as hard for him as you have for me." He turned to Randell. "Robert

Harrison has worked for me since graduating from trade school three years ago and I believe he'll continue to be a good employee for you."

Randell held out his hand. "It's good to meet you Robert. I'm looking forward to working with you. Let's get together in the office later today and chat for a minute. I need to get to know you a little better."

He spent most of the balance of the day getting fully acquainted with the operation of the power tools, and the shop. He smiled to himself as the day progressed. The shop had changed, but in many ways, it was still the same as his old shop. As he moved about the shop he realized that he felt better than he had in many years. He even caught himself humming a little tune as he moved about the shop floor. The smell of varnish, paint and sawdust revived old, and long forgotten memories, and he became conscious of an immense pleasure in cutting and fitting a piece of lumber; in using his hands to fashion and create a cabinet, a useful and beautiful piece of furniture. He hoped he had started down a new road which would bring many changes to his life, and it left him excited, but a little apprehensive. He suspected the next few weeks would bring some challenges. He hoped he was prepared to meet them with honesty and integrity!

Near the end of the workday, he visited with Robert Harrison in his office for about fifteen minutes. Robert seemed a little nervous as he sat across the small desk from him. Randell could understand that he was a little apprehensive at the sudden change in ownership. Randell smiled at the young man and asked. "How old are Robert?"

"I'm twenty-two, sir."

"Are you married?"

A wide smile spread across the young man's face. "No sir, but I'm engaged to a girl, and we'll be married in about three months."

Randell returned the young man's smile. "Congratulations! Who's the young lady?"

Robert set forward in his chair as he spoke with a happy voice. "Her names Betty Flagstaff. We met in high school."

Stewart had reviewed Robert's salary with Randell. "The young man's a good worker and knows what he's doing on the shop floor. He's due for a raise before long."

Randel leaned forward in his chair. "Robert, I want to give you an incentive to help me as I take over this cabinet shop and I'm going to give you an early wedding present. Effective today I'm increasing your weekly salary by ten dollars."

Robert's face lit up with a huge smile. "Thank you, sir. I'll . . . I'll try and do my best for you!"

Randell leaned back in his chair and his face took on a more serious note as he said. "Robert, there's something I need to tell you about myself, so you won't get blindsided and confused." It took Randell only a few minutes to tell him about his previous ownership of the shop, his abandonment of Louise, the woman he had run off with, the bank robbery, and his years in prison. His voice was somber as he concluded. "Robert, I made a terrible and tragic mistake twenty years ago, and I hope to make amends, in some fashion, to the people of this little community for what I did. That's one of the reasons I decided to purchase this shop. I need to make a fresh start!"

Robert had a startled look on his face as he said. "I . . . I understand. I hadn't heard anything about your wife Louise, or you, before today."

"Well, I wanted you to know before you heard it from others." He stood up. "You have a good evening, and when you see your bride-to-be you tell her I think she's made an excellent choice for a husband."

As Robert stood to leave the office Randell remembered one other item he wanted to mention to the young man. "Robert, as you probably know, we have a pretty good backlog of work. If you have a friend, from trade school, you would care to recommend, I think I'll consider putting on another man."

Robert smiled at Randell. "Yes, I . . . I may know someone."

CHAPTER 6

A Challenge

W hen Randell took a chair at the breakfast table, the next morning, Mrs. Herriot appeared in the kitchen door, her arms folded across her ample bosom and her face filled with a heavy, dark, scowl. Her voice was full of venom as she held Randell in a piercing stare. "Well, the truth has come out! Yer not Jimmy Smith, yer Randell Cordell and ya have come back to the scene of yer evil deeds!" She emitted a little snort as she continued. "Ya didn't fool me fer long. I knew I had seen ya before. News gets around real fast here in this small town, and I found out last night that ya are Randell Cordell and ya have bought yer old shop back from Mr. Stewart!"

Mrs. Herriot's other boarder, Michael Kincaid, looked up from his hotcakes with a startled expression, and then quickly averted his eyes, and returned to eating his breakfast. Randell's mouth was dry as he tried to speak. "I'm . . . I'm right sorry, Mrs. Herriot, I . . . I shouldn't have lied to . . .."

She cut him off and her face was red, and filled with loathing, as she spit out the words. "Yer not only a liar, but yer a womanizer and a murderer! Ya took up with that hussy of a woman, and then run off with her, and left yer wife to die all alone out there in that little cabin in the woods! Murder, that's what it was, and ya should be in prison and facin' the electric chair!"

48

"Mrs. Herriot, what . . . what I did was wrong, but it wasn't murder, and I hope to . . . .."

"Ya can call it what ya want, but I call it murder and I won't have the likes of ya livin' in my roomin' house. When yer weeks rent's up, I want ya gone, and I say good riddance!" She stared at him with hard eyes, for a long moment, and then turned and disappeared into the kitchen.

Cordell ate his breakfast in silence, his heart pounding. His past had returned to hound him within a day of his purchase of the cabinet shop! He noticed Kincaid, a middle-aged man, glancing at him from time to time. Mrs. Harriet did not put in another appearance, taking her breakfast alone in the kitchen.

When Randell had finished his breakfast and walked out of the boarding house, Kincaid followed him out onto the porch. He shut the front door and there was a sly grin on his face as he looked at Randell. "Well, the old lady sure didn't cut you any slack! She came down on you like a ton of coal!" He leaned back against the porch railing as he looked at Randell. "Truth is, most of us have made some serious mistakes along the way; I know I have." He paused and glanced at the closed door. "And I'd guess that old lady has made a few mistakes in her lifetime. She's probably not as pure as the driven snow!"

Kincaid paused, looked along the street for a moment, and then continued. "I don't know how much truth there is to what she said about you, but it's none of her business!"

Randell face was filled with pain and shadows. "I'm sorry to say, but it's mostly all true."

Well, even if it's true, it happened many years ago. It should be left to the past." He looked across the little porch at Randell. "Who appointed her as judge and jury over you? She should just keep her crooked nose out of your life and let what happened, those many years ago, lay between you and the Lord!"

Randell looked at his fellow boarder with a heavy face. "I . . . I did make some very serious mistakes here in this town twenty years ago. And it's difficult for me to live with what I did. And I shouldn't have lied to Mrs. Herriot about who I was, but I was unsure when I first got here, and was afraid, and confused."

Kincaid fell silent for a moment as he studied Randell. "I'd like to help. Not sure what I can do, but this old lady will talk this all over town, and who knows when the next shoe will drop on you! I'm planning on being here for several more months, but I'm only paid up through the next four days. I don't care for this old busy body. I think I'll find a new place to sleep and work."

He paused, gazed along the treelined street for a moment, and then continued. "I'm a writer and working on a novel set in a small town in northern Minnesota. I like to pick up some of the local color as I write my books. You need to know the people before you can build their characters, and personalities into a book, so I try and write my books while living in the area where I've placed the novel. That's why I'm here." He chuckled. "Perhaps Mrs. Herriot has provided me with some additional material for my book!" He fell silent for a moment and then said. "If it's all right with you I'll spend some time today scouting about the area and see if I can find another rooming house, or some suitable place for the two of us to light. Is that okay by you?"

"That would be great! I appreciate it very much."

Randell walked from the porch, got into his pickup, which was parked at the curb, drove the short distance to the shop, and he and Robert tackled the construction of three kitchen cabinets for a home in Grand Rapids. The conversation was sparse. as Randell's mind was again a cauldron of emotions following the confrontation with Mrs. Herriot. Kincaid was probably right; within a day everyone in the little community would know he was back in Blackberry and would have heard Mrs. Herriot's version of his sordid past and return to Blackberry.

He didn't have long to wait for the next shoe to drop. At ten-thirty a stout, middle aged, woman walked in the open front door of the shop and stood, hands on her hips, staring across the shop floor. Randell looked up from the work bench and went to meet her. As he approached the lady he was sure he detected a harsh scowl on her face. His intuition told him he was looking at trouble. "Can I help you ma'am?"

Her eyes were filled with fire, as she said. "You certainly can! A couple of week ago I put in an order for two small cabinets to be built along the wall in my den." Her scowl deepened, and her voice took on a high-pitched tone. "I want to cancel the order and I want a refund of my deposit of twenty-five dollars!" She paused and looked at Randell with loathing eyes. "I'll not do business with an adulterer and murderer!"

Randell could see it would be futile to try and explain, or reason, with the woman. He wrote her out a check for her deposit. As he handed her the check he said. "Ma'am, I did make some terrible mistakes many years ago, but I was hoping the people of the community would be willing to forgive me."

She looked at Randell with hard eyes. "Some things can't be forgotten, and I don't believe the people of this town will forgive you for what you did! Abandoning your deathly sick wife and running off with another woman! I'll take my cabinet work to a shop in Grand Rapids. I've heard the owner is a right good Christian man." In a moment she was gone.

Shortly after lunch another woman, tall and slim, her hair pulled back in a hard bun, and with judgmental eyes, withdrew her order for remodeling her kitchen and demanded the return of her deposit. "Yer no good," she had spit out. "And people like you just don't change; once a womanizer always a womanizer!" Randell stood in the doorway to his shop and watched her drive away. He sighed. It was going to be a long day. If this kept up he would be out of business within a week.

They worked until five and then Randell walked to the café. He didn't feel up to facing Mrs. Herriot. It had been a difficult day, but he did chuckle to himself. *Given her temperament, she might put rat poison in his evening meal!* He took his dinner at the café and then drove to the lane which led to the little cabin and then on west for a mile to the Adams dairy farm. When he had visited the cabin, Mrs. Bedford had said she rented the cabin from the Adams family, who lived on the dairy farm. The caretaker at the cemetery had said that a lady by the name of Beth Adams placed the flowers on the grave of Louise. He needed to find out if the lady who lived at the dairy farm was that lady, and if so, why she was placing flowers on his deceased wife's grave.

CHAPTER 7

Beth Adams

He was impressed with the tidiness of the farmyard and the attractive condition of the buildings. He could see two kids, a boy of about ten, and a girl, who appeared to be a couple of year's younger, forking hay to some calves in a small pen. The kids waved to him as he got out of his pickup.

He walked to the front door of the house and knocked. Within moments a neat, and pretty woman looked through the screen door at him. Her face carried a warm smile as she said, "Hello, can I help you?"

Randell looked up at the woman and stammered. "Are . . . are you Beth Adams?"

"Sure am!" She continued to smile at him through the screen door.

He took a deep breath. "Are you the lady who has been placing flowers on the grave of Louise Cordell?"

Beth Adams took a quick step back from the screen door and Randell could see that her smile had vanished, and then she said, "I . . . I think you better come in. We . . . should probably talk!"

She pushed the screen door open for him and he cautiously entered the house. She led him into the living room and motioned him to a wing backed chair, as she took a cushioned chair a few feet away.

53

Randell sat down in the chair, but said nothing, and he was conscious that his breathing had become heavy. He wasn't sure just why, but he had the strange feeling he was about to learn some startling details about the tragic end to his wife's life. He had a strong premonition that the next few minutes were going to be very hard and painful for him!

Beth Adams seated herself in the chair and she couldn't help but stare at the man she had just invited into her living room. He was a stranger, and yet she had a strong feeling she knew quite a lot about this man. If this man was who she thought he was, he and his deceased wife, Louise Cordell, had whirled like a cyclone, through her mind for five years. She was still staring at him as she said. "You're Randell Cordell, aren't you?"

His throat seemed to be filled with a heavy lump. "Yes, ma'am, I am. But . . . but how do you know who I am?"

Randell was relieved when the trace of a smile returned to her face. "Mr. Cordell, it's a rather long and complicated story, but I'd like to tell it to you." She paused as she composed herself. "And I'd like to hear your story as well. I think telling our two stories will be beneficial, perhaps even therapeutic, for each of us!"

She fell silent again for a moment and then she rose from her chair. "Please excuse me while I get a few things before we begin our stories."

She walked across the living room and to a chest that stood against the far wall. Randell's eyes followed her as she made her way across the room. She stood erect and walked with a purpose. And then his heart jumped: an old Remington Rand typewriter sat atop the chest. In an instant he was sure it was the typewriter Louise's girl friends had given her as a wedding present those many years ago. His heart was pounding now, and he watched with gaping mouth, as Beth opened a door on the front of the chest and retrieved a small book, and now he began to experience some trouble breathing. It had been twenty years, but he recognized the book; it was his wife's diary! How

54

had this lady come into possession of these two items? He continued to watch as Mrs. Adams walked to a large credenza, opened a drawer, and withdrew two magazines. What significance did the two magazines carry for him?

She came back across the living room, laid the diary and the two magazines on a small table near her chair, and then seated herself again. Her face was serious, but not stern, as she said. "Mr. Cordell, as I said, we need to talk, and during our conversation let's talk about your wife, Louise, her typewriter you can see across the room on the chest, this little diary that belonged to your wife, and about a short story called *Northern Lights.*"

At the mention of the story, *Northern Lights,* Randell's vision seemed to become slightly blurred, and he felt light-headed. In fact, he was afraid he might faint. He let his head rest against the back of the chair, and closed his eyes, as he tried to control his hard breathing.

The silence continued for a long moment. He slowly lifted his head, forced his eyes open, and stared at the lady. Her face continued to hold a faint smile. The hint of her smile eased his pain a little, but only a little. He forced himself speak. "Please excuse me, Mrs. Adams, but how is it that you have my wife's typewriter and diary in your possession?"

Her eyes were firm, but pleasant, as she said, "It will all come out in a few minutes, Mr. Cordell. Do you want to tell your story first, or shall I go first?"

He knew he couldn't speak coherently, and he mumbled. "Ah . . . please go first Mrs. Adams. I . . . I'm a little confused!"

Beth Adams looked across the few feet of space separating the two of them. She could see that the old typewriter, the diary, and what she had just said, had badly unnerved him. He looked very pale and she was afraid he might faint. She hoped not!

She took a deep breath as she began. "Here's what I know about you and your wife, Louise, and why I'm placing flowers on your wife's grave." She leaned back in the chair, folded her hands, and continued. "My husband and I, and our four little children, came to Blackberry about five years ago. My husband thought he had job lined up, but it didn't materialize. In desperation we moved into the little cabin a mile east of here. It had not been lived in for many years." She paused for a moment and then continued. "In fact, I learned later that it hadn't been lived in since your wife's death some fifteen years prior to our moving into the cabin." She leaned forward in the chair and looked directly at him, and her hands were now gripping the arms of the chair. "Mr. Cordell, it seems that the lonely and tragic death of your wife, in that little cabin, had put a hex on it, and it was viewed by many of the people, who had known your wife, as sort of a haunted cabin."

She relaxed back into her chair as she continued. "We, of course, didn't know any of this when we moved into the cabin. Mrs. Steinhart, who lived on this farm with her husband, Ralph, told me that you and Louise had moved into the cabin shortly after your marriage, and she told me how you had abandoned your wife and ran off with another woman, and that your wife died alone in the cabin."

She paused again, and Randell thought he detected a tremor in her voice as she continued. "Mr. Cordell, I was shocked, and terribly saddened, by Mrs. Steinhart's story about how you had deserted your wife for another woman, and then left her to die all alone. And then, a few weeks later I found your wife's diary in the secret compartment in the rear of the lower right drawer of the oak desk you had built into the wall of the cabin."

Again, a heavy silence filled the room as Randell stared at her, his face a mask of stone. As she spoke she reached and placed her hand on the little diary. "You probably don't know what your wife wrote in her diary. It begins with your marriage and ends just a few days before her death. When I read the diary I was deeply touched, even reduced to tears over the stark tragedy of the last few months, weeks, and days, of your wife's life!"

Beth could see the alarm and hurt in the man's face, but she continued speaking. "In her diary Louise wrote of her heartbreak over losing her husband to another woman, and of her deep and painful loneliness as she lay dying, all alone. In addition, she wrote of her plans to write a short story about a young couple falling in love under the spell of what are known as 'Northern Lights' here in northern Minnesota. Plans which she knew she would never be able to carry out, as she was dying."

Beth fell silent again as she composed herself. Just recalling what Louise had written in the diary was very painful for her, and then she blurted out. "Oh, Mr. Cordell I must tell you, I was very touched, saddened, and hurt, by what I read in your wife's diary. It was all so sad and tragic, but for some reason the part about the short story, she had hoped to write, seemed to distress me the most. Within a short while I took it upon myself to write the story, that I thought she would have written about a young couple falling in love under the enchantment of the Northern Lights. I had found Louise's typewriter in the attic of the little cabin and after my husband oiled it, and I purchased a new ribbon, I wrote the story using your wife's typewriter. I was very pleased that I could write her story on her own typewriter. The story was accepted by the *Saturday Evening Post* and was published shortly thereafter." Beth reached and took up one of the magazines she had laid on the table. She reached forward and held it out to Randell. "This issue of the magazine contains the story I wrote. If you like, you may take it with you and read the story, but I would like the magazine returned when you have finished."

Beth reached for the second magazine on the table and continued. "Several months later I wrote another short story and submitted it to the *Post,* which they accepted and published. This second story is about a young woman, whose husband has run off with another woman, and how she died, heart-broken, and all alone, in a small cabin in the north woods of Minnesota." She handed the second magazine to Randell. "You may also wish to read this story as well, but I must warn you; it may be very painful for you to do so. The story does not treat you very well! In fact, it depicts you as a rather despicable and heartless man!"

She folded her hands in her lap again. "Mr. Randell, that's my story; except for the part about the flowers on your wife's grave." She leaned forward in her chair as she spoke again, and Randell thought he detected tears in her eyes. "Learning of the tragedy of how her marriage to you came to an end, and of her death, all alone, in the cabin, and then, writing these two stories, brought me very close to your wife. I . . . I felt as if I knew her very well. I found her grave in the cemetery and visited it from time to time. Some of the kind people of this community had paid for a headstone for your wife's grave. Mr. Cordell, this may sound a little strange, but I even felt that your wife had become a close, and dear friend to me, and . . . and that's why I place flowers on her grave!"

She could see he was badly shaken by what had transpired over the past few minutes. She stood to her feet. "Let me get you a fresh glass of water before you tell me your story." She turned and walked to her kitchen.

When she returned he took a long drink of the water. Some of the color had come back into his face and he began to speak in a low, and halting, voice. "Mrs. Adams, I . . . I hardly know where to begin. All that you have said about me is quite true. I . . . did abandon my wife for another woman, and I left her to die all alone there in the little cabin. It . . . it was an awful thing to do and I deserve your scorn and even hatred!"

He fell silent for a long moment, and, regaining some of his composure, he continued. "Mrs. Adams, abandoning my wife for another woman eventually led to an attempted robbery of a bank and a prison term, and it wasn't until I read some passages in the Bible, while I was in prison, about how an adulterous woman leads a man to ruin, that I finally began to come to my senses and to accept responsibility for the terrible way I had treated my wife." Tears were running down his face as he said. "I . . . wish there were some way I could undo it all, and . . . and make it up to her!"

He fell silent and stared at the floor, his heart a cauldron of emotions. *Perhaps he should never have returned to Blackberry. He now owned his old cabinet shop, but would he ever be accepted here again?* He was silent for several minutes as he retrieved his handkerchief and wiped the tears from his face.

He looked up at Mrs. Adams and spoke again in a subdued, but firm voice. "It . . . it was all so very stupid of me! I was in prison for ten years and was released about three years ago on the condition that I go straight into the army. I was wounded in the Battle of the Bulge, but I'm fine now, only a slight limp. I was discharged from the army only a few weeks ago. I . . . I had nowhere to go and I hated myself for what I had done to Louise, and, without much thought, I decided to return to Blackberry. I . . . I'm not sure just why I came back here. I . . . I thought perhaps I could . . . make things right if I were able to acquire my old shop. Just, sort of, start over again; if you know what I mean? But that's probably just a pipe dream!"

He looked up into the face of Beth and the tears had returned. "And . . . and Mrs. Adams, I needed to stand at my wife's grave and ask her to forgive me. I went to her grave and that's when I found your flowers. Do . . . do you suppose she's in heaven and could hear me when I begged her to forgive me? I . . . I hope so!"

She spoke in a quiet, but friendly, voice. "Mr. Cordell, I don't know if your wife could hear you, but I'm sure the Lord heard it when you asked Louise to forgive you, and I'm sure the Lord is willing to forgive you if you are truly sorry for what you did those many years ago. And Mr. Cordell, I do believe you are sorry. If you were not sorry I doubt if you would have returned to Blackberry or come to my house today to inquire about the flowers!"

"Mrs. Adams, during those years in prison, I thought a lot about what I had done to Louise. I have prayed many times, over the past few years, asking the Lord to forgive me. I . . . I hope that He will!"

There was compassion and understanding in Beth's voice as she spoke. "You know Randell, we're all sinners, and we all make some serious mistakes as we travel along life's pathways. Some of those mistakes can be very tragic!" She leaned forward in her chair and looked directly into his face. "Mr. Cordell, I'm glad you've come back to Blackberry. I believe it's a significant and genuine gesture on your part to do so! You can't undo what you did, but perhaps you can ease your own pain, and begin a new life again; here where it all began.

She paused and set in quiet contemplation for a long moment and then she continued. "And another thing Mr. Cordell, speaking with you today has helped me understand that I need to forgive you for what you did to Louise. For you see, I have carried a great deal of animosity toward you ever since I learned how you left her for another woman and abandoned her to die all alone. I've disliked you ever since I read her diary! I . . . I believe that our conversation today has been helpful for both of us."

"Yes," he whispered, "It has been very good for me and I'm glad I came to see you. I . . . I remember very clearly that Louise planned to write a story about a young couple falling in love under the spell of the Northern Lights. I'm looking forward to reading the story you wrote."

He had regained some of his composure. "Mrs. Adams, I want to especially thank you for placing flowers on my wife's grave, but you can stop now, if you like, as I intend to make sure there are always some flowers on her grave!"

"I believe that's a wonderful beginning to a fresh start!"

She stood to her feet and extended her hand. "I'm happy that you came to see me, and I want you to know I forgive you for what you did those many years ago. I want to be friends with you. It will not always be easy for me, as I have carried a pretty dark picture of you

60

over these past five years, but I do want to get to know you better." And then she looked toward the kitchen and smiled. "You say you have purchased your old shop back. We have a contract with your shop for some remodeling work in our kitchen. Let's go into the kitchen and I'll show you what we have in mind."

Randell's spirits lifted as they walked to the kitchen. His visit with Mrs. Adams had shown him that she was an unusual and remarkable woman. He was pleased he had come to see her. And, in addition, he was not going to lose her work contract. That also buoyed his spirts.

Their survey of the kitchen was soon interrupted by the boisterous entry of four children, all clamoring for their mother's attention. "Hey Mom," a boy of about ten called out as he and three other younger kids trouped into the kitchen. "Come and see the new baby calf, he's . . ." The lad stopped and stared at Randell. "Hello Mister!" he said in a soft voice.

Mrs. Adams smiled as she glanced from the children to Randell. "Mr. Cordell, these are my children. LeRoy is the oldest at ten, and then Ilene is the oldest girl at eight, and then the twins, Morton and Marie, who are six years old." She turned her attention back to the children. "Can you all say hello to Mr. Cordell. Mr. Cordell is going to remodel our kitchen."

In one voice they chorused. "Hello Mr. Cordell." They stood mute for just a moment and then LeRoy took a step forward and his face was filled with an eager smile, as he looked up at Randell. "Mr. Cordell, would . . . would you like to see our new baby calf? He's real cute! He's in the barn!"

Randell smiled at the beaming faces of the children. They seemed radiant with happiness and very excited about a new calf. "Yes . . . yes," he exclaimed. "I'd like to see your new baby calf!"

Beth glanced from her children to Randell and then down to her children, who had all crowded close to him. "Children, Mr. Randell is a busy man. He may not have time to look at a new calf."

Randell was mesmerized as he looked down into the happy faces of these kids who wanted to show him their new calf, and a sharp pang tore through his heart. Oh, what he wouldn't give for a family of children like these happy kids! He was all smiles as he said. "Yes, I'd love to see your new calf!"

"Oh, good!" chorused the children. Ilene reached up and took his hand. Her long yellow curls swishing as she tugged on him. "Come on! I'll show you our new calf!"

The children led him, at a fast pace, across the yard, into the barn, and to a straw filled stall. As one they pointed to a black and white cow and a tiny little black and white calf that stood very close to its mother as its wide eyes surveyed this mob of people who had suddenly appeared. Ilene looked up at Randell. "That's our new calf. Isn't he cute? He . . . he was just borned yesterday, and . . . and the big cow is his Mommy!"

A man walked up and joined the children and looked at Randell. "Hello, I'm Charles Adams, the father of this troop of youngsters. I see they've hauled you out to the barn to see the latest addition to our dairy herd. This one's a little bull calf so he's not going to add to our milk production!"

Beth smiled at her husband. "Charles, this is Randell Cordell." As she paused for a moment Randell thought he detected a look of astonishment come to his face. "Mr. Cordell has returned to Blackberry and has purchased his old cabinet shop back and he will be remodeling our kitchen."

Randell saw a good looking, square-jawed man, who stood about six-foot-tall with broad shoulder, which carried sturdy and hard muscles. He was clad in slightly soiled work clothing, and Randell detected a slight hesitation as Mr. Adams said. "I'm . . . I'm pleased to meet you, Mr. Cordell."

Beth interrupted as she looked at her husband. "Mr. Cordell came to visit me to inquire if I were the one placing flowers on his wife, Louise Cordell's, grave. We've had a pleasant, but frank visit, about all that happened in our little cabin some twenty years ago. "I'll tell you all about it later!"

She herded her children toward the door of the barn. "Come on kids, it'll soon be dark and I'm sure Mr. Cordell needs to be on his way."

The Adams family were all standing in the yard and the kids were waving at him as he drove out of the farmyard. His mind was filled with wonder as he drove back to Blackberry. *What a loving family! And they had treated him with great kindness: much more than he deserved. He must not let them down!*

CHAPTER 8

Helen Bedford

T he following morning Mrs. Herriot made a brief, grim faced, and silent appearance at the breakfast table, her lips pursed, and her eyes averted. When she had deposited the hotcakes, bacon, eggs, syrup, and coffee on the table, she retreated into the confines of the kitchen, the door shut. She did not return.

An oppressive gloom, an ominous silence, had invaded the rooming house, and held it hostage. Randell and Kincaid ate their breakfast without the usual back and forth banter and talk. The silence was stifling. It reminded Randell of a tomb, or library, with everyone moving on tiptoes. Everything had changed. Randell was deeply troubled by the estrangement, and he blamed himself. If he hadn't lied to her, as to his identity, but had been up-front with her, and told her straight-away who he was, and why he had returned to Blackberry, she may have been inclined to accept him. He glanced up from his breakfast plate at the closed kitchen door. The closed door symbolized a hard, impenetrable, wall between him and his landlady. Lying to Mrs. Herriot had been a bad start to his return to Blackberry.

His breakfast finished; Randall walked out onto the porch. Kincaid followed him and spoke when he had shut the door. "I think I've got some good news. I found a rooming-house on the north edge of town. It's a clean place; the rents the same, with two meals a day at the same price, and best of all, its run by a pleasant lady, who goes about with a smile on her face, in contrast to our present dour landlady. I gave my notice to Mrs. Herriot yesterday afternoon. She was not pleased! But I told her there was a price to be paid for sticking her nose into other people's lives. I'm moving my belongings, and typewriter, tomorrow. I'll see you there." He paused and then continued. "How did things go for you at the shop yesterday?"

"Well, I did lose a couple of orders yesterday, due to Mrs. Herriot's talk about town. However, I had a very nice visit yesterday evening with Mrs. Adams, the lady who's placing flowers on my deceased wife's grave. The visit with Mrs. Adams left me feeling some better." He looked at Kincaid. "And thanks for finding new rooms for the two of us. I appreciate it."

He looked across the porch at Kincaid. "I feel bad about this rupture with Mrs. Herriot. I doubt if it would have happened if I had been truthful with her about my identity from the beginning!" He looked back towards the doorway to the rooming house. "She only has one other boarder and I suspect our leaving is going to put her in a financial bind. I hate for that to happen to an old lady!"

"Well, you may be right that our leaving will bring her some financial stress, but remember, she brought it on herself by throwing you out. Decisions and actions have consequences!" He chuckled. "I need to work that principle into the book I'm writing."

Randell went about his work at the cabinet shop with a new eagerness and spirit. He couldn't quite put his finger on what had happened, but he felt the visit with Beth Adams had somehow "cleared the air." and the first step had been taken towards his acceptance in the community. Both he and Mrs. Adams had been honest with each other during their meeting, and that truthfulness had been very beneficial in establishing a good relationship. A marked contrast to his dishonesty with Mrs. Herriot. But despite the rupture with Mrs. Herriot, his heart was full of the possibilities for his future.

Two days later Robert Harrison introduced Randell to a young man. "This is Todd Bascom, a friend who graduated in the same trade school class as I did. He's been working in a cabinet shop in Ely, but it closed a couple of weeks ago. I told him you might put him on here at your shop. He's a hard worker and will do a good job for ya, Mr. Cordell." Randell wasn't sure if his next move was wise, but his optimism continued, and he hired the young man on the spot.

He visited a small office supply shop in Grand Rapids and had some business cards made up and printed, and then he began a routine of visiting homes in the area, for miles around; leaving his business card and telling everyone about his cabinet shop and the work he could do for them. Within two weeks he had picked up several new cabinet and remodeling orders. This increased his confidence, and even the loss of another contract didn't dampen his high spirits. He planned to begin work on the Adams' remodeling project within a few days.

On a pleasant summer day, he had closed the shop at five in the afternoon and was driving along the street near the Blackberry school, when he spotted Helen Bedford as she emerged from the entrance to the school. He had not spoken with her since his visit to the cabin on the day he had arrived in Blackberry. He had also lied to Mrs. Bedford. On an impulse he pulled the pickup to the edge of the road, got out, and stood by the entrance gate to the school yard. He watched her approach with mild trepidation. Would she respond to his lie in the same way Mrs. Herriot had reacted?

When Helen Bedford approached the gate, she stopped a few feet from him and stood silently, looking at him. Randell spoke first. "Good afternoon Mrs. Bedford. I . . . I hope you're doing well?" He fell silent for a moment and was unsure of himself. "Mrs. Bedford, I . . . I need to speak to you about the first time we met at the cabin!"

She continued to appraise him with her hazel eyes, but her face wasn't hard, and then an easy smile graced her face. "Are you Mr. Smith, or Mr. Cordell today?"

He tried to laugh. "Oh, Mrs. Bedford, it's Cordell, I'm . . . I'm sorry I wasn't truthful with you about who I was when I came to the cabin. I shouldn't have done it, but I had just arrived here in Blackberry, and I wasn't sure how people would accept me, and that's why I told you my name was Smith. It was foolish, and wrong, to lie to you!"

She took a step toward the gate. "I understand, Mr. Cordell, and all is forgiven! I'm pleased we've met again, as I've wanted to speak to you concerning another matter."

"You . . . you do! Well, if you need some help on something I'll be pleased to assist you in any way I can!" He looked about and realized the café was only a few blocks away. "I'd be happy to buy you dinner!" He motioned down the street. "We could go to the Blue Goose Café! Their food's pretty good, and I'll buy!"

He held the gate open for her and she smiled at him as she came forward. "I'll accept your kind offer."

They found a corner table, ordered lemonade, and then scanned the little menu. "The meat loaf and the chicken fried steak are both good," he said. "I eat here pretty often."

The waiter returned and took their orders. Randell looked across the table at her. "Mrs. Bedford, I do want to apologize for misleading you when I visited the cabin." She remained silent and he continued. "I'm sure you know by now why I became so emotional and lost my composure when I stood there in the cabin. You've probably visited with Mrs. Adams about me and she probably told you all about my past!"

There was a trace of a smile on her face as she looked across the table at him. "Yes, Beth and I have visited about you a couple of times and she has told me what happened there in the cabin twenty years ago."

His face fell. "It's . . . it's not a pretty story! I feel very bad about how I treated my wife. What I did was terribly wrong!"

"Well, Randell. If I may call you Randell . . ."

"Yes, please do!"

"Well, Randell, we sometimes make some serious mistakes in the decisions we make, and the actions that follow. Your mistakes happened many years ago, and they're best forgotten now, so we don't need to speak of them again." She looked across the table at him. "I understand you're doing fine with your cabinet shop, and everything I hear about you now is very good."

"Thank you, Mrs. Bedford. Your very kind to forgive me."

They both fell silent for a long moment as they ate their evening meal. Her hazel eyes, bright face, and deep brown hair stirred feelings and emotions within him, which had been absent from his heart for many years. As he looked across the table at her she seemed to be filled with a calmness and serenity he wished he could share. He broke the silence. "Let's change the subject. You know a great deal about me, but I don't know much of anything about you." He leaned forward onto the table. "Tell me about yourself. I know you're a schoolteacher, but I'd like to know more!"

She smiled and there was happiness in her eyes. "Oh Randell, there's not much to tell. I grew up in Minneapolis, took a two-year teaching course, married, and then became a widow, five years into our marriage."

"I'm sorry! What happened to your husband? How did he die?"

A cloud crossed her face. "It was polio! It came onto him during the summer of thirty-five, eleven years ago. It was very serious, and the iron lung couldn't save him. He was gone within a few months."

I'm sorry," he said. "It must have been very hard for you?"

"Yes, it has been difficult for me. I loved him very much! But the passing of the years, and teaching here in Blackberry, have eased my pain."

"I believe you said you've lived in the cabin for three years. Is that when you came to Blackberry?"

"Yes, a friend told me of a teaching position that was open here: teaching the fourth grade. I felt I needed a change; that I needed to get away from my old home and all the memories of my husband. I took the job somewhat on the spur of the moment but have not regretted it. Blackberry's a nice and peaceful place, and it's been good for me. I think I'll stay here as long as the school will have me!"

And then she laughed. "I almost forgot. I told you, there at the school gate, I wanted to speak to you about something."

He leaned forward again. "I'm sorry, I forgot as well. What do you want to talk to me about?"

She was smiling, but there was a note of seriousness in her voice. "Well, you're a carpenter and a cabinet maker, and I thought . . . .. Oh, Mr. Cordell, I shouldn't ask you to do this, but it's for my kids, my students. You see, their desks are all old, worn out, and badly scratched. They all need to be replaced! But the school district doesn't have the money to purchase new desks, and I don't know when they will!" She leaned forward across the table and there was an urgency in her voice. "Mr. Cordell, could you build some new desks for my fourth-grade children before school begins this fall?"

He stifled a laugh, but he did smile. "Of course, Mrs. Bedford, I'll build some new desks for your kids. How many do you need?"

Her eyes were beaming now. "Oh, thank you, Mr. Cordell! I'll be forever grateful to you, and . . . and I know my kids will be as well! They'll be thrilled to have new desks. It's summer now, and school won't begin until shortly after the first of September, so I won't need them until then. Based on the records which I've been given, for the next school year, it appears I'll have ten or eleven students, so If you could make eleven or twelve desks, which would be great! And then she paused, and her face clouded. "But . . . but the school can't pay you as they don't have the money."

He did laugh now. "Don't worry about the money Mrs. Bradford. Your kids will have new desks when school starts this fall!"

Helen glanced at her watch. "Goodness, it's nearly seven and I have a friend to see before I return to the cabin. "I must be going, or I'll keep her waiting." She looked across the table at Randell and her face carried a smile. "Thank you, Mr. Cordell, for the dinner, for the conversation, and most of all, for agreeing to build new desks for my kids!"

He helped her from her chair. "If you're going to be at the school sometime tomorrow I'll come by and take some measurements, so that the desks will be the correct size for the kids. I'll have them for you before school begins."

He walked her to her car and then stood beside the road, watching as she drove away. Despite his lying to her she had treated him with respect and courtesy and had even requested his assistance in building new desks for her school children. He was pleased she had asked him for his help. He stood, looking along the street. He had learned that helping others was always better than taking from others.

CHAPTER 9

The Twins

The Adams twins, Morton and Marie, peered through the split rail fence and across the pasture. They could see the baby calf, and its mother, standing on the far side of the pasture near the edge of the trees. The mother cow grazed along the edge of the meadow, as the calf frolicked in circles about her. This was not her first calf and she was content to let her latest baby run and explore. There was much to explore as everything was new to the little bull calf.

Morton crawled through the fence and looked back at his sister. "Come on! Let's go pet the baby calf!" Marie hesitated. "I . . . I don't think we should! Mommy said for us to stay in the yard and ride our trikes. We . . . better not!"

The twin's father, Charles, and their older brother, LeRoy, had left after breakfast to drive to Grand Rapids. Charles had said to his wife as they prepared to leave. "We'll be gone all day and into the evening. In addition to the cattle and chicken feed, I need to purchase, I want to go to the implement dealer and look over their new tractors. And then I think I'll drive to Deer River to visit with the man who has the bailer for sale. So, it'll be late by the time we return home." He glanced across the seat at his oldest son. "LeRoy and I will have a fun day picking up supplies and looking at farm equipment!"

Beth Adams was busy with her weekly laundry in the small building, which stood adjacent to the house. A Briggs and Stratton gasoline engine powered her washing machine. Ilene was in the living room playing with her kitchen set and dolly.

Randell Cordell and his newest employee, Todd Bascom, were hard at work in the kitchen. It was their third day into the remodeling project. Todd stood back and surveyed a newly installed cabinet. "Wow, it sure looks nice Mr. Cordell! I'll bet Mrs. Adams will love her new kitchen!"

"I sure hope so," replied Randell. "We're going to take our time and make sure we do a first-rate job; not only for Beth, but on every job, we take on. If we concentrate on quality, I believe we'll have all the work we can handle."

Todd looked at his employer. "I . . . I sure do enjoy working for you Mr. Cordell. It's great to turn out first rate cabinets and see the smiles on the faces of the ladies!"

The six-year-old boy, Morton, reached through the fence and tugged at his sister's hand. "Ah, come on, it'll be fun to pet the calf, and we'll be back before Mommy even misses us!" The girl, Marie, glanced back toward the house, hesitated for another moment, and then climbed through the fence. Their eager eyes were on the baby calf, as they made their way across the meadow.

The new-born calf fascinated the two children. It would be great fun to pet him. His black and white fur was so shiny, and he was so cute when he looked at them with his big, dark, eyes, and his ears pointed forward.

The little calf stood, stiff-legged, with his nostrils flared, and his tail up, as the two children approached. When the children were about ten feet away he backed up a couple of steps and let out a little snort. The children advanced slowly; their hands stretched forward. If the baby calf would just stand still they would be able to pet him! Marie hung back a little, as she was afraid of the mother cow, who stood nearby. She glanced at the calf's mother. She was awfully big!

72

Morton continued toward the new-born calf; his hand outstretched in anticipation of stroking the soft fur. Suddenly, the calf snorted again, and with its tail held high in the air, bolted around to the other side of its mother. He stood with his eyes wide, and ears pointed forward, as he looked under his mother's belly at the children.

Morton's face was downcast as he turned to his sister. "Ah baby." He always called her baby. "Ah baby, he's afraid of us and won't let us pet him. I . . . I guess we better go back to the house."

As he turned from the cow, and calf, he heard his sister exclaim. "Look . . . look, see the yellow butterfly! Isn't it pretty; and so big! I'll . . . I'll catch it!"

The large yellow and black butterfly fluttered away from the children, dancing from bush to bush, and flower to flower, as the boy and girl raced in hot pursuit. They were in the trees now and the butterfly continued to fly, just beyond their reach, deeper and deeper into the forest of northern Minnesota. And then the butterfly just disappeared and was gone. The children stopped and looked about in all directions. "Where . . . where did it go?" exclaimed Marie.

"I . . . I don't know!" There was a forlorn look on Morton's face. "It's just gone!" I . . . I guess we better go back home."

The children turned and began to walk through the trees, and then Morton saw the bunny rabbit, as it hopped into view from behind a bush. The little rabbit stopped, its nose twitching, as it sniffed the air. Morton walked slowly toward the rabbit. The little bunny was so cute. Perhaps he would catch it and take it home for a pet! Slowly he advanced, one slow tip-toe step after another. He was within a few feet of the little rabbit when it began to hop away; not too fast, but just fast enough to stay ahead of the little boy and girl. It hopped faster now, and the twins ran through the forest, and around, and through the trees and bushes, in hot pursuit of the little, furry, rabbit. The twins were laughing and giggling as they chased the little rabbit. This was fun! And then the bunny dived under a large bush, and into a hole in the ground, and was suddenly gone.

73

"Ah, it's gone," exclaimed Morton. "I wanted it for a pet!" He knelt at the spot where the bunny had disappeared and pushed the bush back, but all he could see was the hole the bunny had disappeared into. "I guess it's gone into that hole under the bush. That's where the bunny lives; it's his house." He stared at the hole for a moment more, and then stood to his feet. As he stood up a bare branch of the bush caught on his shirt, and he frowned as he pulled the branch away from his shirt.

He turned to his sister. "I . . . I guess we better go back to our house, or Mommy will be upset with us." He turned and began to walk through the woods, past trees, and bushes. Marie trudged slowly along behind him; her little legs were tired from chasing the butterfly and the rabbit.

The two children walked for several minutes and then Morton stopped and looked about. Suddenly, everything looked the same to him. There were trees, and bushes, and shrubs everywhere, in every direction, and they all looked alike. Where was the pasture, and the cows, and the farm? All he could see were trees and bushes, and suddenly his eyes were big, and he was afraid. Marie came to his side and took his hand. She looked up at him and her chin was quivering. "Boy, which . . . which way is our house?"

"I . . . I'm not sure. I . . . I think it's that way," as he pointed ahead into the trees. He turned and looked about. There were trees and shrubs in every direction, and no pathway.

Marie was struggling now to hold back the tears. "Oh boy! Are we lost?" she whispered.

Morton stood very still, his heart pounding, his eyes darting about the forest. He was frightened. And then he saw a tree. It was a crooked tree, with a funny bend about halfway up the trunk. The tree looked vaguely familiar. Had they run past it as they had chased the bunny? His heart full of desperation, he grasped his sister's hand. "Let's go this way," he said, as he pointed past the crooked tree.

74

The two children trudged on through the forest. On and on they walked past trees and bushes, which all looked alike. Morton was sure they would soon come to the pasture where the mother cow and calf, and the dairy cows grazed, and then they would be able to see the house and barn across the pasture. He looked longingly ahead as they plodded on through the never-ending forest. His legs were heavy as he swatted away a cloud of mosquitos buzzing about his head. He turned to his sister, who tagged along beside him, her lips quivering, and dirty tears staining her cheeks. "Let's . . . let's sit down baby. I'm tired!"

"I'm tired too," she murmured. "Oh, boy, when . . . when are we going to get home? I . . . I don't like all of these trees!"

A fallen log lay nearby and the two children climbed up onto it and sat down. Morton looked in every direction, but all he could see were trees and bushes and he could hardly hold back the tears. He looked at his twin sister. "Oh baby, I . . . I think . . . maybe, we're lost! I . . . I don't know which way to go!"

Suddenly Marie jumped from the log and slapped at her leg, and an ant fell to the ground. "Ouch," she hollered. "An ant bit me!" She looked at her brother. "I don't like it here. Let's walk some more. Maybe we can find the pasture and our house!"

Slowly the children resumed walking through the forest, looking forward, hoping to see the meadow. All they saw were trees; lots, and lots of trees. Suddenly Morton gripped Marie's hand and pointed with his other hand, as he whispered. "It's a bear!" From two hundred feet away, the animal stared at the children with dark, searching eyes.

"Oh baby, I'm . . . I'm scared," Morton muttered. He glanced about. Where could they hide from the bear? He noticed a small, four-foot-high rocky outcrop to their left. A large bush grew next to the rock shelf. Gripping his sister's hand, he pulled her around the bush, and then they saw a small overhang, at the base of the rock outcrop. Here was a hiding place! Dry leaves were scattered about the floor of the little enclosure. The children quickly slumped down onto the leaves and leaned against the back wall of the little enclosure.

Morton stared toward the bush concealing their little hideaway. He was sure they were really lost. He didn't know the way home, and he didn't know what to do! They were lost, and a bear was after them! He wished they had never left the farmyard. He should have listened to his sister! His head slumped forward, and he rubbed his eyes with his little fists, as sobs racked his little shoulders.

Marie reached and placed her hand on his knee. "It's . . . it's all right boy. Mommy will find us! She'll come soon!"

Morton's voice was barely a whisper. "I . . . I hope so!"

The two children didn't realize it, but the bear was leaving the area as fast as he could run. He was just a yearling and very unsure of himself. He had seen the children. They were humans and he knew he should always avoid humans. He was moving away as fast as his four legs would carry him.

The two little children sat, slumped against the small rock wall at the back of their little hideaway. Marie whispered again. "Mommy will find us soon!" Slowly she laid her head on her brother's shoulder and he encircled her with his arm and pulled her close.

The twins were inseparable, and in the stress of being lost, they instinctively clung to each other. "I . . . I hope so," he whispered back to her. They were very tired from chasing the butterfly and rabbit, and trudging through the forest. Slowly their heads began to nod.

Beth Adams was breathing hard as she burst into the kitchen. "Mr. Cordell, can you please come and help me? I . . . I can't find Morton and Marie. The last time I looked they were playing in the front yard and riding their trikes. The trikes are there, but I've looked all about the yard, and buildings, and I can't find them. They sometimes play hid-and–seek from me, and make it hard for me to find them, but they usually giggle, which gives them away."

A sudden fear gripped Randell. They were just little kids! He dropped his tools. "Sure, Mrs. Adams, we'll help you find them!" He turned to Todd. "Come and help; we'll all look for these youngsters!"

As they stepped out the front door Beth looked at Randell, and her eyes were filled with alarm. "I sometimes find them asleep somewhere in the barn, or in one of the sheds, but . . . but, I've looked everywhere, and I can't find them!"

They stood in the yard for a moment as Randell surveyed the farm and its buildings. There were a lot of places two little kids could hide. He looked at Beth. "You stay here with Ilene; Todd and I will go through all the buildings. We'll see if we can locate your two kids!"

An hour later Beth found the two men standing near the barn. Randell looked up and then walked to Beth. "I'm sorry, Mrs. Adams, but we've gone through all the buildings and looked in all of the machinery and have been unable to find them. In addition, I drove out the driveway and along the county road both ways. I even went as far as the little cabin and checked with Mrs. Bedford on the off chance they had walked the mile to the cabin, but there's no sign of your kids!" Randell paused and looked at the anguished face of Beth. "I'm worried Mrs. Adams, it'll be dark before long!"

He stood silent, as he looked about the farm, his mind a whirl of emotions, questions, and possibilities. He had to find those two children! Where should he look for them? Where were they? Had some harm come to them?

His eyes roam about the farmyard again, and then beyond to the pasture and the far trees. Where were these two little children? He noticed the cows grazing in the pasture and along the tree line at the far edge of the meadow, and then he saw the cow and baby calf standing a little apart from the rest of the cattle. He turned back to Beth. "Beth, do you suppose the twins may have gone into the pasture to get close to the new calf, perhaps to see if they could pet it, and then wandered into the woods and became lost?"

77

Beth stared across the meadow. Her face full of anguish. "Oh .
. . oh, I hope not!"

Randell stood, his eyes sweeping the meadow and far tree line.
"Beth, I'm going to take Todd and go across the pasture and into the
trees and search back in the woods for a good distance."

Her face was filled with fear, as she exclaimed, "Yes, please do!"

"Beth, in the meantime, I suggest you telephone the sheriff in
Grand Rapids and see if he, and some men, can come to your home.
They can help us search the entire area, including the forest on all
sides of your farm. He needs to come as soon as possible. I'd sure hate
for the kids to be lost in the woods overnight!"

She stared at him with wide and frightened eyes; like a deer
caught in the high beam of a car. "Yes . . . yes, I'll telephone the sheriff.
I'll do it right now!"

Randell reached and placed his hand on Beth's shoulder, and
he tried to fill his voice with conviction and certainty. "Beth, I'll do my
best to find your two babies!"

Some of the anguish left her face, and her voice was barely
audible. "Thank you, Randell!" She started toward the house, and then
turned back. "After I telephone the sheriff I think I'll take Ilene to the
cabin, and leave her with Helen, and then come back here. As you said,
it'll be dark before long and I'll get a couple of lanterns filed with oil
and then carry them across the pasture to the tree line. If it gets dark
and you haven't found the children, you come and get the lanterns. I'll
be waiting with them!"

"That's a good idea, Beth!" He turned to Todd. "Come on, let's
go and search back in the woods on the other side of the pasture!"

The two men walked across the pasture and entered the trees:
a thicket of pine, spruce, aspen, and brush. The northern half of
Minnesota was covered with a heavy forest of trees. The locals referred
to these forests as "the woods." The two men spread out as they
advanced into the woods. Each began to call out "Morton, Marie, can

you hear me?" They walked deeper into the forest, calling the names of the twins as they advanced. They kept this up for well over an hour, but no answering call came back to them. The bear did hear them, and he turned and ran again. *Humans everywhere; could a bear have no peace to find an evening meal of berries!*

Dusk was falling, and the forest was now filled with darkness as the two men made their way back to the edge of the pasture. They could see Beth making her way across the pasture, carrying two lighted lanterns. Beth held up a lantern and in the light cast by the lantern Randell could see that her face was a mask of fear and anxiety. "You . . . you didn't find them?"

"I'm afraid not, but . . . but we'll keep trying!"

"I . . . I telephoned the sheriff and he said he would get several men and be here within an hour or two." Beth stood in silence, her eyes darting about. She was having trouble controlling her breathing and was afraid she would break down in tears again. She looked at Randell "What . . . what are we going to do? My babies: we must find them! They can't be left all alone, all night, in the woods! Oh Mr. Cordell, we must find them!"

Randell took the two lanterns from Beth and handed one to Todd. He stood silent for a moment, as he surveyed the tree line where the heavy forest began. "We may be looking in the wrong area. I think we'll move a little further west and then search that part of the forest. It'll be slow going in the dark!"

He looked at Beth, and then on an impulse of compassion, and understanding, he put his arm around her shoulders and pulled her close for a moment. She burst into sobs and buried her head in his shoulder. She continued to sob for several moments and then she lifted her head, took a step back, and wiped the tears away with her sleeve. "I'm . . . I'm sorry Randell," she whispered. "The thought of my babies lost in the forest is just too much for me!"

"It's okay. I understand!" He glanced across the meadow toward the house. "I suggest you return to the house and wait for the sheriff."

"Yes . . . yes, I'll do that."

The two men walked along the tree line for some distance and then stopped. Randell turned to Todd. "Let's spread out and go into the woods here, perhaps we'll have better luck this time." Once again, they advanced into the heavy forest.

The sun had long since fled below the western horizon and the forest was now filled with darkness and gloom. The lanterns cast only a faint light into the inky blackness, which pushed in against them from every direction. Carefully, and slowly, they walked into the darkness, as they called out the names of the twins. They heard nothing, except the chirp of crickets, as they played their nightly music, and the occasional lonesome hoot of an owl.

They had walked for several minutes, when suddenly, Randell's heart caught, as the beam from the lantern sent back a reflection to him. Something that didn't belong in a forest was lying on the ground near a bush. He stepped forward and knelt. It was a button, perhaps a button from a boy's shirt. A button was out of place here in the forest! Had the children passed this way! And then he smiled as he noticed the rabbit burrow dug into the base of the bush. Perhaps they had chased the rabbit here to its burrow? Hope sprang up in his heart as they pushed on into the black of the night. His voice rang loud in the dark and oppressive silence of the north woods of Minnesota. "Marie, Morton, can you hear me!" The only sound was the echoing voice of Todd, as he called out the same message.

Beth walked slowly across the pasture, her footsteps heavy and weary; her mind filled with terror for her babies. She entered the house and went into the kitchen, sat down at the table, and buried her head in her hands. Once again sobs racked her body and tears flowed freely down her cheeks. The thought of her two youngest children, wandering lost in the dense darkness of the forest, pierced her heart with uncontrollable fear.

Too distressed to remain in one place for long, she left the kitchen and walked through the house. She paused at the chest which sat along the side of the living room and her eyes fell on a recent photo of her family. The twins stood, beaming up at the photographer. Marie was dressed in a blue skirt and Morton in blue pants, and each were wearing matching white shirts with blue trimmings on the collars and sleeves. She grabbed the picture and held it close to her breast, her head bowed with fear and her eyes filled with tears. How had she let this happen? It was her responsibility, as a mother, to always keep track of her children. If they came to any harm, how would she ever live with herself, or how could she ever face her husband again, and her other two children?

She heard a car drive into the yard. Perhaps it was the sheriff, or Charles and LeRoy returning? They should be home anytime. She dreaded to face her husband and tell him the twins were lost. It was too awful to even think of telling him. She steeled herself and walked out the front door. Ilene came bounding from the car to her. "Mommy, have you found Morton and Marie!" Beth knelt and clasped her daughter close. "No, . . . no, not yet, but Mr. Cordell and Todd are in the forest looking for them." She tried to put conviction into her voice. "They . . . they'll find them!"

When Beth stood up Helen drew her close and held her tight as the tears came once again. When the sobs ended she held Beth at arm's length and looked into her anguished and tear-stained face. "I thought it best for me to come to your home and be with you. Let's go inside."

Beth hesitated, and then she said, "I . . . I can't just set in the house. I must do something!" She paused and looked at Helen. "We have another lantern. I'll light it and let's walk back across the pasture and wait for Mr. Cordell and Todd."

In the little cave Marie slowly raised her head from her brother's shoulder. She opened her eyes and stared into the darkness. She could see nothing, but she had heard something. Some sound had awakened her! She nudged her brother and whispered. "Boy, I . . . I think I heard something!" The two children sat in hushed silence. Listening! Marie whispered. "Oh boy, maybe the bear has come back!" It was very dark in the small cave as the two little children huddled in deathly silence, hardly breathing. And then they heard the cry, "Morton, Marie, can you hear me?"

Marie turned to her brother. "It's . . . it's not Mommy! It's a man! Oh, boy, I'm . . . I'm scared!"

Several moments passed as they sat, staring into the void of black. And then they heard the voice again, and it was closer now. "Marie, Morton, this is Mr. Cordell; can you hear me?"

Morton jumped to his feet and tugged at Marie. "It's Mr. Cordell; he'll take us to Mommy!" The darkness was dense, and they could barely see as they stepped out of their little enclosure and past the big bush. They stood just beyond the bush, gripping each other's hands, as they stared, with hopeful eyes, into the gloom of the night.

Suddenly, Morton pointed. "Baby; see the light!" It seemed to be a long way off and very small, but Morton was sure it was a lantern, like his Daddy used at night in the barn. He yelled as loud as he could. "Mr. Cordell, help . . . help us! We're over here!" And then both children, boy and girl, were yelling at the top of their lungs. Within moments Randell Cordell had a child in each arm and they were clinging to him with a death grip.

The two women and the little girl, Ilene, stood at the edge of the woods. The flickering light of the lantern cast long, dark, shadows into the forest. Beth shivered. It was a little chilly, but she knew she was shaking with fear. Helen stood at her side, holding Ilene's hand as they peered into the dark forest. Beth's voice was filled with anguish, as she cried, "Oh, Helen, what . . . what will I do if they can't find my babies?"

82

Helen moved closer to Beth. "Don't lose hope Beth. They'll find your twins! Just have faith!" Silently, the two women, and Ilene, stood, at the edge of the woods, waiting, watching, and hoping! And then Beth's heart jumped as she detected a faint light flickering through the darkness of the forest. And then she could make out the light from two lanterns. It was the two men, Todd, and Randell, walking through the trees, toward her and Helen. She watched, barely breathing, as the two lights grew larger, and nearer. And then her heart was bursting. Each man was carrying something in his arms! Yes . . . yes, she could see now; each man was carrying one of her babies! Mr. Cordell was carrying Marie and Todd was carrying Morton. She started to rush forward, but Helen restrained her until the men walked out of the trees and into the pasture.

Beth ran forward, and Randell placed Marie into her outstretched arms. His voice was full of warmth and compassion, as he said, "We found your babies, Mrs. Adams!"

Beth was beside herself with relief and joy as she smothered her daughter in hugs and kisses and then she knelt and took Morton into her arms. Morton looked at his mother and his voice quivered as he said. "We got lost Mommy, but Mr. Cordell found us!"

Marie tugged at her mother's dress. "When we got lost I told boy that Mommy would find us, but it was Mr. Cordell who found us, but that's okay, he's a nice man, and I like him a lot."

Beth looked up and she could see Randell's face in the light from the lantern as he stood looking down at her and the twins, a broad smile spread across his face. Beth slowly rose to her feet, as she held the hands of her twins. She took a step forward, as she looked at him with tears in her happy eyes. "Yes, Marie, he is a nice man, a very nice man! And . . . and I like him a lot too!"

CHAPTER 10

Mrs. Herriot

The brisk, cool days of spring gave way to the long, and warm, days of summer with their never-ending daylight and sun. The profusion of colorful flowers continued to bloom in the yards and gardens of Blackberry, and few would fade before the advent of fall.

The coming of summer brought a whirlwind of busy activity for Randell Cordell and his two employees. Only one contract was cancelled by a lady who held his past against him, and he was very pleased to have picked up several new cabinet and remodeling contracts. His rescue of the Adams twins was widely heralded throughout the town and community, and congratulations from people he knew, and even from complete strangers were frequent. Randell always responded to these accolades by replying that anyone would have done the same, but his actions, in rescuing the children, did much to enhance his standing in the community. From that day forward, many of the people of the area saw Randell Cordell in a new, and different, light, and much of the old stigma seemed to have faded away. In addition, it seemed to Randell that his cabinet business began to pick up shortly after the rescue of the twins.

Randell continued to live in the boarding house he, and Kincaid, had moved into following the tiff with Mrs. Herriot. Kincaid continued to spend long hours each day pecking away on his typewriter, as he spun out his novel. It was taking much more time to complete than he had expected because of all the new characters, he kept inserting into the plot. He had told the lady who ran the boarding house. "I like to write my books while living in the area where the story is taking place. It helps me pick up on the culture and personalities of the local people." However, it seemed to him that Blackberry, Minnesota had more unusual characters than most small towns, and it was taxing all his writing skills to work these diverse personalities into the plot of his book. But the writing wasn't a bore, in fact, it was quite interesting, even exciting.

Randell didn't intend to continue to live in a rooming house indefinitely. In fact, he had come across a house, located near the edge of town, and on the shore of a small lake, which had caught his attention. The owner had told him he was considering selling the home sometime during the next year. If his cabinet business continued brisk Randell intended to seriously consider purchasing the property.

By chance, he drove by Mrs. Herriot's rooming house on a warm summer day. She was in the front yard, pruning shears in her hands, straining to prune some of her unruly shrubs. On an impulse he pulled the pickup to a stop, got out and approached her. Several months had passed since he had lied to her about his identity, and he felt he should offer his apologies to her, again, for this deception. Would she accept his attempt at reconciliation, or reject him?

She ceased her pruning and watched him as he advanced across the lawn. He was relieved that she didn't greet him with hard, and hostile, eyes. He tipped his hat. "Good morning Mrs. Herriot. I've been intending to come by and see you."

She looked at him with eyes that seemed to be filled with hurt and pain. "I'm . . . I'm pleased, Mr. Cordell, that you have come by. I've wanted to speak to you."

"Mrs. Herriot, I am very sorry that I lied to you when . . ."

She broke in. "Mr. Cordell, there's no need to apologize to me, as I'm the one who was at fault and should offer an apology. I . . . I shouldn't have called you a womanizer and murderer. Such language was very harsh and unkind of me! What you did happened many years ago, and I shouldn't have been judgmental of you, either for your actions those years ago, or for using an assumed name when you returned to the community. I should have been much more understanding and forgiving!"

As she stepped toward him, the trimming shears slipped slowly from her hands and dropped to the ground. Her face was filled with distress as she spoke. "Mr. Cordell, it's difficult for me to admit this to you, but my past is not as free of mistakes as my harsh words to you implied. For you see, Mr. Cordell, I . . . I also have a past that I'm not proud of, and wish I could undo, and make right. I should have remembered my own mistakes before I spoke harshly of you! Unfortunately, I have become a grumpy, and unhappy, old woman, and it came to the forefront that morning at the breakfast table!"

She stared, with shadowed eyes, down at the ground for a long moment, before looking back up at him. "Over forty years ago, I left a good husband, and a little boy, and married another man, who made a lot of starry-eyed promises to me, and who I thought was much more exciting and appealing than my husband. But the man turned out to be a fraud and a cheat, and of course, the marriage didn't last. It was a terrible mistake to leave a loving husband and my little boy! What foolishness, especially for a mother! And I have only seen my boy a few times since then. It was a very bad mistake! A tragedy I've had to live with all these many years!"

Randell was shocked that she would make this personal confession to him, and he was uneasy as he muttered. "I . . . I'm sorry about what happened to your marriage and that you haven't seen your son."

"Thank you for your consideration, Mr. Cordell. As you can see, I should have been much more considerate and understanding of your past mistakes."

"Mrs. Herriot, I accept your apology and I'm very sorry that we got started off on the wrong foot when I first came back to Blackberry. I feel it was mostly my fault, and I do want to apologize for lying to you." His voice was filled with emotion as he continued. "Oh, Mrs. Herriot, I . . . I think that many of us have made some terrible mistakes we wish we could undo and make right. I guess that's . . . that's one of the reasons I returned here to Blackberry. I . . . I hoped I could do something to overcome those dreadful things I did when I lived here before!"

She looked at Randell with a haunting gaze, and her eyes were filled with sadness, as she said. "When my second marriage ended my first husband had remarried and had custody of our son. It was impossible for me to make amends for my terrible error, and I have had to live with that awful mistake for these many years. It haunts me to this day! I never married again, and have no children, and am all alone in this world." She looked up toward her home. "This rooming house is all that I have. And . . . and it's not doing very well . . .."

Randell stood in silence as he observed her anguished face. "I'm sorry, Mrs. Herriot, about the mistake you made and for losing a good husband, and . . . and especially your little boy. I wish there were something I could do to help!"

Mrs. Herriot had regained some of her composure. "There's nothing you, or anyone else can do. It's too late now and many, many, years have passed. What's done is done, and it can't be undone. It'll go with me to the grave!" She paused and looked at her boarding house and then back at Randell. "What I need now are some boarders. I only got one! If I don't get more I'm going to be in financial trouble before long!"

Randell stood in silence for a long moment as he looked at the elderly lady. This conversation with her had not gone at all as he had envisioned. Her face was filled with sadness and pain, and in the warmth of the afternoon her forehead was covered with beads of perspiration. He was struck with how tired and worn she looked.

His gaze swept across the shabby rooming house and yard. It was close to becoming the neighborhood eye sore. He should assist this old woman! He turned back to her. "Mrs. Herriot, my rents paid up at the boarding house, on the north end of town, for five more days and then I think I'll just move back into your rooming house. That is if you'll have me? And besides, your cooking is better than what I'm getting now!"

He took a step forward, stooped and picked up the pruning shears. "In the meantime, let me finish trimming these shrubs and bushes for you." He looked about the yard. "I can see you could use a gardener to mow the lawn, spruce up the flower beds, and someone to shovel the snow from the drive and walks when winter comes on." He looked up and surveyed the house and then smiled at the old lady. "Your rooming house could also use a little fixing up and a new paint job, perhaps a light grey with white trim. That would look nice! I'll bet a new paint job would even attract some additional boarders for you?" He had a big smile on his face as he continued. "I think one of my employees, and I, will work during the evenings and on weekends, and we can have the house repaired and painted in a short while. I think I'll just take on those jobs, and whatever else you need done here at your rooming house, to keep the place in decent shape, inside and out." He laughed and smiled at her. "In exchange for lunch now and then if you don't mind?"

She stood, staring at him. Astonishment splashed across her face! "You would do these things for me? Especially after all the things I've said about you, all around town! And . . . and I don't have the money to pay you! It'll take more than a few lunches to make things right!"

He smiled at her. "There will be no charge for our labor and you can pay me for the paint and materials when you can afford it. Until then it's on me; that is if you don't mind!"

She drew herself up to her full five and half feet of height as she said, "I don't mind a bit. I'll have lunch waiting for you in half an hour." She laughed as she turned to return to her house. "And mind, don't you be late!"

Randell watched her march into the house. It was nice to see the old lady smile, and laugh, and walk with a spring in her step. He attacked the shrub with the shears. As he worked he began to understand that as he helped others with their needs and problems -- such as rescuing the twins and aiding this elderly lady -- he was also helping himself recover from the wounds and trauma of his own past.

That evening Randell cornered Mr. Kincaid. "I've got some local color, background, and personality for you to include in your book. You'll need to disguise the identity of the individual very well, and never tell anyone what I'm about to tell you, but it may be something you'll want to work into your book." He then filled Kincaid in on the conversation with Mrs. Herriot earlier in the day. "Your right, she's not as pure as the driven snow, but it's all in the distant past. She's an old lady now and she needs some help. I'm going to move back to her rooming house when my rents up here. I'm going to try and help her some with repairing and painting her boardinghouse, inside and out, and keeping up the yard. Hopefully, I can make things a little easier for her in her old age." He placed his hand on Kincaid's shoulder. It's something I can do to make amends for my own past mistakes." He shook his head. "It's a strange world isn't it? I've made a new friend in Mrs. Herriot!"

He paused, and his face took on a serious note. "You know, there's something to be learned here. The Good Book teaches us that if we treat others as we would like to be treated, most of the problems in this world can be solved!"

Kincaid was shaking with laughter. "Wow, I think I just got some more good material for my novel! I may never get this book finished, and it will probably be too long for anyone to read!"

CHAPTER 11

The Old Man

Randell eased the heavily loaded pickup along the highway between Grand Rapids and Blackberry. The bed of the pickup was heavily loaded with top grade pine, spruce, and oak lumber. Within a few weeks the lumber would be transformed into beautiful cabinets. He held his speed to thirty-five miles an hour and tried to avoid the few potholes scattered along the road. He didn't want to blowout a tire or break a spring.

He had driven into Grand Rapids early that morning and signed a contract to build and install the kitchen and bath cabinets in the homes the Pierson Construction Company were building on the outskirts of Grand Rapids. The war was over and there was a mini housing boom going on. It seemed as if all the returning soldiers had married, were having babies, and needed a place to live. Ralph Pierson had walked into Cordell's shop yesterday and had stayed for nearly two hours, reviewing house plans and cabinet designs with him. "We're building a variety of quality houses, at affordable prices, for the returning veterans, and the wives love well-built, attractive, cabinets. We've found that nice cabinets sell houses!"

He had smiled at Randell as he looked up from the floor plan of a house. "Mr. Cordell, I've picked up a number of good reports on the quality of your work, so I decided to come and see your shop and review our cabinet designs with you. I like what I see, and if you're satisfied with the pricing, then if you'll come up to my office in Grand Rapids tomorrow we can sign the contract and get the ball rolling. How does that sound?"

Cordell had been a little stunned and had instinctively run his hand through his hair and stood to his feet. It was a large contract: kitchen and bath cabinets for over seventy-five homes! Pierson had said they were planning on building four to six homes a month, depending upon demand and the availability of labor and carpenters. "We're going to work hard to get many of the homes up and closed in before winter sets in, so we can do the inside finish work, and you can install the cabinets, during the cold, and inclement, winter weather."

His head had cleared, and he had reached across his desk and shook Pierson's hand with a firm grip. "It's a deal! I'll be in your office first thing in the morning!"

He was now on his return trip to Blackberry and his mind continued to be filled with astonishment at his good fortune in landing this large contract. Upon signing the contract, he had immediately driven to the lumber yard and purchased the load of lumber. With the signing of this contract, he would need to put on some additional help; at least one seasoned cabinet man, and he would like to find an older man to keep the shop swept and tidy. These were his first priorities.

He leaned back in the seat, as the pickup continued along the highway, and his mind roamed over the past few months, He had arrived in Blackberry in early spring with a vague, and uncertain, hope of turning his life around. An aspiration that the future offered something better for him than the pain and heartache, which had filled most of his life over the past twenty years. Beyond that ambiguous hope there had been no real plan as to how he was to accomplish this turnaround in his life. In a startling turn of events, he had purchased his old cabinet shop. And even more surprising, the volume of business had been very good, even before signing the contract today.

Sure, he and his two men never cut any corners and worked very hard to turn out high quality cabinets, and he was sure that accounted for much of the growth in his business. Word of mouth was the best advertising! But there seemed to be more at play here than attention to quality control. He sensed that the people of the town had forgiven him for his past indiscretions, and they now accepted him as a member of the community, but what had brought about this gracious acceptance?

He smiled to himself as he drove the pickup along the road. A few days ago, the lady who had stormed into his shop, and had told him, in no uncertain terms, that she wouldn't do business with a womanizer and murder, had suddenly appeared in his office. Randell had offered her a chair, and with downcast eyes, she had looked across his desk at him. "Ah . . . Mr. Cordell, ya may remember I got my deposit back from ya and took my work to a cabinet man in Grand Rapids. Well, he built and installed the cabinets, but it's a right poor job. I . . . I need for ya to come and see if ya can sort of fix the mistakes he made. Can ya do that? I . . . I'll pay ya for yer troubles!"

Randell had assured the lady he would come to her home, that very afternoon, and look over the cabinets and see what could be done to fix the problems. "Oh good," she had exclaimed. And then she had looked across the desk at him. "Mr. Cordell, I'm right sorry about how I treated ya when I came here to your shop and cancelled my order. Mrs. Herriot had told me about your leaving your wife and running off with another woman, and all. I . . . I think I came on too strong and shouldn't have judged ya for what happened all those years ago!"

She fell silent for a moment and then her eyes brightened, as she continued. "Mr. Cordell, everybody I speak with tells me you're a real fine man! I heard about your rescuing them sweet little Adams twins, who was lost, at night, in the woods. Everybody is talkin' about it! And . . . and now we all can see that your fixin' up, and paintin' Mrs. Herriot's rooming house. And she told me you won't take any money for doing it. She says you've treated her mighty fine, especially after all the bad things she said about ya, an orderin' ya to leave her boarding house. I'm askin' for yer forgiveness for the things I said about ya!"

He had smiled across the desk at the lady. "All is forgiven and forgotten!" She had left with a smile on her face.

He had recently finished building the school desks for Helen Bedford's pupils. Helen, and the school officials, had been lavish in their praise of the sparkling new desks. The head of the school board had even told him they would somehow find the money to pay him. Randell had replied, that if they could reimburse him for the lumber and hardware, it was all he needed, the rest was a donation to the school. In addition, he had finished the needed repairs to Mrs. Harriot's boarding house and the painting of the house would be completed within the next few weeks. People who were driving by sometimes stopped and commented on how nice and fresh her boarding house looked. And, as sort of an "icing on the cake," Mrs. Harriot had rented out almost all her rooms. "If I weren't so old I'd kiss you!" she had exclaimed, "But I will give you a hug." She had pulled him close for a fleeting moment. "Randell, I'm thinkin' your return to Blackberry has changed many things for this old woman!" Randell had thought he detected a tear in her eye as she had said, "Thank you for being so kind to this old lady who treated you so badly when you first returned to our town!"

He drove the loaded pickup on along the highway, pondering all that had happened to him. One thing stood out. Now that he endeavored to help others, instead of taking from them, undreamed of blessings had come to him. He believed this was the key to his good fortune. Mrs. Herriot's life had changed for the better, due to his kindness toward her. He had rescued the Adams twins from the darkness of the forest. New desks had been built for Helen Bedford's pupils. He had rebuilt the lady's poorly made cabinets. It seemed that the more he gave of his time and means, to aid others, the more he received in return. In addition, he was attending church each week and he had recently started paying a tithe. But strangely, giving ten percent of his earnings away didn't seem to hurt him financially. Blessings seemed to be in abundance in his life now.

He had noticed another change. He seemed to feel better than he had in many years. The stoop seemed to be mostly gone from his shoulders and back. Even the limp seemed to have subsided. He looked forward to getting up and going to his shop each morning.

He was very thankful for these multiple blessings, but his heart was still filled with a void, an ache, a longing. It hung, heavy, and burdensome, on his soul. He stared ahead, along the road, as he drove. He was lonely and all alone. Yes, he had made many new friends, Mr. Kincaid, Charles, and Beth Adams, and even Mrs. Herriot, but a large void remained. He wanted, he needed, someone to share his good fortune with. He craved someone to love, care for, hold close, and look after. Who! Who would love him again, as Louise had once loved him?

The road slipped by beneath the pickup as he drove on toward Blackberry. He guided his heavily loaded pickup around a sharp bend in the road and nearly ran into an old, dilapidated, car that sat, immobile, near the center of the road. He slammed on the brakes and brought his pickup to a shuddering halt a few feet short of the decrepit vehicle. A whiskered man stood at the front of the car, the hood up, and scratching his scraggily head. Randell opened the door and got out. Something looked vaguely familiar about the scene, both the man and the beat-up old car.

The whiskered old man–it was difficult for Randell to tell just how old the man was with his disheveled hair, heavy whiskers, and untidy clothing–looked up at Randell as he approached the front of the car. A smile gradually came through the whiskers. "Well, it's you! Yer the guy I hauled into town a few months ago. It was early last spring! I . . . I see yer still here!"

Randell walked forward and held out his hand. "Yes, I'm still here in Blackberry. It's good to see you again.!" The hood was open, exposing the engine of the old car. Randell glanced down at the ancient power plant. "What seems to be the problem here?"

The man peered in under the hood of the car for a long moment and then turned to Randell. "The engine's died, kicked-the-bucket, that's what she's done!"

Randell smiled at the old man. "I'll be happy to look at the engine. Perhaps I can get her up and running."

The old man shook his head. "It would be nice if ya could, but I doubt it. I think the guts of the engine have busted. I believe the crankshaft has broken or somethin' real serious! She's dead; nothing will move. She's locked up tightern' a drum!"

The engine crank hung, at its place, just below the radiator. Randell grabbed the crank, pushed it forward into place, and gave a hard pull. Nothing moved. The old man was right, the engine was frozen tight. Not a good sign! He peered inside the engine compartment again. The old engine sat mute and silent. Randell doubted if it would ever come to life again. He stepped back and surveyed the rickety piece of machinery that at one time, many, many years ago, had been a rather nice car. He suspected it was now time for this old rattletrap to go to the graveyard for dead cars. He turned back to the whiskered old man, who stood silent, and somewhat crestfallen, near the front of the relic. Randell broke the silence. "My names Randell Cordell, I'm sorry but I can't remember your name."

The old man looked up, but Randell couldn't detect much of a smile, as the man said, "I'm Barnhart Jorgensen." He paused for a moment. "Could I impose on ya to give me a lift to my son's place? It's on the way into town; only a couple of miles on. I guess my boy can come back here with his tractor and tow my car home."

"Sure, you bet!"

With a few hard shoves and heaves, Randell, and the old man, pushed the derelict car to the side of the road where it would be out of the way of the traffic. "There, it'll be all right until your son can tow it off!"

Once they were inside the pickup, and moving on down the road, Randell spoke. "What are you going to do for transportation, now that it appears your old car has died!"

The whiskered man looked across the seat at Randell. "Oh, my son will get me something better. He's been after me to get rid of the old clunker." He smiled at Randell through his whiskers. "I'm sort of a stubborn old cuss and I liked the old car. I've had it for many years. I just enjoyed driving it. No fancy gadgets ta worry about or figure out how to make them work; it didn't even have a radio." He smiled at Randell, through heavy whiskers. "But I did install a heater some years back. It got a bit cold driving about during the winter with no heater!"

Randell looked across the pickup at the man. "What do you do with your time all day? You got much that keeps you busy?" An idea had suddenly come to him.

"Oh, I just mostly putter around my son's place, but sometimes I just sit on the front porch and watch the world go by along the highway."

Randell slowed the pickup a bit as he looked across at the old man again. "I have a cabinet shop in Blackberry. Would you be interested in coming into my shop, about the middle of the afternoon, each day, and sweep up the sawdust, small pieces of lumber lying around, and such. Just keep it in a clean and tidy condition. I'd pay you, and it would sure be a help to me and my men!"

The whiskered old man sat in silence for a moment and then looked across the pickup at Randell. "Well, . . . yes, I just might do that! It would change my routine and I could use a few extra bucks; don't have much comin' in! When do ya want me to start?" He paused, "I can't get into town 'till I get somethin' ta drive!"

Randell smiled back at the old man. "You come in as soon as you get new transportation. Do you know where my shop is located?"

"Yeah, I think so. Did ya purchase Stewart's shop?"

"Yes, that the shop."

Within a few minutes Randell had dropped the old man off at his son's home and was backed up to his shop unloading the lumber. Harrison assisted him in carrying the lumber into the shop and stacking it along the back wall. He told Harrison about signing the new contract. "It's a lot of new work for us. You got anymore friends who are good cabinet makers? I think I need to hire another man!"

CHAPTER 12

Stella Cunningham

The long days, and short nights, of summer passed quickly for Randell, as he and his three employees, worked to stay ahead of a multiplicity of contracts to build and install cabinets. Under the heavy load of work the weeks flew by and soon summer gave way to a rush of cool weather and a menagerie of colors as fall descended across the forests and meadows of Northern Minnesota.

Randell had forgotten the serene beauty of a fall day in Northern Minnesota. The aspen, poplar, and birch trees painted the hillsides in brilliant gold, red, and ochre, which reflected the bright autumn sun against an azure blue sky. The rich red leaves of the oak and maple trees reflected their crimson patterns into the blue waters of the abundant lakes of Minnesota. Honking geese and ducks passed overhead, in graceful V patterns, as they made their way south. As spring gave way to summer, and summer to fall, Randell was sure that his decision to return to the place, where his downfall had begun, had been a good decision. The beautiful fall weather made his spirits sore.

The delightful fall weather passed all too quickly, and within a few fleeting weeks the trees had shed their leaves under the onslaught of ever heavier frosts. Soon the residents of the community began to wake up to cold mornings; many accompanied with harsh winds and blowing rain. Within a few weeks bitter winter weather began to grip the land. The inhabitants of the community were forced to pull out their long underwear, heavy coats, caps, gloves, and boots as armor against the god of winter, who quickly took control of all Northern Minnesota, holding the land in his ridged grasp. There was no escape from this frigid world, except to stand close to the pot-bellied stove, or the fireplace!

On this early February day, a bitter, cold, wind blew straight from the North Pole as it howled along the ice-covered streets, tugged hard at coats and caps, and sucked all the warmth from the body of anyone who was forced to be outside on this bitter winter day. Heavy banks of snow lay along the streets and roads of Blackberry and no one ventured out into the beastly weather unless there was no alternative.

Robert Harrison ushered the woman through the door leading from the shop into Randell's office "A lady's here to see you, Mr. Cordell." With a puzzled look on his face, Harrison cast a quick, sidewise, glance at the woman. She was a poorly dressed stranger! He doubted if she had come to the shop to purchase cabinets. With a fleeting glance at the woman, he shut the door, and retreated into the shop.

Randell was surprised that any woman would venture out in today's ghastly weather to come and discuss new cabinets or remodeling. He looked up from his desk and was, indeed, surprised at what he saw. The lady stood, just inside the door, clutching a tattered coat close about her shivering body. Her eyes darted about the room, and then down at the floor. Randell was so surprised at her shocking appearance that he was at a loss for words. When she glanced up at him, her eyes seemed to be filled with fear and a weariness of body and soul. The picture of a hunted and frightened animal flashed through his mind.

The bedraggled appearance of this woman startled him, and he quickly stood to his feet and walked around the corner of his desk. Her head was covered with a tattered stocking cap, pulled down tight over her ears. A few scraggly strands of hair protruded from beneath the edges of the cap. She stood just inside the door, her body shivering from the cold, as she clutched a thin, and ragged, summer coat to her frail body. He glanced at her feet, and saw a pair of badly worn summer pumps, heavily encrusted with snow and ice. Her sox, which had originally been white, were now very wet and very dirty.

His eyes drifted back up to the woman's face. Her lips were blue from the cold and were trembling. Her face was heavily lined, pale, hard, and drawn. As he stared at her Randell remembered a comment horseman would sometimes make when they saw a poorly fed, worn-out old nag of a horse, that had been badly neglected. *"The poor horse has been ridden hard and turned out wet!"* That phrase came to his mind as he looked at the woman who had just been ushered into his office. Her tired, searching, frightened, eyes unnerved him.

He stared at this apparition, standing inside the doorway of his office, and suddenly, his mind became a cauldron of emotions. Had he seen this woman before? If so, where? An oppressive silence filled the room, like a surreal and haunting ghost. With an effort he cleared his throat and broke the heavy silence. "Ma'am can . . . can I help you?"

When she spoke, her voice was trembling and barely above a whisper. "My, it sure feels good to get out of that wind and come inside!"

His heart jumped, as if stabbed with a knife! He'd heard that voice before!

He stood, speechless, at the edge of his desk and stared at the woman. He should say something, but his voice seemed to have deserted him. A faint smile crossed the woman's haggard and drawn face. "You . . . you don't know me, do you?"

It took Randell a long moment to find his voice, as his mind raced, and then he blurted out. "No ma'am, I'm afraid I don't." But the sound of her voice again, brought the stab back to his heart, and old and nearly forgotten images were churning through his mind.

Once again, the semblance of a smile returned to the gaunt face of the woman, and then she spoke again. "Randell, I'm Stella, yer old flame!"

A long, and poignant, silence ensued as he fought to regain his composure. With a slow movement of his hand, he pointed to the chair across his desk. His voice was broken, and cracked, as he said, "Please . . . please have a seat Stella." She stepped forward and slumped into the chair.

He turned back to his own chair and slowly sat down. He had oiled the chair, but in the silence, it gave off a faint squeak. He stared at her for a long moment, as his mind raced. He finally found his voice again. "Stella, why . . . why are you here? What has happened to you? How . . . how did you find me?"

She sat in silence as she fumbled, with numb fingers, at the buttons of her coat. The front of the tattered coat was held together by only two of its five buttons; the other three were missing. When the coat was finally unbuttoned it revealed a faded, and badly worn, light summer dress.

She slowly lifted her head and looked across the desk at him. Her voice was trembling, and her eyes were filled with anguish. "Well, finding you wasn't easy, but I ran into a man in Kansas City, who said he knew you while you were in the army. He told me you had gone to Blackberry, Minnesota. I . . . I used up almost all of the little money I had for a bus ticket and got here about an hour ago." She tried to smile again, but her face seemed frozen from the cold. "That walk from the bus stop, at the filling station, to your shop nearly did me in! I'm right near frozen to death! That wind just went right through this coat! I . . . I wasn't sure I'd make it here to your shop!" She leaned forward a little in the chair, and her pain-filled eyes shifted from Randell and down to the floor, as silence returned to the room.

Randell found his voice again. "Stella, what has happened to you? Why have you come back here, to Blackberry?"

She slowly looked back up at him. Her voice was barely above a whisper and her eyes were full of pleading. "Randell, I'm . . . I'm at the end of my tether. I . . . I'm dying, and I need your help!" And then she slumped back into the chair, averted her eyes and looked out the small window at the blowing snow. Her body was shaking, her lips were trembling, and he could see fear, pain, and hopelessness in her leaden eyes.

Before he could find his voice again, she looked back at him and continued her narrative in a faint and barely audible voice. "Randell, I'm all in, and . . . and, I'm dying! I . . . I need someplace to spend my last days! Can . . . will you please help me? I'm desperate Randell, or I wouldn't have come . . . !"

Pain filled memories flooded through Cordell's tumultuous mind. The woman seated across the desk from him bore only a faint resemblance to the Stella Cunningham he had once known. But it was her! The woman he had ran off with twenty years ago. He was shocked. She had stumbled out of the bitter cold and snow, and back into his life again, under vastly different circumstances. The old Stella was gone, and had been replaced with this tired, worn, and gaunt woman. He found his voice. "Where . . . where, have you been these past years? I guess you've been out of prison for a few years?"

She continued to fiddle with the front of her coat with her stiff fingers. "Yes, I've been out of prison for a while." She looked across the desk at him with frightened eyes. Eyes that reminded him of a cowering and beaten dog. "Randell, those years in prison were hard on me; nearly killed me. They worked me like an animal there in the laundry for over twelve years! When I was finally released from prison I did find some work during the last couple of years of the war in a munitions plant but was laid off when the war ended."

She looked at him with a face filled with anguish, fear, and pain. "And . . . and Randell, I've had a tough time finding any work since. There's not much use for a woman with a hard past, and a prison record!" She tried, but failed, to laugh. "Randell, I've . . . I've had to

102

make a living any way I could. The oldest profession, that's how, . . . and . . . and it's worn me out, near killed me, it has! Randell, I . . . I need your help, . . . real bad!"

Her haunting eyes fell away from him, and once again she stared at the floor. Randell knew he should say something, but he sat, silent, flabbergasted, and tongue-tied, unable to find his voice, as tumult tore through his mind and heart.

Slowly she looked back up at him. Her forlorn eyes sent shivers racing up his spine. "Randell, a few months ago I began to have dull pains in my gut, and after some tests the doctor told me I've got a tumor low down in my belly, and he says it's most likely cancerous. He . . . he said I've only got a few months to live. He told me to go home to my family and let them take care of me, until I died."

Her eyes were filled with pain and pleading. "Oh Randell, I . . . I don't have any family to go to! My younger brother was killed a few months before the war ended, and my parents are gone." She fell silent as she glanced about the little room. "Randell, no one cares about me! I'm all alone, and . . . and I need help!"

Her eyes were haunting as she continued. "Oh, Randell, I . . . I did you wrong those years ago, but you were always kind, and nice, to me, and . . . and I've got no one to turn to. Will . . . will you please help me? I . . . I need someplace to sleep and a couple of meals a day until I'm gone!" That's . . . that's all I need! Will you please help me?"

Cordell stared across his desk at this tragic spectacle. He was stunned and speechless. The pain filled past had come full circle and was now setting across the desk from him. What he saw, setting there, staring at him, with scared and pleading eyes, was a sad and tragic vision. It was a shadow of the past; come back to cast a dark stain across his life again. He was shocked! In his wildest dreams he had never expected anything like this!

He knew he didn't want anything to do with this woman, who, with red lying lips, and flirting eyes, had enticed him into adultery. She had led him along a pathway of pain and ruin, like a lamb to the slaughterhouse! Somehow, he had to get her out of his office, and out of his life. He wanted nothing to do with her! She was poison, pain, sorrow, and ruin! He could never trust her. She would do something to destroy his life again! The possibilities for hurt and pain from her were endless.

His mind was a whirl of emotions as he stared at her. What should he do to get rid of her? He glanced out the frost shrouded window. He could hear the bitter winter wind as it blustered, in hard gusts, blowing snow past the window, and along the street. His heart was as full of squalls as the wind, which raced along the street outside his shop.

The past spring, summer, and fall flashed through his racing mind. So many good things had happened to him over these months, and now she had come back to cast a pall, a dark shadow over him. She would ruin, and destroy, everything he had accomplished and was working toward. He must get rid of her!

His mind was racing and filled with upheaval! If he turned her back out into this weather, she wouldn't last long. In those torn, and tattered, summer clothing, it would be a death sentence. It would border on murder! What should he do? His mind continued to churn, and his breathing was heavy, his heart pounding!

And then a startling, and sobering thought, flashed through his troubled mind. Mrs. Herriot, Mrs. Adams, and Mrs. Bedford had all given *him* a second chance. These wonderful people had forgiven *him* for his past mistakes. He looked across the desk again at the shivering and emaciated woman, her eyes filled with fear, uncertainty, and pleading. Should he do less for her? Could he forgive her for her past mistakes; for the pain she had caused him?

No, he couldn't just swat her away, like an annoying fly, out of his office and back out into the bitter cold, sub-zero wind of a northern Minnesota winter. He couldn't and wouldn't do that to her! He had to help her! It was the right thing to do! How would he want to be treated if their roles were reversed? He had gone willingly along the pathway of degradation with her! And . . . and perhaps his response to her plea for help, was a part of his own redemption from his tragic and sordid past!

He slowly leaned forward across his desk, and looked into her pleading eyes, and his voice was now filled with compassion, and understanding, as he spoke. "Yes, I'll help you Stella. You come with me and I'll get you a nice warm place to sleep and something for you to eat, and then we'll see where we go from there!"

He stood to his feet and walked around the desk. He helped her up from the chair, and taking her arm, he led her from his office and across the shop floor. He stopped and spoke to Robert. "Harrison, I'll be out for a couple of hours. This lady needs some assistance." He continued to hold her arm as he escorted her to the door of the shop. He paused in thought. "Wait here, you need a heavy coat." He returned to his office and retrieved one of his extra winter coats. When he returned to where she stood, waiting for him, he helped her into the coat and belted it tight about her. It was far too large for her frail body and hung nearly to the floor. "The wind is still up, and my pickup will be cold," he said. "You wait here while I go and start the pickup and give the heater a few minutes to warm up the inside of the vehicle. I won't be long."

Stella Cunningham stood just inside the shop door and waited, clutching the coat to her body. The coat felt good, even here inside the shop where it was warm. She looked about the large room. It was bustling with activity, with three men all working on cabinets. Randell had his old shop back and many tomorrows to look forward too. She had nothing and was dying! There was no future, no "tomorrow" for her, only death and a cold grave! Would her grave even have a headstone marking her resting place? She thought of Louise Cordell. She had died a lonely death and now lay in a snow covered grave. Perhaps justice was now being carried out! She leaned against the wall, closed her eyes, and a heavy sigh escaped her lips. *Randell was going to help her! Perhaps things would be a little easier for her until she died.*

105

Within a few minutes Randell had bundled her into his pickup and within a couple of minutes he pulled up in front of Mrs. Herriot's rooming house.

Stella looked along the car seat at him. "Isn't this the rooming house of Mrs. Herriot? If it is, she won't want me to stay here in one of her rooms."

Randell smiled at her. "I've become a good friend of Mrs. Herriot, and I'm sure there won't be any problem."

Randell pushed the door open to the rooming house and ushered Stella through the foyer and into the living room. Fortunately, it was empty. He helped her out of the heavy coat and into an overstuffed chair near the blazing fireplace. As he looked up, Mrs. Herriot walked into the living room from the kitchen. She stopped and stared at the bedraggled woman, and then turned to Randell. "Who . . . who is this lady?"

Randell turned to Stella. "Wait here and I'll be right back." He turned and walked to Mrs. Herriot. "Can I speak with you, in the kitchen?"

Mrs. Herriot had a startled look on her face as she said, "I . . . I guess so!"

When they were in the kitchen Randell looked at Mrs. Herriot "Perhaps you'd better take a chair, as what I'm about to tell you is going to come as a quite a shock!" He pointed toward the living room. "Mrs. Herriot, that woman out there is a shadow from the past." He paused, as he glanced through the kitchen door at the forlorn figure huddled in the chair, and then back at Mrs. Herriot. "That bedraggled woman you see out there, in your living room chair, is Stella Cunningham! She's the woman I ran off with twenty years ago!"

Mrs. Herriot bolted upright in her chair. "No! It can't be her!"

Randell shut the door to the living room and it took him only a few minutes to relate to Mrs. Herriot all that Stella had told him. "She just walked into my office an hour ago, nearly frozen to death! She's not wearing winter clothing, just an old summer dress and a worn-out summer coat! Believe me; it was quite a shock to look up and see her standing in my office, and I'm sure it's quite a surprise to you to see her setting in your living room!"

Mrs. Herriot sat in stunned silence as she looked at him from across the kitchen table. Her voice was full of irony. "As you and I know, it's right hard to escape the past! It . . . it has a way of comin' back to haunt you again and again. Believe me, I know from experience!"

Randell took a seat across the kitchen table from her. "Mrs. Herriot, Stella's past isn't very pretty, and she says she's dying of cancer, but as you can see, she needs help. I'd like to put her up here in your rooming house and then have a doctor examine her. I . . . I hope you'll consent to her staying here? I'll pay for her room and meals; three meals a day."

Mrs. Herriot's face carried a faint smile. "It's a strange world Randell. A few months ago, I would have tried to run her out of town or let her freeze outside in the cold! That's probably what I would have done!" Her eyes leveled on Randell. "But you and I understand these things better, now that we've each spoken of our past with honesty."

She stood to her feet. "Yes, of course, she can stay here in my rooming house. I'm nearly full now, but I've got a couple of rooms." She paused as she glanced from the kitchen and along the hallway leading away from the living room. "I'll put her in the south room on the ground floor. No stairs that way, and the room gets some winter sun, and is cheerful. I . . . I think she'll like that!"

They returned to the living room. Randell sat down beside Stella. "Stella, Mrs. Herriot will help you to your room and show you the bath. Do you have a suitcase?"

Stella looked up at him and then at Mrs. Herriot, and there were tears streaming down her face, as she said. "Thank you, Mrs. Herriot, I'll try and not to be a bother to you." She turned back to

Randell. "I left my little suitcase at the bus stop. Could you get it for me?"

"I'll go and get it right now and have Mrs. Herriot bring it to your room." He paused as he looked into her forlorn and tear-filled eyes. "You take a hot bath and have a good evening meal, and I'll look in on you this evening, after I close up the shop."

She reached and placed her hand on his arm and her voice was choked, and very soft, as she said, "Thank . . . thank you Randell for helping me!"

Twenty minutes later he delivered Stella's small suitcase to Mrs. Herriot.

The long, and bitter, winter night had descended across the town when Randell locked the door of the shop and returned to the rooming house. Mrs. Herriot met him at the door. "She's resting in her room. A hot bath and a good supper of potato cream soup, and some hot tea, has helped her some, but I think she wants to stay in her room for now. Her rooms just down the hall; room number three. I suggest you go and visit with her there." Mrs. Herriot paused and then whispered. "I . . . I don't think she's got much in the way of clothing, and nothing suitable for this bitter winter weather!"

Randell knocked on the door and heard a faint, "Come in." He slowly pushed the door open. She was setting in a reclining chair beside the bed. Her hair had been combed and she was wrapped in a nice, dark blue, robe. Her face was drawn and tired, but she looked much better than when she had appeared in his office. "Hello Stella. I'm sure the bath got you warm again and the supper took away your hunger. I hope you're feeling much better now. And you look nice in the robe!"

She patted the robe with her hand. "It's Mrs. Herriot's. She insisted that I use it, as I don't have one." She pointed to a chair. "Won't you have a seat, and thanks for coming back to see me tonight."

He sat down in the chair. "Stella, in the morning, when the clothing store is open, I'll go and buy you a robe and a few other things I'm sure you need. I'll have them here for you before noon. I'll pay for everything."

Her head was resting on the back of the recliner, and she looked tired and worn. She spoke slowly. "Thank you, Randell. I would appreciate that very much, but don't go to much bother, as I won't be around much longer. It's . . . it's awfully kind of you!"

He knew he shouldn't ask, but he felt that sometimes it was good to just talk and get things out in the open. Many times, it helped to ease the hurt and pain. He tried to smile as he said. "Stella, I'm sure it's a long story, but how did things come to this for you? What wrong turn did you take that started you down a pathway of pain and degradation?"

She was silent, and her face an impenetrable mask for several minutes, as she continued to rest her head against the back of the chair. Her eyes were shut, and he thought she wasn't going to respond, and then she raised her head and looked at him. "Randell, it's not such a long story, but I run from it, and rarely admit the truth to myself." She sighed and then continued. "I'm near the end now and perhaps it's time I came clean; was honest with myself." She looked at him with sad eyes. "You know Randell, it's hard to be really honest with yourself. You always make excuses, or blame others for your problems, when all along the problem is actually yourself!"

"Yes," he said. "I . . . I know what you mean!"

She eased the chair up to a more upright position and looked at Randell with heavy eyes. "As I look back, I think I had pretty good parents, but when I was a young teenager I thought they were awful. My parents were very strict and strait-laced, especially my mother. My mother rarely smiled or let her hair down, and she seldom enjoyed a good laugh. Her attitude was that if it was fun, it was probably sinful, and wrong. I wanted to have fun, have a good time, and my mother would never let me do it; instead, she criticized, and questioned, almost anything I wanted to do. As I grew older it just seemed to me that the church, we attended, was made up of a lot of old people who wanted to tell me what to do. They wanted to run my life! My parent's rules never troubled my younger brother very much, but they angered me, and I rebelled as soon as I was old enough to leave home. I left home when I was seventeen and never returned very often. My parents tried to reason with me, but I never listened to them; I just did what I wanted to do without much thought for the consequences, or the future!"

She paused and stared at the dark window, of her room, for a long moment. "But nothing ever went well for me, and I thought it was because of what other people did to me." She raised her head from the recliner and a little chuckle escaped her forlorn face. "You know Randell; I used to wake up in the morning and lay there wondering what dirt others were planning to do to me today? Randell, I've come to my senses, and I now realize no one was scheming to do anything bad to me. My own conduct was the source of my problems. It's been hard for me to admit it, but I've come to realize it's true!"

She fell silent again as her eyes roamed about the little room, and then her face took on a painful expression. "I've never told you this, but before I met you I was married, for a short while, to a good man, and I believe I loved him a great deal, and that he loved me. But, when he tried to talk to me about some of the foolish things I did, about my headstrong ways, I wouldn't listen to him and become angry with him, and within a short while I left him. As I look back now I realize leaving him was a very foolish mistake, which I will always regret, for he was a good man. If . . . if I had listened to him I believe my life would have turned out very differently. Things never went very well for me after I left him!"

She leaned her head back in the recliner and sighed. "It's . . . it's too late now for me!"

Randell's voice was filled with compassion as he said, "Perhaps not: over the past few months I've learned it's never too late to come to the Lord and ask him for forgiveness, and then work to make things right again in your life." He leaned forward in the chair. "Stella, as you know, I've also made some foolish mistakes, but I'm trying to face those past demons here in the town where it all began to unravel twenty years ago. In addition, I'm now attending church each week. It's been a real blessing to me. Would . . . would you want to attend church with me next week?"

She lifted her head and looked at him, and he could see a bit of a smile on her haggard face as she said, "I suspect it's far too late for me to begin church attendance, but, as the saying goes, 'better late than never.' Yes . . . yes Randell, I think I would like to go to church with you. I guess it can't do me any harm!"

With a soft sigh, she laid her head back onto the chair and closed her eyes, and after a few moments Randell quietly slipped out of her room and silently closed the door.

He was badly shaken as he climbed the stairs to his own room. He hung his coat and cap on a wall peg and sat down on the chair and took off his shoes. He lay down on his bed with his hands behind his head. He'd go down to the kitchen in a few minutes and ask Mrs. Harriot to make him a sandwich, and some hot chocolate to drink, but right now he needed to think.

He stared at the far wall for a long time, and once again his mind was a cauldron of emotions, and questions. Stella Cunningham, the woman who had enticed him to his downfall of infidelity, abandonment of his dying wife, into a failed attempt to rob a bank, resulting in a long stretch in prison, had suddenly come back into his life. Stella was a very troubled, and degraded, woman, and perhaps, a dying woman! He had never envisioned anything like this happening! What were the consequences of this august event, for him, and for Stella? He lay on his bed for a long time, just thinking, as he tried to calm his churning mind.

CHAPTER 13

The Blue Goose Café

The next morning Randell made a brief stop at his shop to go over the day's work schedule with Bill, Todd, and the new man he had hired. "I've a few errands to run for the lady who came by yesterday. I should be back by ten o'clock. You men carry on until I return." The three men exchanged quick glances as Cordell left the shop. Their talk during the morning was filled with speculation. Who was this bedraggled woman, who had suddenly appeared in the shop yesterday?

Stella's suitcase had been small and light. It was obvious her wardrobe was meager, worn, and totally unsuited for harsh winter weather. Randell had made the difficult decision yesterday to help her. He was unsure how far that commitment went, but she obviously needed some winter clothing, a robe, and some personal items. Purchasing these few items would make her life more comfortable, especially, if she were dying. He would do this for her!

He drove to what he thought was the best dress shop in town, and with the help of a kindly sales lady he selected several skirts and blouses, two dresses, a pair of slacks, and an attractive, warm, lady's hat. In addition, he purchased a long winter coat, two pairs of attractive shoes, a pair of winter gloves, a colorful winter scarf, a warm robe, and a nice pair of women's winter boots. He also asked the lady to put together a selection of under garments. He then had the items wrapped into six separate packages.

His arms were full as he carried the packages to his pickup. As he laid the multiple packages on the seat he grinned to himself. He had gotten carried away and had purchased considerably more than he had intended. It was a little strange. Making the gift selections had made him feel good.

When he arrived at the rooming house he carried the packages along the hallway and knocked on the door of Stella's room with the toe of his boot. Once again, he heard a soft voice call out. "Come in."

She smiled at him as he entered the room. "Good morning," he said. Two books were laying on the little table, next to the recliner, and Stella was looking through a copy of the weekly, *Grand Rapids Herald* newspaper. He surmised Mrs. Herriot had brought her some reading material. She was also attempting to make Stella's life as comfortable as possible. She watched, with startled eyes, as he laid the several packages on her bed.

He took a seat on the edge of the bed. Her hair was nicely combed and the harsh lines, which had etched her face yesterday, were now subdued. "I hope you're feeling better this morning?"

"Yes. I'm much better! I was very cold and about done in from the long bus trip here from Kansas City. A good night's rest in a comfortable bed and some good food, have all helped to make me feel much better." She waved her hand at the packages spread out across her bed. "Randell, I know I asked you to help me, but I . . . I didn't expect you to purchase a lot of new clothing for me!" She was silent for a moment and her face was full of sadness. "I'll probably not be able to wear most of what you've purchased, as I'll soon be dead!"

"Stella, I could see yesterday you didn't have any winter clothing, and I want to help you. And besides, I enjoyed buying these clothes for you. I hope everything fits. If not, I'll exchange them for a different size. And these winter clothes will allow you to get outside occasionally and take in some fresh air. I . . . I hope you'll like what I bought for you!"

Once again, her eyes were brimmed with tears as she looked up at him. "I . . . I don't deserve this kindness but thank you! I'm sure I'll like everything you've purchased."

He stood up from the bed. "I've got to get back to my shop, but I'll stop by this evening. You can open the packages after I've left." He walked to the door and looked back at her. It was strange, but he felt concern and compassion for this woman who had caused him so much pain and grief. Now, she was all alone and desperately needed help! He was surprised at himself, but he wanted to help her. On the spur of the moment, he said, "Stella, if you feel up to it I'll take you out to dinner this evening. There's a café in town that has decent food. Would you like that?"

She sat in silence for a moment as she gazed up at him. Her face had softened, and the heavy lines were less pronounced. "Yes, I think I'd like that. I'll look forward to getting out and having dinner with you tonight. Thank you for asking me!"

He thought of her illness. "Stella, if it's all right with you I'd like to stop by Doctor Jensen's office, when I leave here, and make an appointment for you to see him. You can go over your symptoms with him and tell him what the other doctor diagnosed. Perhaps he'll have some comments and suggestions, or he may feel you should have some more tests. I'll pay for his fees. Is that okay by you?"

"Yes . . . yes, I think that will be fine, but I doubt if seeing the doctor will change anything."

As he turned to leave she called to him. "Come here, Randell."

He stepped to the recliner. With a quick motion she grabbed his hand and pulled him down toward her. Her eyes were brimmed with tears as she whispered. "Thank you for helping me! You . . . you, and Mrs. Herriot, have been very kind to me, and are doing much more for me than I deserve!" She motioned toward the packages. I . . . I don't deserve all these gifts!"

"Stella don't give me too much credit. I'm just doing what's right for a change!"

"Perhaps, but I do wish to thank you!" I'll be forever grateful to you for your kindness!"

The bitter sub-zero cold continued to hold the town in a firm grip. Late in the afternoon it began to snow, and a sharp wind tugged at coats and hats, as it cut through a body like a piercing knife. Randell would need to get up early the next morning to shovel the walks around the rooming house and along the front of his shop. To keep the shop warm, Randell, or one of his men, fed a steady stream of coal and waste wood into the big, black stove, which stood near the center of the shop. It was mostly a losing battle, as it was difficult to get the temperature in the room much above sixty degrees. The shop windows were shrouded and etched with frost and snow.

Randell, and his three employees, worked all through the day, finishing out several cabinets for installation in one of the contract homes in Grand Rapids. Just before three in the afternoon Bernhard Jorgensen drove up in the new car his son had purchased for him shortly after his old clunker had died. It wasn't a new car, but it was new to him. He glanced back at the car as he walked toward the cabinet shop. It was a nice car, with a good heater, and even a radio, but he missed his old car. It was an old friend he had driven for many years. He immediately set to work sweeping and cleaning the shop floor. He hummed an old tune, as he worked. *"She'll be coming 'round the mountain when she comes! She'll be driving six white horses when she comes!"* It was an old English Ballad, made popular by railroaders in the late 1800's. He had learned the song when he was just a lad, and the tune had never left him. Funny, but he usually thought of his departed wife, whenever he hummed the catchy little song. He smiled to himself. To his knowledge, his wife had never driven six white horses, or even two.

115

At five o'clock Cordell's employees left the shop, and Randell shoveled a goodly amount of coal into the big stove and banked it for the night. It would be cold when they returned to the shop in the morning, but the lingering heat from the stove would keep the shop above freezing during the night. He tugged on his heavy coat and pulled the collar up around his neck. He took his cap from the rack near the front door and pulled on his fleece lined gloves. He knew he would be hit by a frigid blast of sub-zero wind when he stepped outside. He locked the shop door, and with his head arched into the stinging wind, made his way to his pickup truck. He got in and started the engine. It grumbled and growled in protest at being called into service in these low temperatures. He retrieved a long-handled brush from under the seat, got out, and brushed the two-inch accumulation of new snow from the windshield. It was bitter cold in the vehicle and he sat for several minutes, the engine at fast idle, as it warmed up sufficiently for him to turn on the heater.

Fifteen minutes later he brought the pickup to a halt near the front of the rooming house. It had been dark for nearly two hours. The wipers swished back and forth across the windshield as he watched the wind blow the falling snow across the glow of the corner streetlight. It was a bitter, frigid, winter evening. Not a good night to be out. He had promised Stella he would take her to the café for dinner, but he questioned if he should take her out into this winter night. Perhaps it would be better if they took their evening meal in the rooming house. No, he thought, she'd been cooped up all day in the rooming house. The winter clothing, he'd purchased for her would keep her warm, and it would be all right to take her to the café. They wouldn't be out in the cold wind for long, and it would be warm in the café. He was sure she would be pleased to get out for an hour or two. He needed to keep the pickup warm for Stella, and he left the engine running, with the heater going full blast, when he went into the rooming house.

When he stepped into the foyer, Stella was seated in a chair in the living room. She was wearing the new coat he had purchased for her. She looked up at him and smiled. "Hello Randell, I'm ready to go to the café." She paused and looked at him. "I can see that it's beastly weather out, and you've probably had a long, hard, day at the shop. Perhaps we should just eat here at the rooming house?"

She looked nice in the new coat. "How are you feeling Stella? Did you have a pleasant day?"

"Yes, I feel much better, thanks to some rest and good food."

He stepped forward as he spoke. "Yes, it's cold, and snowy out, but the pickup is warm, and I think you'll enjoy getting out for a short while and eating at the café, rather than here at the rooming house. I . . . I think it'll be good for you to get out for an hour or two. And don't worry about me; I'm not worn out from working at the shop."

She stood to her feet. "If you think it's all right I'd like to go." She pulled the coat open reveling the dark blue dress he had purchased for her, and she pushed out her foot showing him the new boots he had given her. Her face took on some radiance. "I love all of the clothing you purchased for me, and everything fits very well. I don't think I'll get cold with this nice winter coat." She chuckled. "You're actually very good at selecting clothing for a woman!"

She took his arm. "Randell, this illness I've got has sapped most of my strength, so I need to lean on you some. I spent most of the day in the recliner reading, but I'm looking forward to getting out for a short while. I need a break from reading and doing nothing."

Within a few minutes Randell pulled the pickup to a halt in front of the *Blue Goose Café*. He quickly assisted Stella from the vehicle, and taking her arm firmly in his, he helped her across the icy walkway and into the eating establishment. He guided her to a table, near the stove. She would be warmer here than near a window. The café was nearly deserted, with only three other customers on this cold and snowy winter evening.

When they were seated Stella looked about the little café. It was neatly arranged with nicely appointed wooden tables and chairs, and pretty tablecloths. "It's a nice little place," she exclaimed. "I don't remember it from twenty years ago."

"The building was here, but the waitress told me the café has only been here for about three years."

She pointed to the small kerosene lamp setting near the center of the table. The lamp cast a soft glow across the table. "The lamps are sure pretty, and they make the place feel romantic." She looked across the table at him. Her eyes had lost the haunted look they had carried when he had first seen her in his office. She laughed. "Not that I'm feeling very romantic. I . . . I think that's all in the past for me!"

He had no desire to speak of romance. That subject was filled with pain and hurt. "It's a well-run café and I think you'll find the meals especially good. During the summer months the lamps are replaced with vases of flowers. The owner works hard to keep the place attractive for his customers."

She looked across the table at him and smiled. "Thank you, Randell, for bringing me here this evening. It's been a long time since I've been treated to dinner by a *nice* man, who wasn't looking for *more* than a meal."

Randell thought it best not to respond directly to this statement. The waiter appeared, and they each ordered a cup of hot chocolate and then reviewed the menus the waiter had left with them. "I don't have a very strong appetite and my stomach is pretty tender," she said. "I think I'll just get a salad and a bowl of tomato soup." Randell decided on a salad and a chicken fried steak.

When the waiter returned she surveyed the two of them. "Good evening Randell, nice of you to come in during this awful weather." She glanced down at Stella. "And who's yer lady friend?"

Randell looked up at the waiter. "Betty, this is Stella Cunningham. She's . . . she's, an old friend."

The waiter's eyes shifted from Randell to Stella, and she fell silent, as her eyes darted back to Randell. When she spoke, her tone was crisp. "Have ya decided on what ya want to eat?"

When the waiter had taken their orders and left, Stella looked across the table at Randell. "I vaguely remember her. I think she worked at the feed store twenty years ago, and by the look on her face I'm sure she recognized my name. I think she knows who I am, and that I enticed you to run off with me!" She leaned back into her chair. "I . . . I don't think she was happy to see me, although I hardly knew her." She sighed, as she looked at Randell. "It's awfully hard to escape your past, isn't it?"

Randell chuckled, but then his voice took on a serious note. "Stella, unfortunately, we're both prisoners of our past. We can't completely escape our foolish mistakes, and it seems as if those mistakes are always lurking just around the corner. They are there, whether we like it or not, ready to jump out and leer at us at any time!" He paused and then continued. "The waiter's name is Betty. I told her, a short while after I returned here, who I was and after some scowls and frowns she seems to have accepted me, but I'm sure it came as quite a surprise to her, when she heard your name."

Betty delivered their food in silent efficiency, and they both ate in quiet reflection, savoring the hot food. Randell looked up. "Oh, I almost forgot! I stopped in at Dr. Jensen's office and you have a ten o'clock appointment with the doctor a week from Friday. I'll come by and take you to his office and then wait and bring you back to the rooming house."

She stirred her soup and then looked across the table at him. "That will be fine. I'm not looking forward to a visit with the doctor, but I suppose its best. I'm pretty sure he'll most likely confirm the previous doctor's diagnosis of cancer."

She returned to her soup and ate in silence for several minutes. Randell said nothing. It had been twenty years since they had spent any time together, and it felt strange. They were each lost in their own painful reflections on the past.

Presently she laid down her spoon and looked across the table at him. "I suppose it's a silly question, but I wonder where we would each be, and how our lives would have turned out, if I hadn't enticed you to run off with me, and rob the bank? I . . . I think running off together may have been a 'fork-in-the-road' day for both of us. And . . . and we both chose the wrong fork, although I was pushing you hard down the wrong road!"

Randell was thoughtful for a moment. "It's hard to say how things would have turned out for each of us. I . . . I have asked myself the same question many times. Would Louise still be alive if I had been here to care for her? It haunts me almost every day, and especially when I take flowers to place on her grave." He looked across the table at Stella. "But don't be too hard on yourself! I was as much to blame for our affair as you. It took the two of us to make those bad decisions years ago!"

"It's rather sad, isn't it! We only get one crack at the life our parents give us, and some of us just throw it all away, with foolish decisions and crazy actions. It's taken me a long time to learn this, but our decisions and actions have consequences. I'm sure things could have turned out much better for both of us if I hadn't been so rebellious, had stayed with my first husband, and you had remained faithful and supportive of your wife."

She grew silent for several minutes as she finished her soup, and then she looked across the table at him again. "But we made our impulsive decisions and we must live with them now, these many years later. I'm dying of cancer and you're trying to put your life together again here in Blackberry. Based on what little I've seen; it appears to me you're doing a decent job of it! I'm . . . I'm not so sure about myself! But it won't make any difference, as I'll soon be gone!"

His voice was full of compassion. "Don't think about dying Stella. Just take things a day at a time! Don't give up hope! Perhaps you'll be surprised at how things turn out for you!"

Betty appeared with the check. She looked down at Stella. "I . . . remember you now. You ran off with Randell twenty years ago, and Randell left his ailing wife for you. It was a terrible thing for both of you to do!" She looked at Randell. "But I know Mr. Cordell is trying to make a new go of it here in Blackberry, and I've given him the benefit of the doubt. I'll . . . I'll do the same for you Miss Cunningham. I'll not judge ya for what ya did all those years past, and I'll wish ya good luck!"

Stella looked up at the waiter. "Thank you, Betty, I appreciate your thoughtfulness, very much."

When the evening meal was finished, they did not linger. "I'm tired Randell and need to get another good night's rest. It would be best for you to take me back to the rooming house."

"You stay seated here for a few minutes, while I pay the check and get the pickup warmed up."

She watched him walk across the café. She noticed he had a slight limp, and she wondered what had caused it. She would ask him sometime, but not tonight. She leaned back into the chair. She was tired, and anxious to return to her room, but her heart felt better than it had in many years. Mrs. Herriot had been very nice to her, even lending her personal robe to her. A very kind gesture. And Randell had rented her a room and even purchased a lot of clothing for her, including some nice underclothing, which she desperately needed. She was touched by his thoughtfulness toward her. She closed her eyes. He had changed and was not the same man she had ran off with.

Randell touched her shoulder. "I can see your tired. The pickup's warm, and I'll take you to your room."

Within a few minutes they stood in the doorway to her to her room. As he helped her out of her coat, he said, "I'm going to be busy for a few days installing some cabinets in Grand Rapids, so I may not see you, but I'll take you to church on Sunday."

She stood leaning against the door. Her face was pale and tired as she said. "The little outing has worn me out. I don't have much strength anymore, but thanks for the new clothing, and for the evening out at the little café." There was a faint smile on her face as she said. "Randell, it's been a long time since I've been treated like a real lady!" She reached and placed her hand on his arm. "Thank you again for being so kind to me these past two days. And I'm looking forward to attending church with you. I hope you don't mind setting with me. It may invite some hard looks!"

He smiled down at her. "I believe I can handle the stares, and the questions!"

CHAPTER 14

Susan

Charles Adams stepped back from the cream separator and gave it a long, hard, stare. His ten-year-old son, LeRoy, who stood nearby, looked up at him. "What's the matter with it, Daddy? Can you fix it?"

He turned to the boy who stood peering at the machine. "I'm afraid it's kicked-the-bucket LeRoy. I think the gear box has stripped." He looked down at his son. "Well, I guess we shouldn't complain. I'm not sure how old this cream separator is, but it was here when Mrs. Steinhart died five years ago, when we inherited this farm, and I'm sure it had been in use for many years before that, so I guess we shouldn't be surprised it has finally died." He put his hand on his son's shoulder. "It's a mighty cold and snowy day, and we can't do much, except work on some machinery in the machine shed. I need to pick up the parts I ordered for the binder, a few weeks ago, so I think we'll go into town, pickup those parts, and then check out a new cream separator. That sound okay to you?"

LeRoy looked up at his father and shook his head up and down. "Yeah, that will be fun!"

They stepped out of the milk shed and Charles looked up at the lowering, snow-leaden, skies. It had begun snowing again yesterday and was still snowing lightly. In addition, the temperature was well

123

below zero. It was a frigid winter day but nothing unusual for northern Minnesota. He turned to his son. "Let's get the hay and grain put out for the cows and horses, and then we need to spend a little time clearing the snow from the walks around the house. After breakfast we'll drive into town and pick up the parts for the bailer, and then we'll look for a new cream separator."

Both the man and the boy were bundled up well against the bitter cold. LeRoy wore a heavy winter coat, rubber overshoes pulled over his work shoes and buckled up the front, and a woolen cap, with the flaps pulled down over his ears and tied under his chin. In addition, his hands were encased in heavy wool mittens. Charles was clad in work boots and a winter coat, although the collar wasn't pulled up against the wind. He wore a winter cap, but his ears were not covered, and he wore a light pair of gloves. Charles was a rather handsome man with a firm jaw, bright eyes, and a ready smile. He was friendly to everyone he met. He stood six feet tall with broad and muscular shoulders and arms. The cold had never bothered him, and he rarely covered his ears against the winter blasts of wind, snow, and ice.

As they pitched the hay to the cows, Charles mind drifted back over the past few years and to their journey from Colorado, to the cabin, a mile down the road, and then to this farm. He loved the farm and dairy, as it provided an ideal environment in which to raise his large family of four kids. In what had been an unpredictable turn of events, he and his wife had inherited the farm a little over five years ago from an elderly lady, Bertha Steinhart, when she had died.

The Steinhart's had no children, and Beth and Charles had been shocked, and surprised, a few days after Bertha's funeral, when her lawyer had arrived at the dairy, while they were milking the cows, and informed them that Bertha had bequeathed all her possessions: the dairy farm, including the cows, horses, and chickens, to Charles and Beth. It had been a bolt out of the blue, which had changed their lives forever. That night, as they lay in bed, discussing their good fortune, Beth had exclaimed. "The Steinhart's helped us with milk for our children and food for our family, and we helped them get in their crops and care for the dairy during their last days. We helped each other!" She had sat up in bed and her face had been filled with wonder as she had continued. "Oh Charles, if you live the Golden Rule and help others, as you would have them help you, then the more you give the more you receive in return! We must never forget that wonderful truth!"

During the year they had lived in the old abandon cabin, they had grown to love the tiny home, tucked back into the pines, spruce, and aspen, of the Minnesota north-woods. They didn't want to part with the cabin and they had talked the owner into selling the cabin and a few surrounding acres to them. During the following two years they had made some repairs to the cabin and had then rented it out. Mrs. Bedford was the latest occupant of the cabin.

Charles thought on these things as they shoveled the walks around the house. He had married a very unusual woman and she was the light of his life. He loved her dearly! Beth had attended college for several years, although she had never received a degree. In addition to her responsibilities as a mother and housewife, she had become an accomplished writer. The diary of Louise Cordell had inspired her first two short stories, Since the sale of those first stories Beth had written many short stories, which had been published in several of the popular magazines. Her agent was now pressuring her to write a book, a full-length novel. Yes, she was, indeed, a very unusual woman, in many ways!

During their family breakfast Charles informed Beth that the cream separator had died, and that he and LeRoy were going to drive into town to pick up some parts for his bailing machine and look for a new cream separator.

Beth looked across the table at Charles. "I think I'll take the twins, and Ilene, and go in with you." She laid her fork on the table and her face took on a look of concern and seriousness. "Charles, another chapter in the history of the little cabin has come out of the

125

shadows. Helen Bedford told me the other day the woman Randell Cordell ran off with twenty years ago, a Stella Cunningham, rode the bus into Blackberry a few days ago. Helen said she didn't know many of the details, but she understood the woman was penniless and very ill, and she had appealed to Randell for help. Helen said that Randell has put her up at Mrs. Herriot's boarding house."

Charles looked across the table at his wife. "Well, that is interesting news. I never thought we would lay eyes on either Randell, or the woman he ran off with, and now they've both returned to Blackberry! It's all very interesting!"

Charles concentrated on his breakfast for several minutes, and then said. "Randell has his old shop back, and it appears, he's working hard to do what's right by everybody." He smiled as he looked across the breakfast table at his wife. "Rescuing our two youngest kids sure went a long way toward refurbishing his reputation. I believe he has a lot of friends now! But it's very strange that the woman he ran off with has also returned to Blackberry! I suspect it will be hard for the people of the community to forgive her."

Beth looked across the table at her husband. "You know Charles, after finding the diary of Randell's wife, Louise, I painted the woman he ran off with, as a wicked woman in the short story I wrote for the *Saturday Evening Post*." She brushed back a strand of hair from her forehead. "Charles, what I wrote about her may be quite true, but there's probably another side to the story I wrote. Her side of the story! And Charles, I suspect it's a sad and poignant tale! And I also suspect this woman, Stella Cunningham, needs a friend right now, especially if what Helen tells me about her condition is true. She needs someone to give her some comfort and support, especially if she's seriously ill, perhaps dying! Every sick person needs a friend to give them support, encouragement, and understanding. Tragically, Louise Cordell didn't have that support when she lay dying twenty years ago!"

Beth's face was full of determination as she continued. "I believe I should hear her side of the story; hear what she has to say and get to know her! Despite her past we should be willing to forgive her and help her. Yes, I think I'll go into town with you, and call on this woman; not to condemn her, but to see if I can be of some assistance to her. Perhaps there's something I can do to make her life a little easier!"

An hour later Beth and the twins got out of the car in front of Mrs. Herriot's rooming house. As they had driven into town Charles had said, "You take the twins with you and I'll take LeRoy and Ilene with me. With just the twins with you her room won't be too crowded. The twins are usually well behaved, and she may enjoy them."

Mrs. Herriot greeted Beth at the front door. "Why, Mrs. Adams, I haven't seen you in ages! And I see you have your twins with you." She glanced down at the two youngsters and smiled. "And I guess these are the two little ones Mr. Cordell found lost in the woods! It was very nice of him to hunt for them in the dark!" She looked back up at Beth. "I'm sorry, do come in out of the cold!"

The twins crowded close to their mother as Beth unbuttoned her coat. "Mrs. Herriot, I've come to visit with one of your boarders, a Stella Cunningham. She doesn't know me, but I want to see if there is anything I can do to assist her. I . . . I think you probably know all about her and Randell, and the little cabin of ours, two miles out of town."

Mrs. Herriot's face held a sly smile. "Yes . . . yes, I know all about what took place in the cabin twenty years ago, and about Stella and Randell's past. Come, I'll show you to her room."

When Beth knocked on the door she heard a faint voice call out. "Come in."

When she opened the door, Beth saw a frail woman, she guessed was only a few years older than herself. The woman was seated in a recliner and holding a book she had been reading. Beth pushed the twins into the room and closed the door. "Miss Cunningham, I'm Beth Adams and these are two of my children." Beth could see a look of astonishment come across the woman's face. "You

127

don't know me, and this may sound strange to you, but I feel as if I've known you for several years."

Slowly the book fell from Stella's hands and onto her lap. She stared up at Beth, and then she stammered. "I . . . I know who you are. Randell Cordell has told me about you. You're . . . you're the lady who lived in the cabin where Louise Cordell died, and who wrote the story about her dying all alone in the cabin, and you go to the cemetery and place flowers on her grave!"

"Yes, you are quite correct, so I guess you know quite a bit about me." She paused for a moment. "Miss Cunningham I would like to visit with you for a few minutes. Not to condemn, or censure you, but to get to know you. I understand you are ill!"

Stella looked up at Beth, but remained silent, as if considering how she should respond to this stranger, who had made a sudden appearance into her life, and then she said in a soft voice. "Yes . . . yes I would like to get to know you." She motioned toward a chair. "Please be seated, and your two cute kids can set on the bed. What are your children's names?"

Beth helped the twins out of their winter coats, took off their overshoes, and got them seated on the bed. "The boy's name is Morton and the girl's name is Marie." She looked at the twins. "Can you say hello to Miss Cunningham?"

"Hello, Miss Cunningham," they chorused.

Stella smiled at the two shy youngsters, who sat staring at her with wide eyes. "How old are you?"

Marie spoke up. "I'm six, and boy is six, and . . . and we're twins!"

Stella smiled at the two children. "Thank you for coming to visit me."

Beth turned to Stella. "Miss Cunningham, I've been told things have not gone well for you and that you are seriously ill. I've come by to visit with you, and to ask if there is anything my husband and I can do to make things a little easier for you."

"Please, Mrs. Adams, just call me Stella." She looked about the room, her eyes glancing from the twins and then back to Beth. "It's very kind of you to offer to help me. But why do you wish to help me? I'm sure you know about my past, and the kind of woman I've been, and that I was in prison for some years. Why . . . why should you want to help me?"

Beth pulled her chair a little closer to Stella. "Stella, five years ago I wrote a short story for the *Saturday Evening Post* about a woman who died a lonely death in a little cabin, all because a loose woman had run off with her husband. In my story, I painted her as a scarlet woman, and I was sure she deserved everything I wrote about her! You, of course, are that woman!"

Beth ceased speaking and grew silent for a long moment. She wasn't sure what she should say next. Talking with people about their mistakes is not easy, or usually even wise. Beth was, by nature, an optimistic person, and she was sure that hidden deep within this woman's heart was a longing for something better than what had happened to her over the past twenty years. Perhaps it was foolish of her, but Beth carried a hope that she could be of some assistance to Stella in finding a new, and better, pathway for her life.

Beth spoke again. "Stella, sometimes we get off on the wrong foot in life. We make a first mistake and it just seems to snowball, and then one mistake leads to another." Beth reached forward and placed her hand on Stella's arm. "But Stella it's never too late to begin anew, to try and right the mistakes of the past. Your mistakes took place twenty years ago, and I believe its time to forgive and forget! There's no reason for me to hold a grudge against you! So, if there's something I can do for you, that will make your life a little easier, I would be pleased to do so."

Stella face was full of astonishment as she looked at Beth. "Randell told me about the story you wrote! What you wrote about me was harsh, but quite true." She looked up at Beth and then she began to sob. "Oh, Mrs. Adams, I've made so many mistakes in my life! I . . . I wish I could just start it all over again. But I can't; and now I'm dying of cancer."

She fell silent for a moment, as she struggled to gain control of her emotions. "That's what the doctor in Milwaukee told me. He said I'll soon die from this cancer I have." She looked at Beth with anguished eyes. "Oh Mrs. Adams, I have no family. My younger brother was killed in the war and my mother and father are deceased. I'm all alone, but Randell has been so kind and helpful to me, and so has Mrs. Herriot, and a Mr. Kincaid. They've all been very kind!"

To Beth's surprise, when Stella had started to sob, Marie had scooted across the bed and began patting her on the shoulder. "It's all right, Miss Cunningham. Don't' cry!"

Stella reached up and took Marie's hand, and squeezed it. "Bless you Marie. You're such a sweet little girl!"

Beth was silent as Stella found a hanky in the pocket of her robe and dried her eyes. What could she do, or say, that would bring some hope, and change, into the tragic life of this woman? And then she remembered something her father had said to her many years ago. She had also remembered it when they had inherited the dairy farm. *"The more you give the more you receive. It's a great eternal principle of life. You cannot give yourself into poverty!"*

"Stella, did Randell tell you about our visit when he came to my home to inquire about who was putting flowers on the grave of Louise? Did he tell you how Bertha Steinhart had given us milk for our children and how my husband and I had assisted Mr. and Mrs. Steinhart during the months before they died? Did he tell you how we each desperately needed help, and how we each helped each other?"

A faint smile came to Stella's face. "Yes . . . yes, he told me about the milk, and about your helping the old couple with their dairy. It was very nice to help each other!"

130

"Stella, the lesson here is that as you help others, many blessings come back to you in return. Seeking the good of others is the way in which true happiness is found. Our experience in helping the Steinhart's taught my husband and I that there is a great principle at work here. It's a wonderful wellspring that brings happiness and contentment to each person who helps, and gives, to others. As a person gives of the blessings, they have received, their capacity for receiving is enlarged and increased. Room is made for fresh supplies of blessings they can then bestow on others. And Stella, that's why I'm here today, inquiring as to how I can be of some help to you."

Stella sat in the recliner; her face full of questions as Beth continued. "Stella, this may be hard for you to accept, especially in your present circumstances, but I believe you should try and find someone you can assist; someone who *needs* your help very much!"

Stella looked at Beth and her face was covered with a frown. "I . . . I see what you mean, but how can I help anyone. I have nothing; no money, nothing to give, and I'm very ill. I'm . . . I'm dying!"

"Stella, it's not the amount of money you can give that counts, it's the giving of yourself that really matters most. And Stella, you may have more to give than you realize. When my husband and I came here to Minnesota five years ago we were dead broke. We had absolutely nothing and were forced to live in the little abandoned cabin. Mrs. Steinhart gave us milk for our children, and bread for our table, yet even in our poverty we were able to help the Steinhart's and others. Stella, the most valuable gift any of us can give comes from our hearts. We can give of our love and our time. Stella, giving to assist others is a state of mind. It's a lifestyle which we choose!"

Beth paused and smiled at Stella. "It really comes down to this! Do we see our place in the world as an opportunity to give, or as an opportunity to take from others? I don't want to be judgmental Stella, but I suspect your past life has been one of taking, instead of giving. That's what needs to change! When you find a way to give help, comfort, and love, to others, I believe a great measure of peace and happiness will come to you!"

Beth stopped speaking and then blurted out. "Forgive me Stella; I've probably said too much! Perhaps I've gone from visiting with you to meddling and preaching!"

Stella glanced at Marie, who continued to pat her shoulder, and then back at Beth. "No, you haven't said too much, and what you have said is the sad truth. I've wasted my life feeling sorry for myself and trying to take as much as I could from others, for my own benefit. I even did that to Randell twenty years ago, but despite how I treated him then, he's been very kind and helpful to me. Randell has heavy responsibilities at his shop, but he's been very generous in giving of his time, and money, to help me. Mrs. Adams, I believe Randell has been living the principle of giving to help others, and . . . and I think it has changed him a great deal. He's not the same selfish man I ran off with years ago!"

She wiped away her tears with her hanky as she looked at the twins, who sat in silence, as if they understood the pathos which held the little room. "Oh Beth, I would give anything to have a loving husband, and two wonderful children like these twins of yours, but . . . but I will never have those blessings . . .!"

At that moment a wild and outrageous idea raced through Beth's mind, and she spoke without further consideration, or thought. "Stella, I've just thought of something. I believe there is a way you can give to help someone who genuinely needs help. You . . . you can give care and love to a little girl, and I'm sure she will give love and happiness back to you. Let me tell you what I am thinking!"

Stella leaned forward in the recliner. "What . . . what do you mean? What little girl?"

"Stella, there's a little four-year-old girl here in town who lost both of her parents in a tragic car accident a few months ago. She's all alone and living in a foster home with an elderly couple. It's not a very good situation for the little girl, and no one has come forward to adopt her. Stella, this is a sweet little girl who desperately needs someone who will play with her, and her dolly, read children's books to her, and be her friend. She needs someone to love her and be a mother to her."

Stella sat up straight in the recliner as Beth continued. "If . . . if I were to bring this little girl to this rooming house, for a few hours, three or four times a week, would you be willing to read children's stories to her and play with her?"

The tears were back in Stella's eyes as she whispered. "Yes . . . yes, I would like to meet the little girl. What is her name?"

"Her name is Susan, and I believe if you meet her, before long the two of you will be the best of friends. If it's all right with you I'll see if I can bring her here to you later today. I'll bring some of her things and she can stay overnight with you."

"Yes, I . . . I would like that! I hope I can meet her today!"

Beth leaned forward and Stella's hand. "I'll go and get Susan as soon as my husband returns for me." She looked at Stella. "Stella, before I go, and if it's alright with you, I would like to have prayer with you."

Once again, Stella's face was full of astonishment and her eyes were brimmed with tears, as she whispered, "No one has ever prayed for me before! Please pray for me!"

Beth bowed her head and the twins, seeing the actions of their mother, instinctively clasped their hands together and bowed their heads. Stella saw this action and the tears came again. What wonderful children! Beth's voice was soft as she prayed. "Dear Lord, I pray that you will bring comfort and peace to Stella. And Lord if it is your will, I pray that you will intervene and heal her from her illness. And we also request that you guide her, and little Susan, as they get to know each other. Thank you, Lord. Amen."

Within moments Beth and her children were gone. Stella leaned back in the recliner and picked up the book she had been reading. She slowly opened it to where she had left off. She looked at the printed words, but her thoughts were not on the book. Beth had said that she would bring Susan today! Her mind was now racing. Her heart was filled with a vision of a little orphan girl. What was the color of her hair, and her eyes? Would the little girl be shy and quiet, or would she be friendly, with a gregarious and infectious smile!

She quickly laid the book on the small chest beside the bed and sat forward in the chair. There were things she needed to do! She must prepare for the arrival of this little girl! She needed to take a bath, comb her hair, and then dress in one of the new dresses Randell had purchased for her. Other thoughts raced through her mind. She should purchase some children's story and picture books, and a coloring book and some crayons. As soon as she was dressed she would go to Mr. Kincaid and inquire if he would drive her to a store, so she could purchase these gifts for the child. She hoped she had enough money to make these purchases. If not, she would borrow from Mr. Kincaid and then ask Randell to reimburse him.

With surprising agility, she jumped up from the recliner and went to her closet. She selected a dress and laid it on her bed. Quickly she took up her toilet articles, left her room, and walked along the hallway to the bathroom. She was smiling as she ran the bath water. She was not thinking of her past mistakes and her illness. All her thoughts were focused on meeting a little orphan girl.

CHAPTER 15

Jimmy Branson

Hartsell looked across the counter at Charles. Here's the binder parts ya ordered last month. The total is forty-nine, fifty. It seems as if everything cost more these days!"

Charles reached to his shirt pocket for his checkbook. "Yes, you're right, these parts are expensive, but I think they'll keep the binder going for another year, or better."

As Charles wrote out the check, Mr. Hartsell, the owner of the implement shop, cleared his throat. "Charles, I picked up some disturbing news yesterday. I'm not sure just what I should do with it?" He paused and looked at Charles through thick glasses. "As ya know, Randell Cordell, the man who deserted his wife and ran off with another woman years ago, came back to town last spring and bought his old cabinet shop back. And then, the woman he ran off with returned a short while ago. They're both stayin' at Mrs. Herriot's boarding house."

Charles looked up from writing the check. "Yes, I know; they're both back here in Blackberry. I told my wife they're Shadows of the Past. Interesting how things go around and then return to where they all started!" Charles looked across the counter at Hartsell. "I understand Cordell's shop is doing well, and from what I can see he's

135

attempting to put his life back together again. I can tell you he did a great job remodeling our kitchen! I don't know much about Cunningham, but I understand she's quite ill and may not live."

Hartsell cleared his throat again. "Charles, I assume you've heard of Jimmy Branson, that fire and brimstone preacher up in Grand Rapids. He's no big deal, only got a small bunch of hot heads a following him. Well, here's what I heard. The missis was in Grand Rapids yesterday, and a friend told her this group is all agitated and worked up into quite a lather over Randell and Stella. It seems these people are sure Stella and Randell are sleeping together there in the rooming house. In their minds they're just continuing what they were doing years ago; living in sin! Now I doubt that's true. I don't think old Mrs. Herriot would put up with that for a minute! Well Charles, my wife says those folks are up to something! The lady told her these people are planning on taking matters into their own hands, so to speak. Her friend think's they plan on setting fire to the rooming house and burning it down." He paused as Charles handed him the check. "It's probably just idle talk, but ya never know with that bunch of do-gooders, and rabble rousers!"

Charles picked up the box of parts for his binder. "Interesting! Perhaps I should speak to Mrs. Herriot and to Randell Cordell. Sort of give them a heads up on what your wife heard."

CHAPTER 16

Church

By ten thirty, on this Sabbath morning, the temperature had risen to a benign ten degrees above zero. It had stopped snowing and the sun made fleeting appearances through a mostly overcast winter sky. In addition, the wind had died to a gentle breeze.

Beth and Charles Adams herded their four children along the center aisle of the church toward an empty pew, Beth could see about halfway to the front of the sanctuary. As they neared the empty pew she glanced to her right and saw Stella, Randell, and the orphan girl, Susan, seated in a pew. Little Susan was snuggled in between Stella and Randell and Beth could see that her face was filled with a happy smile.

Within a few hours of her conversation with Stella, Beth had returned with Susan and a small suitcase containing most of the child's clothing and meager belongings. The elderly lady, who was caring for the child, had said to Beth. "If the little girl is happy, and content, there in the rooming house with this Miss Cunningham, just let her stay as long as she likes. I suspect she'll be better cared for, and much happier, with someone who is younger than my husband

and me. We've gotten along in years, and the little girl needs someone much younger to care for her."

The elderly lady had paused from her dusting and looked at Beth. "Mrs. Adams, this little girl needs a younger couple to step forward and become her a new mother and father. Most of all she needs a real 'Mommy' to hold her, love her, and correct her, if necessary. She's a sweet little girl and my husband and I care deeply for her wellbeing, but we're just old folks, and it's different than the love and care of younger parents."

Beth paused in the aisle and looked along the pew toward Stella, but before she could speak the twins recognized Stella and they both waved their hands, and chorused, "Good morning Miss Cunningham!"

Stella leaned forward and smiled at the twins. "Good morning Morton and Marie. It's good to see you again!" She looked up at Beth. "I see you have your whole family with you today!"

Beth smiled at the trio. "Good morning, Stella, Randell." Beth looked at the shining face of Susan, and then continued. "Susan, have you made friends with Miss Cunningham?"

The little girl looked up at Beth from her place between Randell and Stella. Her face was covered with a shy smile as she said. "Yes, Mrs. Adams. I . . . I like Miss Cunningham." She turned and looked up at Stella and then back to Beth. "I think Miss Cunningham is going to be my new Mommy!" She glanced at Randell. "And . . . and maybe Mr. Randell is going to be my new Daddy!"

A startled look flashed across the faces of Stella and Randell. Beth saw Stella glance down at the little girl, and then encircle her with her arm and pull her close in a warm hug.

When Beth and her family were seated in the empty pew, she leaned toward Charles and whispered. "What have I done? Did you hear little Susan say that Stella was her new mommy?"

Charles just smiled and whispered back. "Ah, don't worry about it, Beth! It'll all work out just fine!"

A lady began playing soft organ music and a hush descended across the little church as almost all conversation came to an end. Beth leaned back in the pew, her mind a whirl of conflicted feelings. The little orphan girl had just said, *"I think Miss Cunningham is going to be my new Mommy!"* Was Charles correct that it would all work out just fine. Stella was dying and would never be able to become a real mother to the little girl! What she had done, in bringing Susan to stay with Stella, might crush the little girl. Get her hopes up, and then have them dashed to pieces when Stella died! She bowed her head. *"Lord, help me out of this terrible mistake I've made!"*

Stella's arm continued to encircle the little orphan girl. She liked holding her close. The presence of the child brought warmth and comfort to her. She had someone to love and she was overjoyed when the little girl returned her expressions of love and care. It was a new experience for her and she longed to hold on to it.

Stella sat quietly as the soft organ music filled the little church. It had been a long time! She hadn't heard such music since her teenage years. In fact, she hadn't been inside a church since she had left home when she was seventeen. Yes, it had been a very long time! Her eyes roam about the little sanctuary. Soft light filtered in through the frost covered windows, bathing the church in a mellifluous glow, as if it were filled with the presence of God. Except for the soft music, the sanctuary was enveloped in a reverential peace and quiet. Even the children seemed to set in awed silence.

A large, fifteen-foot-high cross, made of a dark wood, had been built into the front of the sanctuary. Stella had a vague memory of being taught, as a child, that Christ had died for our sins on a cruel cross. Her eyes continued to dwell on the cross. Had He died for *her* sins; her many sins?

She closed her eyes for a few minutes and listened to the organ. The music washed over her troubled mind, through her soul, and a peace and calmness engulfed her heart. Slowly, the ever-present, shadow of her sordid past, and the anxiety of her cancer, faded into the background, and seemed to drift far away.

She opened her eyes and glanced at Randell, and he smiled back at her. He had told her he had been attending this little church since shortly after he had returned to Blackberry. He had said to her. "Although I was not fully conscious of it at the time, I guess that one of the reasons why I returned was to make a new beginning to my life. And when I saw this little church I realized a new beginning should also include church attendance. Attending church has been a real blessing to me!"

Little Susan had watched as Stella had shut her eyes and relaxed. And she had noticed when Stella had glanced at Randell, and they had smiled at each other. She was only a small child, but she discerned that these actions indicated contentment and love, and instinctively she had scooted a little closer to Stella and had been overjoyed when Stella had hugged her a little tighter. It felt good to be hugged. Susan liked the peace and quiet of the little church, but most of all she basked in the love and acceptance these two people had extended to her, since the day Mrs. Adams had brought her to meet Miss Cunningham. This love and acceptance brought back happy memories of her deceased parents.

The organ music stopped, and a man announced the opening hymn. "Our hymn today is an old favorite. Please stand and join me in singing *Amazing Grace.*"

Randell helped Susan to her feet and she stood in the pew between Randell and Stella. Randell took the hymnal from the back of the pew and opened the song book to the old hymn. Stella glanced at the hymnal, but the words were blurred by the tears in her eyes. She looked up from the book and fixed her eyes on the cross at the front of the church. The words of the hymn filled her with wonder, as she and listened to the congregation sing the beloved hymn with loud and happy voices.

Amazing Grace! How sweet the sound,
That saved a wretch like me!
I once was lost, but now am found,
Was blind, but now I see.
Twas grace that taught my heart to fear,
And grace my fears relieved.
How precious did that grace appear.
The hour I first believed!

Stella had a vague memory of the hymn from her childhood. Would God really save a wretch such as she? It would be wonderful, a miracle, if He would!

When they had finished singing the hymn the congregation sat back down in the pew and the minister began his morning sermon. Instead of seating herself between Stella and Randell, Susan sat down on Stella's lap, smiled up at her, and then laid her head on Stella's shoulder. Stella wrapped her arms about the child and held her close. Within moments she had drifted off to sleep, her long golden curls splashed across Stella's dress, and a look of contentment on her little face.

Following breakfast, Stella had combed and curled the little girl's hair. Susan had stood in front of the mirror, turning to the left and then to the right, admiring herself. "Oh, don't I look pretty!" she had exclaimed.

Stella thought back to when Beth had brought Susan to the rooming house. The child didn't know her, and Stella had assumed she would be shy, and even afraid. Beth had knelt beside the little girl as she said, "Susan, this is Miss Cunningham. She wants to get acquainted with you and be your friend. Miss Cunningham will read to you from a picture book and help you color some pictures in a coloring book. Would you like that?"

Susan had her thumb tucked firmly in her mouth and her eyes were filled with apprehension as she looked from Beth to Stella. Stella had picked her up and they had sat down in the recliner. Stella had hugged her as she said. "Hello Susan, I'd like to be your friend. Would you like to live here with me for a few days? I'll read to you from a picture book, play some games with you, and help you color some pictures in a new coloring book I've purchased for you." The thumb had come out of her mouth, and she had looked at Stella with sparkling eyes as she had exclaimed. "Oh . . . oh, yes, I would like that!"

Stella glanced down at the sleeping child. The little girl had accepted her outreach of love and care without fear or question, and was sleeping contentedly, snuggled against her breast. As she looked at the slumbering child she was suddenly overcome with warmth and love for this helpless little orphan girl, who needed someone to love and care for her. In that tender moment Stella Cunningham knew she wanted to be that person. She wanted to be Susan's new mother; to care for her and to love her! She wanted this desperately!

Hope filled her heart as she closed her eyes and murmured in a soft voice. *"Please Lord; give your grace to this little girl. I've only known her for a very short time, but I . . . I believe I love her. I want to love her. Lord, I . . . I need someone to love and for someone to love me! Oh Lord, I've never really cared for anyone before, and I believe she needs me. She needs a mother to love and protect her. And Lord, will you forgive my many sins?"*

She paused as a startling thought came to her. It was an impetuous and sudden thought, and then she continued with her silent prayer. *"And . . . and Lord, could I ask you to please heal me of this illness which I have. Please heal me so that I can be this little girl's mother for many years. I . . . I know I'm asking a lot, but I'm asking it for this child and not for myself. I . . . I want to help her, just like Mrs. Adams said. She said we should give to others and not take from them! That's what I want to do! I want to give my love to this little girl, and care for her!"*

She opened her eyes and glanced toward Randell. She could see he was listening to the sermon, and she turned her attention to the preacher, as she heard him say, "We should each live in the sunshine of love and giving. Kindness is a product of love, and kindness and love toward others will be repaid with kindness and love, which will return to enrich the lives of both the giver and the recipient. Let's read what Paul says about this in the book of Ephesians." The minister thumbed through his Bible for a moment, and then began to read. "Be kind and compassionate to one another, forgiving each other, just as in Christ; God forgave you."

Stella glanced again at Randell. He had been very kind, compassionate, and forgiving, when she had come to him for help a few days ago. She strongly suspected he had not wanted to become involved with her again. She had discerned his hesitation when she had begged him for help. Why had he agreed to help her? Twenty years ago, she had brought him nothing but pain and heartache! But in her heart, she knew why. He had agreed to help her because he had changed. He was not the same selfish man who had abandoned his ailing wife twenty years ago. Returning here to Blackberry, and attending this little church, had changed him, and he was now a loving, and kind, man who gave of himself, and his means, to help others, instead of taking from others. Could she become a loving and kind woman, who helped others? Would she live long enough to become such a person?

Fifteen minutes later they were filing out of the church. Little Susan walked between them, her little hands held by the hands of Stella and Randell. The minister stood in the foyer, greeting each person as they left the church. "Good morning Randell. It's great to see you on Sunday mornings!" He looked at Stella and then down at Susan. "And who are these two, pretty ladies?"

"This is Stella Cunningham, an . . . an old friend, and this little girl is Susan. Susan is an orphan that Stella is looking after."

The minister beamed. "It's good to meet you Stella. I hope you'll join us again in our worship service" He turned to the little girl and extended his hand. "My, you look nice today!"

Susan looked up at the minister, and her eyes were sparkling as she spoke. "Miss Cunningham is my new Mommy. I like her a lot!"

The pastor smiled back at the little girl. "I'm sure Miss Cunningham is a wonderful mother to you!"

They started to walk on, and then, on an impulse, Stella stopped and turned back to the minister. "Sir," she blurted out. "Sir, would . . . would you be willing to help me learn about kindness, love, helping others, and about forgiveness. Could . . . could you do that for me?"

The pastor quickly turned to her and his eyes were filled with understanding, as he took her hand in both of his. "Why yes, Miss Cunningham, I can do that. If you like I would be most pleased to give you Bible studies. You can learn all about giving, love, and kindness to others, and how Christ died for your sins. If you'll tell me where you and Susan are living, I'll come by, and we can begin studying from the Bible this week!"

"Thank you, Pastor. I live at Mrs. Herriot's boarding house. I'll look forward to the Bible studies."

As they turned to exit the foyer Charles Adams, who had walked up behind them, called out. "Hold on Randell, Stella, I need a word with the two of you." They waited just outside the church in the early afternoon sunshine. It was cold, but the sun cast warm rays on their faces. Within a moment Charles and Beth walked up to them. Charles looked at both Stella and Randell as he_spoke. "We heard Susan say she hopes the two of you are going to be her new parents." He looked directly at Stella as he continued. "Beth's concerned that she may have made a mistake in suggesting you care of this little girl. She's worried the child may be hurt if something should happen to you."

Charles' eyes were full of compassion. "Stella don't worry about it! I believe it will turn out just fine. You just be a loving mother to the child and accept her love in return. The love you have for each other will overcome anything which may happen, and you'll both be enriched and blessed. You just go forward and take it a day at a time."

Stella was silent for a moment. "Thank you, Mr. Adams. I . . . I'll try to be a loving mother to Susan, and I appreciate your faith in me."

* * * *

Stella lifted the little girl from the bathtub, stood her on a chair, toweled her dry, helped her into her panties, and pull her nighty over her head. She smiled at the little girl. "This is such a pretty red and blue nightgown! You look so nice in it. Who gave it to you?" Instantly she bit her tongue. She shouldn't have asked. Perhaps the child's Mother had given it to her, and to respond to the question would be painful for the little girl.

Susan was silent for a moment as she looked down at the gown and then back up at Stella. Her little eyes were clouded with uncertainty as she spoke. "My Mommy made it for me, and . . . and then she went away, and . . . and never came back!" The little girl stood in silence for a long moment as her eyes flickered about the small bath, and then she stared into Stella's face with a painful expression of wonder and questioning. "Why did my Mommy and Daddy go away and not take me with them? Didn't they want me anymore?"

Stella was bewildered and speechless by the little girl's profound and penetrating question. With trembling hands, she finished tying the bow on the night gown, her mind a whirl. She must answer this child's question. But how? *Please help me Lord!* she whispered to herself.

She took a deep breath, picked up the child, sat down on the chair, and seated the little girl on her lap. She tried to keep her voice calm as she began. "Susan, your Mommy and Daddy didn't leave you because they didn't want you. I know it's hard for you to understand,

145

but sometimes bad things happen to good people, like your Mommy and Daddy, and they can't come back to those they love." She paused. Would the child understand about death? She plunged on. "Susan, your Mommy and Daddy were killed in a car wreck and are dead. They are buried in the cemetery, and they can't come back to you!" A haunting silence filled the bathroom as Susan stared up at her. Stella's answer had been blunt. She had been truthful in her reply to the child's question, but was it the right response?

The little girl's eyes were now even larger, and brimmed with tears, as she looked at Stella with questioning, eyes. "If Mommy can't come back, who will be my Mommy?"

This question was even more difficult to answer than the child's first question about why her parents had gone away. Again, she sent up a silent prayer. *"Oh Lord, please help me here!"*

Before she could answer, the little girl spoke again. "Miss Cunningham. If Mommy can't come back, will . . . will you be my new Mommy? I want you to be my new Mommy!"

Tears were now sliding along Stella's cheeks, and she remembered what the child had said in Church, and what Charles Adams had said to her following the church service. She swallowed the lump in her throat, and then she swept the little girl into her arms. "Yes," she whispered. "Yes Susan, I would like to be your new Mommy!"

The child's arms were now tight around Stella's neck as she whispered. "Oh goodie! I . . . I love you Mommy!"

CHAPTER 17

The Doctor

Randell eased the pickup into a parking space in the parking lot adjacent to Dr. Harold Jenson's office. He let the engine continue to idle and the heater to run. He was pleased the temperature had warmed up to a few degrees above zero. The winter sun cast pale shadows across the mostly deserted parking lot.

He looked along the seat toward Stella. She sat in silence, her head resting on the seatback. She had made no move to open the door and get out of the pickup. She lifted her head and looked at him with shadowed and distressed eyes. "I'm . . . I'm scared, Randell!"

He reached along the seat and took her limp hand. "I understand Stella. I'm sure a visit with another doctor will not be easy for you."

She squeezed his hand. "Oh, Randell, it's all kind of strange, and crazy. I've been feeling quite a bit better since I arrived in Blackberry." Her eyes were filled with a mixture of hope and anguish as she said, "This is probably just foolishness, but I've gotten my hopes up that maybe the doctor will find that I'm *not* dying!" Her eyes drifted from him and she fell silent as she stared out the pickup window. "But I'm sure that's just a false hope, just foolishness on my part! I'm probably feeling better because I'm eating and resting better!"

Randell had never inquired about her cancer and the doctor's diagnosis. "How did you learn that you had cancer?"

"Well, I began to feel poorly and heavy in my lower abdomen. So, I went to see a doctor in Kansas City. I didn't have a regular doctor, so I just went to a doctor who had an office nearby. He ran some tests and did a fluoroscope. He said I had a large growth, or mass; a tumor is what he called it, in my lower abdomen. He also told me the tumor was most likely cancerous. I asked him if they could operate and remove the tumor. He said it was too late for an operation. He told me the tumor was too large to remove without serious damage to other vital organs."

Randell continued to hold her hand in his. "I'm .sorry Stella. I . . . I don't know anything about tumors and cancers, but regardless of what the doctor told you, I believe it's probably a good idea to get a second opinion. It may be a long shot, but perhaps, when the doctor examines you, he'll have a different opinion than the Kansas City doctor and will suggest a different course of action for you."

She sat in silence as she looked out the windows of the pickup at the snow and ice covered parking lot. Several sparrows, their feathers bunched up against the cold, had alighted in front of the pickup and were hopping about in search of crumbs and tidbits. She watched the birds for a few moments and when she spoke again her voice was flat, and without conviction. "Well, perhaps he'll see things differently than the other doctor, but I doubt he will." Slowly she released his hand and reached for the door handle. "Well, let's go in and hope for the best!" She paused and looked back at him across the pickup. "I . . . I hope I can handle it if he confirms the other doctor's diagnosis. I know it will be hard for me! I shouldn't have gotten my hopes up."

"Stella, when you came into my shop and asked for my help, I told you I would give it to you, and that's a promise I intend to keep. I'll be here to look after you, no matter what the doctor says today. You can count on it!"

A faint smile came to her face as she looked back at him. "Thank you, Randell; that means a lot to me." And then she emitted a light laugh. "You know Randell this is all sort of crazy isn't it. We ran off together twenty years ago for passion, and the money we thought we would get from robbing a bank. What we ended up with was heartache and prison! And now, we're both back here in Blackberry, where it all started, and you are helping me, and it's certainly not for passion, or money!"

"It is rather nuts, isn't it!" he laughed. "Our lives take us along some strange pathways, with some bizarre, and unexpected, turns and twists!" He looked along the car seat at her. "But Stella, you keep your hopes up. I've come to believe those crooked turns and twists of life can be made straight, and a person can get back onto the high road of life again."

He quickly left the pickup and walked around to her door. He took her arm to assist her from the pickup and across the ice covered parking lot. They had taken only a few steps when she stopped and looked up at him with eyes that were, once again, filled with fear and concern. "Randell, I told you about the conversation I had with Susan in the bathroom, about the death of her parents and why they never returned to her. I promised her I would be her new Mommy! But Randell, if I die, I can't be her mother!"

Her voice was choked as she continued. "I've only known her for a short while, but she has brought so much happiness to me. Oh Randell, I've never had anyone to really love and who returned my love. I . . . I love her so, and I really do want to be her mother." Her voice was filled with emotion, as she continued. "If I die; who . . . who will care for her? She'd be taken back to live with the old couple! I . . . I think it would break her heart!" Her face was filled with anguish as she looked up at Randell. "It was probably a mistake for me to have agreed to care for her! I'm not sure I thought it through very well when Mrs. Adams suggested I look after the little girl!"

In an instinctive action Randell put his arm around Stella's shoulder and drew her close. "Stella, I . . . I don't believe it was a mistake for you to take-in little Susan. I suspect Mrs. Adams suggested you look after the child because she believed it would be a wonderful way for you to give love, and care, to this little orphan girl. And Stella, more importantly, I believe Beth understood that you would receive a great blessing from caring for her."

Randell turned and faced Stella as he continued. "Stella, I believe we have both learned how Charles and Beth Adams feel about helping others. It's sort of a way of life for them. I guess it's something they learned while they lived in the little cabin during that first long winter they were here in Blackberry and Charles was out of work. You know how they believe our acts of love, mercy, and assistance to others, make-up no small share of the blessings and happiness of life. And Beth is right! Taking in Susan has brought you much happiness and many blessings!

"And Stella, you should also remember Charles told you not to worry about taking Susan. He said everything would work out just fine. I'm not sure just what he had in mind, but let's just take him at his word until we know otherwise!" He looked at her and smiled. "Stella, I've been praying for you. I've been praying everything will turn out all right for you. So, let's go into this meeting, with the doctor, with the faith that everything will turn out okay; just as Charles said it would!"

She leaned heavily on him as they negotiated the icy walk to the entrance to the building. As they stepped into the warm foyer she stopped and looked up at him. "I . . . I do have much to be thankful for! Randell, I'm just a tramp, a fallen woman, and yet you, Beth, Charles, Mrs. Harriot, and others, have been very kind to me! And the Bible studies, with the minister, have been such a blessing to me. Nothing like this has ever happened to me before. And I . . . I do want to be a better person, and . . . and most of all, I want to be a loving mother to little Susan!" She lifted her chin. "Let's go see the doctor!"

Randell sat in the waiting room, thumbing through a magazine, while the doctor examined Stella. They had left Susan with Mrs. Herriot. Randell had knelt and spoken to the little girl. "Susan, your new Mommy needs to go and visit the doctor. We won't be gone very long, and Mrs. Herriot will look after you until we return. I think she will help you with your coloring book. Is that all right with you?"

Susan had looked up at Randell. "Does Mommy have a tummy ache?"

"Yes, she has a pain in her stomach."

The little girl had smiled. "That's okay; the doctor will take it away!"

The voice of the nurse brought Randell back to the present. "Mr. Cordell, Miss Cunningham, and the doctor would like for you to come into the examination room. Please come with me."

Dr. Jensen was a tall man of over six feet, with heavy black hair, bushy eyebrows, a big smile, and a firm handshake. With long strides he stepped across the examination room and extended his hand to Randell. "Come in Mr. Cordell. I've completed my examination of Miss Cunningham and she asked that you be present to hear my comments." Stella sat on a chair and the doctor motioned Randell toward an adjacent chair. "Have a seat; I believe I have some good news!"

Randell glanced at Stella. She sat in a chair, ridged and tense. He looked back at Dr. Jensen. "Thank you, doctor. I'm anxious to hear your comments."

The doctor leaned his long frame against the wall of the little examination room. He glanced at Randell and then turned his attention to Stella. "Miss Cunningham, you definitely have a rather large growth in your lower abdomen. I've confirmed this with the fluoroscope images which I made a few minutes ago. You told me that the physician in Kansas City said you were suffering from an inoperable, cancerous, tumor." He cleared his throat. "The good doctor is correct that you have a growth in your lower abdomen, but I'm puzzled as to why he believed the tumor is inoperative. Lower abdominal surgery used to be rare, but that has changed in recent years and such procedures are now quite common. There is really no way of determining if his diagnosis of cancer is correct short of surgery, and lab tests of the tissue from the tumor. This is what I strongly recommend."

Stella glanced at Randell and then looked across the little room at the doctor. She appeared more relaxed as she said, "Doctor, if you operate on me do you believe you can remove the tumor?"

"Yes, I believe the tumor can most likely be safely removed. However, if the tumor is cancerous then the challenge is to remove all the cancerous tissue, and it's possible the cancer may have spread. That's the stickler here!"

He stepped forward from the wall, where he had been leaning, and took a chair directly in front of Stella. "Miss Cunningham, we need to take your illness one step at a time. As you know, I've taken some blood samples which I'll send to the lab in Grand Rapids. I'll have the report sometime next week. An analysis of your blood will give me some additional information relative to your tumor. I plan to then telephone a Dr. William Blackstone at the University Hospital in Minneapolis. He's an old colleague of mine, and I will value his opinion as to how to proceed with your tumor. I'll review my findings with him. If he agrees, I'll want you to go and see him, perhaps for some further tests and another fluoroscope of your abdomen. I suspect he will then recommend that you undergo abdominal surgery to remove the tumor. If so, he'll most likely refer you to one of the very fine surgeons at the hospital."

Stella's face now carried a faint smile. Doctor, are . . . are you saying that I might not die from this tumor?"

Dr. Jensen reached and took her hand in his. "Miss Cunningham, I can't say for certain you don't have a fatal cancer, but it's my professional opinion there is at least a fifty-fifty chance you do not as these large tumors are seldom, cancerous. We must finish the tests, conduct the surgery, and send the tissues to the lab for analysis, and then we'll know for certain. A few months from now you may be as healthy as any person on the street! I'm hoping it will turn out that way for you!"

Stella gripped the doctor's hand, with both of hers, as she said in a voice that was barely audible to Randell. "Thank you doctor; thank you so very much for this wonderful news!"

The doctor stood to his feet and looked at Randell. "Mr. Cordell, I suggest you return Miss Cunningham to her rooming house, and to the little orphan girl she told me about."

He looked again at Stella. "Miss Cunningham, you try and put all conjecture about the tumor from your mind. It won't do you any good to worry the problem to death!" He smiled at Stella. "You give all of your attention to that little girl. One thing I've learned in my years of practice is that a good frame of mind is very therapeutic, and sometimes can even be a strong factor in bringing healing. You just spend your time loving that little girl and let her love you back! That will be excellent medicine for you!"

153

CHAPTER 18

Daddy

T he winter sun was making its appearance above the eastern horizon as Randell drove his pickup into Grand Rapids. The days were very short this time of year, and daylight didn't chase away the winter darkness until after eight o'clock. Following an inquiry at a furniture store, he was directed to an establishment specializing in furniture for children. With the assistance of a pleasant clerk, it took him about an hour to select a child's bed, mattress, sheets, and quilt. He was very pleased to find a colorful bedspread, and matching pillowcase, decorated with a variety of cute baby animals. He was sure the little girl, Susan, would especially like the bedspread and pillowcase. In addition, he purchased a child's table and chair. Susan could set at the table and color in her coloring book.

Strange feeling coursed through his heart as he paid for his purchases. He was startled and filled with considerable astonishment. In making these purchases he was fulfilling some of the responsibilities of a father! Susan had blurted out in church that she hoped he was going to be her new Daddy. The thought of being a father to this little girl filled his heart with wonder, questions, and some trepidation.

He knew Susan's avowal came from the heart of a lonely little girl. He suspected far-reaching events had been set in motion when Stella had agreed to care for the little girl. What did the future hold for the girl, Stella, and for him? He was startled to realize he would most likely have never met the little girl, if Stella had not come back into his life. A sobering thought!

With the help of the clerk, he loaded his purchases into the bed of his pickup. They carefully placed some old blankets around the furniture to assure it wouldn't be scratched, or damaged, during the drive back to the rooming house. He then tied a tarp down over the pickup bed to further protect his purchases from rain or snow.

He was smiling to himself, as he drove south toward Blackberry. He was sure Susan would be excited to have her very own bed, table, and chair. What was happening was all very strange. He had only known the little girl for a short while, and yet he could not resist her unconditional expressions of love for him and Stella; two, badly flawed, adults, who had suddenly come into her life. She knew nothing of their troubled past and readily accepted them as her new parents. It was all a little scary, but it gave him a warm and happy feeling to buy things for this little waif.

Susan sat on Stella's bed and watched, with big eyes, as Randell and Mr. Kincaid placed the bed and table in the room. Kincaid chuckled to himself as he left the room. What was happening here with Randell, Stella and this little orphan girl was all very interesting, and more gist for his book.

When Stella unwrapped the colorful bedspread, and laid it out across the bed, the little girl couldn't contain herself. She jumped from Stella's bed and flung herself onto the new bed. She sat in the middle of the bed and her face was beaming as she exclaimed. "Oh Daddy, this is my bed, and I like the animals!"

Stella spoke to the little girl. "You should thank Mr. Cordell for the bed and desk."

The little girl's eyes were aglow as she jumped from the bed and flung herself into his arms. "Thank you, Daddy, for the bed and desk. I . . . I like the animals best of all!"

Randell and Stella stood in the middle of the room and smiled as they watched the happy little girl examine the various baby animals. Stella turned to Randell. "She loves both the bed and table, but especially the bedspread!"

In an involuntary, but instinctive action, Stella moved close to Randell and her arm encircled his waist. "It's very good of you to purchase the bed and table for her." She looked up at him with a sly grin on her face as she continued. "I hope you understand what this means? Purchasing these gifts for her only reinforces her belief that you are her new father. Are you prepared to accept that?"

"I . . . I think so," he stammered.

Randell was conscious of the presence of Stella's arm about his waist, and this action by Stella was almost as unnerving as the thought of taking on the responsibilities of being a father to Susan.

They stood in silence as Susan hopped off the bed, gather up her coloring book and crayons from the stand beside Stella's bed, and seated herself at the little table. Within moments her head was bent forward, in childish concentration, as she colored in her coloring book. Randell said, "Stella, I'm not sure just where this is all going to end up. I believe this little girl has adopted you and I as her Mother and Father! How are we going to manage this new responsibility?"

Stella stood in silence as she watched Susan, head bowed in childish concentration, over the coloring book. "I don't believe either of us ever thought we would be taking on parental responsibilities when we came back here to Blackberry; I know I didn't! I came here only for help, and to die! But if the doctor is right, I may be here for a good long time." She looked up at Randell. "Can we, two tarnished individuals, really be good parents to this little girl?"

"It's a little frightening isn't it. I . . . I hope so!"

156

Randell's heart was full of strange emotions as he drove to his shop. Could he really be a good father to the little girl? Was he prepared to accept this responsibility?

CHAPTER 19

Todd Bascom

It was a little past eleven-thirty when he parked his pickup and walked into his shop. Robert, and the new man, were working together, assembling a cabinet. Randell looked around. "Where's Todd; is he ill?"

Robert looked up from his work and swallowed hard. "Ah, Mr. Cordell, I . . . I think Todd is about to leave town."

"He's what? What do you mean, he's leaving town? He's never said anything to me about quitting his job and leaving Blackberry!"

Randell could see that Robert was uneasy and unsure as he spoke. "Well, ya see, Mr. Cordell, I think it's this girl he's taken up with!"

"Well, what's wrong with that? He's young and not married. And what's the girl got to do with his not coming to work?"

Robert leaned back against the cabinet he was working on and ran his hand through his hair. "Ah, Mr. Cordell, I don't think this girl is exactly a nice girl; if ya know what I mean!"

Randell's heart leaped, and he looked at Robert with a face full of fear. "Robert is . . . is he sleeping with this girl?"

"I . . . I think so. I'm pretty sure he is!"

"What's this about his leaving town?"

Robert stood silent for a moment; his expression unsure. "Well, I've only picked up a little, but I think he's going to Chicago with her. I think they're leaving on the bus at twelve thirty today. I . . . I think he was afraid to tell you and was just going to leave. I . . . I think this girl has promised him something when they get to Chicago; some kind of a deal with some of her friends, where he can make a lot of money, or something like that!"

Randell turned and ran toward the door, calling out over his shoulder. "I'm going to the bus station. When I return I'm going to have Todd with me, even if I have to hog tie him and throw him in the back of the pickup!"

Robert smiled to himself. He was sure Todd Bascom, and the girl, were in for a big surprise in a few minutes.

It took Randall only three minutes to drive to the service station, that also served as the bus stop. The bus was parked in front of the station, its door open. He could see Todd, and a young girl, standing in line, each with a suitcase, waiting to board the bus.

He swung the pickup to a halt at the curb, jerked on the brake, shut off the engine, and leaped out of the pickup. He strode to the bus with long, quick, steps. When he was within fifty feet of the bus Todd saw him, and Randell could see his eyes widen in surprise and apprehension. Randell never broke his stride. Without as much as a "hello" he reached and grabbed an arm of both Todd and the girl. "Both of you! I want you to come with me!"

The girl scowled at him as she yelled. "Let go of me! Who are you?"

Randell pulled the two reluctant young people out of the line of people and toward his pickup. "You're both coming with me! Don't put up a fight!"

The girl continued her attempt to escape his hard grasp. "Let me go, you beast!" She turned and yelled at Todd. "Do you know this man? Help me!"

"Yes," he said, in a meek voice. "He's . . . he's my boss; Mr. Cordell."

She turned and glared at Todd. "Well, make him let go of me! He's no right to force me to come with him! Where's he taking us?"

They were at the curb beside the pickup now. Randell continued to hold both the girl, and the boy, in a firm grasp, as he spoke to the girl, whose face was contorted in anger. "I'm taking you to my cabinet shop. I want to talk to both of you about what you're about to do. After I've spoken with you, and if you insist, I'll bring you back here to the bus stop and you can catch the next bus." The girl continued to glare at him as he pushed them both into the pickup. He tossed their suitcases into the back of the pickup. Within a few minutes he was herding them into his shop.

He led the young couple through the shop and into his office. Robert looked up from the cabinet he was assembling, watched as they disappeared into Randell's office, and the door was shut. He smiled to himself. It would be fun to be a fly on the wall of Mr. Cordell's office and listen to the conversation. He was sure it would be a very interesting exchange!

Randell motioned for Todd, and the girl, to each take a chair. He took his chair at his desk and looked at the girl. "What's your name, young lady?"

She continued to glare at him, and for a moment he thought she was going to refuse to answer. With pursed lips she replied, "My names Marjorie; what's it to you?"

"Marjorie, I'm sorry we've met under these circumstances, but I hope you won't think too harshly of me after I've explained why I've brought you here."

Randell fell silent for several moments as he looked across his desk at the two young people. They sat in silence, staring at him. Todd's face was full of fear and concern, and the girl's face was full of anger and defiance. Randell leaned forward in his chair and spoke in a soft voice. "I have a story I want to tell both of you. It's a true story, and it's a sad and tragic story. I hope you will listen very carefully to what I'm about to tell you!"

He spoke in a soft, but firm, voice. He began by telling Todd and Marjorie about his marriage, twenty-one years ago, to a beautiful and wonderful lady. He told them of their first home in a little cabin two miles south of town. He told of the cabinet shop, they were setting in, and of Louise's job as a schoolteacher. And then his voice took on a grim tone as he related to them how he had met Stella Cunningham in a bar, and of his unfaithfulness to his wife. And then he told the two young people how he had abandoned all that was good in his life and had left Blackberry with Stella, when she had promised him some easy money. And with a voice that was filled with emotion he told the two young couple of the heart-breaking death of Louise, all alone in the cabin. He took a moment to regain his composure and he then told them of the bank robbery and of the many years in prison for Stela and himself. He acquainted them with how hard Stella had been worked in the prison laundry, and of his own backbreaking labor breaking rock, and hand grading roads.

He brought his rather long story to a close by telling them of the return of Stella to Blackberry. With a grim face, which was riveted on Marjorie, he told her of Stella's degradation in selling her body for money for the past few years, and that she was now a broken, sick, and perhaps, a dying woman.

Todd and Marjorie sat in stunned silence as his story came to an end. Their eyes were now downcast and staring at the floor. The anger had left Marjorie's face, and it was now pallid, and devoid of expression. Randell leaned back in his chair as he regained his own composure. It had been painful for him to relate this sad story to this young boy and girl.

He let Todd and Marjorie contemplate what he had told them, for a long moment, and then he spoke again. "Stella and I both made a terrible mistake twenty years ago when we ran off together, and it destroyed our lives." He looked straight into the eyes of Todd and Marjorie. "I believe the two of you were about to make a serious mistake today!" Randell's face was full of pain as he continued. "You can take it from someone who's has been down that road! You can't build a happy life on an illicit relationship, and by running away from your jobs and family, and attempting to make some easy money! It can't be done! You'll only end up hurting yourselves, and your parents! I hope the two you will think very carefully about what I have just told you!"

A pin drop would have sounded like an explosion in the stillness of the room. Randell broke the silence. "Todd, I hope you'll go back out into the shop and take up your work building cabinets for me. I would like that very much and I believe, with all of my heart, that it will be best for you."

He shifted his gaze to the girl. "Marjorie, I'd like to take you to your home, or place of work."

The silence continued for a long moment and then the girl looked at Todd. "I . . . I think what Mr. Cordell has suggested is probably a good idea." She looked back at Randell. "I worked at the drug store until I quit my job two days ago. Perhaps they'll take me back? I think I'll go and speak with the owner."

Todd stood to his feet. "I'll . . . I'll go out to the shop right now and get to work." He stopped at the office door and looked back at Randell. "Thanks,' Mr. Cordell for telling us your story." He turned and looked at Marjorie. "I . . . I think this is best! I'll see you in a few days, and . . . and we can talk then."

Randell held the pickup door open for Marjorie, and then walked around the vehicle and slid in under the steering wheel. He glanced at the young girl. She looked at him for a long moment, with anguish filled eyes, and then her composure crumbled as she burst

162

into tears. Within a moment her head was laying on Randell's shoulder as sobs racked her body. "What a fool I've been!" she murmured between sobs.

It was cold in the pickup. Randell reached and turned the key on with his left hand and then pushed the starter with his foot. The engine came to life and within a few minutes he began to feel some warmth from the heater. The sobbing of the young girl slowly subsided, and she lifted her head and looked up at him. Her face was full of anguish, and her voice trembled, as she said, "Stella had . . . had to sell herself, her body, for . . . for money! How awful!"

She slowly scooted across the seat to the other side of the pickup. Randell spoke to her in a soft voice. "Yes, it's very sad isn't it? I don't know you Marjorie, but I . . . I wouldn't want that to happen to you, and I know your parents wouldn't want it to happen. That's why I was so frank with you when I told you, and Todd, my story."

She sat in silence as she looked out through the frost covered window of the door of the pickup, her lips quivering. Slowly she turned and looked across the pickup at him. Her voice was cracked as she said, "Thank you, Mr. Cordell." She blushed as she continued. "I . . . I should never have let Todd sleep with me, but it wasn't all his fault. I . . . I'm to blame as well! I encouraged him! I led him on!" She paused, chewed on her lip for a moment, and then looked across the pickup at him. "Oh, Mr. Cordell, I see now that Todd and I were about to make a terrible mistake! Do you suppose I can get my old job back?"

Randell dropped the pickup into gear and eased forward away from the curb. "I'll take you to the drug store. I've become acquainted with the owner, and perhaps if I speak with him he'll give you your job back." He smiled at her as he glanced across the pickup. "I won't give him any of the details. I'll just tell him you're a friend of mine and that you have changed your mind and would like to have your old job back. I suspect it will all work out."

"Thank you," she whispered.

As they neared the drug store she turned to him. "Would it be all right if I went and visited Stella sometime, at the boarding house? I'd . . . I'd like to get to know her, and . . . and perhaps there is something I can do to help her?"

Randell smiled as he replied. "I believe Stella would be happy to have you call on her."

CHAPTER 20

The Arsonists

It was very dark, and very quiet, in his office adjacent to the work floor of the cabinet shop. The only sound was the low moan of the winter wind as it blew along the streets and alleyways of the town. Things always seem worse at night, and any sort of trouble is magnified in the melancholy of darkness.

The cot was uncomfortable and cold, and the night seemed endless. Randell couldn't help but feel that everyone else in Blackberry was soundly asleep, safe, and comfortable in their own bed. He pulled the blanket up tight around his shoulders against the penetrating cold of the night. This was his second night in his office, waiting in the cold for arsonists to show up to attempt to burn down his shop. He didn't want to keep this up for many more nights!

After Beth and Charles had returned to the rooming house with little Susan, Charles had driven to Cordell's shop. He had told Randell what Hartsell had told him about Jimmy Branson, and his concerns that Branson, or some of his followers, might attempt some foolish action against Randell and Stella.

"Hartsell thinks these people may attempt to set fire to the rooming house, but I tend to think your shop is a more likely target. There are a goodly number of people at the rooming house and it would be much more difficult to set fire to the house, undetected, than to your shop, which stands empty and unguarded through the night. Hartsell's wife picked up this information, and who knows if it's something these people would do? It's hard to believe anyone would attempt to burn down the rooming house, or your shop, just because of what you did twenty years ago, or even for what they think you're doing now!"

Randell had concurred with Charles' belief that the likely target would be his cabinet shop. As an extra precaution, he had also gone to Mrs. Harriot and told her of the possible threat. "I'm going to call Marshal Johnson and ask him to have some men patrol your rooming house each night."

When he had called the marshal, he had replied. "Thanks for the tip. As you know, our law enforcement here in Blackberry is mostly voluntary and we don't normally have anyone out all night. I'll get a couple of men to drive by the rooming house, and your shop, several times each night for the next few weeks. We'll try and keep an eye out for any suspicious activity!"

Randell had told the marshal. "Just so you'll know, I plan on sleeping at my shop for the next few nights. I'll be on guard there in case anyone shows up and attempts to set it on fire."

"You be careful, these people could be dangerous!" the marshal had replied.

He lay on the cold cot and wondered about Branson and his followers. Why would those strangers, from Grand Rapids, have any interest in what he and Stella had done twenty years ago, or even what they were doing now, either good or bad? Some people take it upon themselves to be both judge and jury of the conduct of others! He could understand their condemnation of his actions twenty years ago, but setting fire to his shop, or Mrs. Herriot's rooming house, was a violent response, and would most likely get Branson or some of his followers in serious trouble with the law! Not a smart move!

The ever-present winter winds had blown large drifts of snow up against the sides of the cabinet shop. It would be difficult to set fire to the building from the outside, especially in the bitter winter wind. It was much more likely any attempt to set fire to the building would be made from inside the building, where there would be a large supply of dry wood to use in starting a fire. The three doors, leading into the shop, from the outside, were all locked, and Randell had made sure that all the windows were secured. He was in his office, but he had left the door, leading out into the shop, open a few inches. It was likely that anyone attempting to enter his shop would make some noise, either in prying a door open, or in breaking a window.

He didn't know the time but felt sure it was well past midnight. The thermometer on the porch at the rooming house had read ten degrees below zero when he had left to come to his shop shortly after eleven that evening. It was a bitter cold winter night! No one in his right mind would be out on such a night!

When he had told Stella of his plans to sleep overnight at the shop for the next few days, her face had filled with concern, and she had reached and placed her hand on his arm. "I . . . I understand, but Randell, do be careful! It would be terrible if something were to happen to you. What . . . what would I do? And what would happen to little Susan if . . ..?"

He was fully dressed, including his coat. He wanted to be ready for action in case an attempt was made to break into his shop. He had no weapon, except for a three-foot-long two-by-four, which lay beside the cot. When he had told them marshal of the threat, and of his plans to sleep at the shop, he had said. "If someone tries to break onto my shop, I'll give you a call as soon as possible."

He stared into the darkness and his mind drifted back across all that had happened over the past weeks. The little orphan girl, Susan, had entered their lives only a few days past, yet it seemed as if they had known her much longer, for she had captured his heart, as well as Stella's. The little girl was very young, and dependent on others for her care and wellbeing. At the suggestion of Beth Adams, Stella had agreed to keep the little girl. No strings had been attached, and if she so chose, Stella could ask Beth to come, get the child, and return her to the elderly couple who had been looking after her. But Randell was sure that such an action would break the child's heart.

He had purchased a bed and a desk for this little girl, and he understood these purchases indicated the child was not going to be returned to the elderly couple. The truth was, both he and Stella were now firmly committed to the care of the child. He was sure the coming of this little girl into their lives portended momentous change.

Randell stared into the inky blackness of his office, and his heart was startled and troubled. Stella's decision to take the child, and his actions in purchasing furniture for her, evidenced their shared commitment to the child. Did that commitment include marriage to provide a real home for the little girl? Considering their past, marriage seemed outrageous and absurd!

He pulled the blanket up about his shoulders to ward off the penetrating cold. He wished it were daylight. He could think better in the daylight and when he was working, as against laying here in the cold, still, darkness of this little room. What was it Charles had said about not worrying about the future? He had said. "Everything will work out all right. Just take it a day at a time."

Randell had become well acquainted with Charles and Beth Adams, since that first visit with Beth in her home, and he had learned they were both upbeat and optimistic persons. Beth and Charles always looked on the bright side of every problem. They believed if you addressed a problem with love and kindness, it could usually be resolved. That's what he needed to do! Love and kindness would overcome all the problems associated with their commitment to the little girl. It would all work out!

He felt better now, and he relaxed into the cot. He was tired, and he snuggled down into the make-shift bed and the blanket seemed to hold off some of the cold. He slowly drifted into an uneasy slumber.

A hazy vision drifted through his mind. A golden-haired little girl was seated at a small desk. Her head was bent forward in concentration as she colored pictures in a coloring book. Slowly the little girl looked up from her coloring book and smiled at him and Stella. Her bright eyes were filled with love and joy as she exclaimed. *"Thank you, Mommy and Daddy, for my coloring books and for the bed and table. I love you both!"* Together, he and Stella were about to step forward and sweep the little girl into their arms, when the sound of breaking glass shattered the dream.

Instantly he sat upright, shaking his head, and the dream was gone. He quickly rose from the cot and slipped to the slightly ajar door. He slowly pulled the door open another few inches, pressing his face to the open space between the door and jamb. There were several windows in the shop and it was slightly lighter in the shop than in his office, which had only one window. A full minute passed, as his eyes roamed across the shop. He could see no movement, and a heavy silence held the room. And then, there was another crash of glass being broken and falling to the floor. The sound was coming from the window at the rear of the shop, abutting the alley. Silently he picked up the two-by-four, pulled the office door open, and eased out onto the shop floor. He slipped behind a large stack of lumber, where he knelt, peering over the lumber toward the window. In the pale light, he could see that the entire window had been bashed in, and he could feel the cold draft spilling in through the open window.

The shop was shrouded in a deep silence as he watched two men come through the window and drop the two feet to the shop floor. One of the men carried what appeared to be a two gallon can. Randell suspected it was filled with either kerosene or gasoline.

Both men had flashlights, which they directed about the shop floor until the beam of one of the lights came to rest on a pile of waste lumber. One of the men spoke. "That's what we need! Let's find some sawdust and then pile some of these small pieces of lumber, and some sawdust, up against the front and back walls of the shop. We'll douse the two piles with gasoline, and when we put a match to 'em, this place

169

will go up like dry brush in a lightnin' storm! Old Branson will be pleased; indeed, he will! Come on, let's find some sawdust. A shop like this should have lots of sawdust!"

The two men spread out across the shop floor looking to locate a container of sawdust. One of the men began searching along the back wall of the shop and the other wandered toward the stack of lumber where Cordell crouched.

Randell watched the man cross the shop floor toward his hiding place. When he walked by the end of the stack of lumber Randell made his move. In one swift motion he stood and swung the two-by-four, catching the stranger just above his ear. The man went down with hardly a grunt.

Randell grabbed the man's flashlight, which had fallen to the floor with a loud clatter; the sound echoing across the shop. He quickly pushed the switch, turning off the beam. He had stuffed some short lengths of rope into his pockets and he quickly knelt and tied the man's hands behind his back.

The second man's voice came from the other side of the shop. "Yeah, Mack, did ya trip and fall?"

Randell muffled his voice. "Yeah, I've stumbled over something. I've hurt my leg. Ya come an' help me!"

Randell slipped back behind the stack of lumber and watched the man's flashlight bob up and down as he walked across the shop floor toward the spot where his partner lay. He knelt at the man's side. "Mack, can ya get up? Hey, what's this? Yer hands are tie . . .!"

Randell's assault from the pile of lumber sent the man sprawling onto the shop floor. Within moments he held the man in a vice-grip, with his arm twisted hard behind his back.

"My arm! Yer breakin' my arm!" the man screamed.

"Stop struggling and I'll let up on you!"

The man was breathing hard. "Okay, okay, I give up!"

170

Randell loosened his grip on the man as he pulled his other arm behind his back and quickly tied them together with a length of rope. He walked the few steps to the door of his office and flipped on the light switch, flooding the room with light.

He returned to the two men and checked to make sure their hands were securely bound. He stood to his feet and looked down at the second man. "Your partner will come around in a few minutes. You come with me into my office." He reached down and grasped the unconscious man's collar and dragged him into his office. He motioned for the second man to take a chair. Randell sat down at his desk and dialed the phone. In a few moments a man's voice answered. "Hi, Marshall," said Randell. "I've got a couple of would-be arsonists tied up here in my shop. I'd like for you to come and take them off my hands!"

"I'll be there in ten minutes!"

Randell put down the receiver to the phone and looked at the man who was lying on the floor. He was beginning to stir. Randell knelt and helped him up and into a chair. The man shook his head, looked at his partner, and muttered. "What . . . what happened?"

The other man's voice was grim but did have a trace of humor in it. He glanced at Randell as he spoke. "I . . . I think he hit you with a two-by-four!"

"I believe ya, My head hurts like hell!"

Randell left the two men and walked to the front entrance of his shop. He flipped on the outside light and unlocked the door to allow Marshal Jackson entry when he arrived. As he walked back across the shop floor he wondered just how he should deal with these two men. He knew from personal experience the harshness and degradation of a prison, and he hated to have any part in sending anyone to a similar fate.

He returned to his office, took his chair, and looked at the two men. "Breaking and entering, with the intent to set fire to my shop, is a serious offense. It's pretty clear, what you had in mind." He motioned toward the can he had retrieved from the shop, and which now sat against the wall in his office. It was solid evidence of their intent. He suspected a jury would quickly convict the two men of attempted arson.

"Your actions tonight will probably land both of you in prison for several years!" He studied at the two men. They looked to be ordinary men; nothing special, good, or bad. Prison would be hard on them. It was a heavy penalty for a few minutes of foolishness! He knew he was right; he had been there! He leveled a steady gaze at the two men. "You guys interested in a deal, if I don't press charges?"

The man he had hit with the two-by-four spoke. "What . . . what ya got in mind? I ain't ever been in jail."

His partner chimed in. "Me neither!"

Randell continued to study the two men and then an idea came to him. He was thinking as he spoke. "I'm willing to make a deal with the two of you, in return for my dropping all charges against you. First, you agree to sever all connections with this guy, Branson, and his group of rabble rousers. Second, you give me some evidence, within two weeks, that you are both gainfully employed. Third, you keep out of trouble with the law for two years. And fourth, you both show up for church at the little church, down the street, at least twice a month for the next year. If the two of you will agree to these conditions, I'll not press any charges against you for breaking and entering my business, with the intent of burning it to the ground." He paused and looked at the two men. "Is it a deal?"

The men eyed each other for a few moments and then the one with the knot on his head spoke. "Rob, it sounds better than a stretch in prison to me!" He glanced at his partner. "This whole thing was a fool idea. I . . . I think we should get shut of Branson! That's what we should do! Branson's a little wild, and sort of led us on some to get us to burn down this place!"

172

Rob looked at Randell. "Mister, I think we'll just take you up on your offer!"

"It's a deal then! Marshal Jackson will be here in a few minutes and I'll tell him of our understanding. I'll not press charges if you keep your end of the bargain."

Within a few minutes the marshal walked across the shop floor and entered the office. He glanced at the two men and then looked at Randell. Randell pointed to the can which stood against the shop wall. The marshal walked to the container, removed the cap, and sniffed. "Gasoline," he snorted. "This place would have gone up like dry tender if doused with this stuff!"

The marshal turned to the two men. "You two men are in a lot of trouble! I hope you understand!"

Randell motioned to the office door. "Marshal, if I could have a word with you!" They stepped out into the shop and Randell quickly explained the deal he'd outlined to the two men.

"Very interesting!" the marshal exclaimed. "I want to speak to them."

They stepped back into the office. The marshal looked at the two men as he spoke. "Rob, Mack, I know both of you and I don't believe either of you have ever been in trouble with the law before. What in the world ever induced you to try and set fire to Mr. Cordell's shop?"

Rob spoke. "We're right sorry about this! I. . . I guess we both sort of got carried away with what old man Branson said about Cordell, and that woman, Stella; I guess is her name." He paused as he glanced from the marshal to Randell. "Branson said that Cordell and this woman was livin' in open, and blatant, sin, and somethin' needed to be done about it. He said the Lord expects us church people to put a stop to such goings-on, as an example to the community. He said we got to keep the standards up, or the country will just go to pot!"

The marshal eyed the two men. "I suspect the two of you didn't actually have any proof that what Branson told you about Mr. Cordell, and Stella Cunningham, was true?"

The two men looked at the floor for a long moment and then back up at the marshal. Mack found his voice. "Na, not really, we just took Branson's word for it!"

The marshal continued. "Well, I've gotten to know Mr. Cordell pretty well over the past months, and I don't believe what Branson claims is true. In fact, Miss Cunningham is a very sick woman and Mr. Cordell is helping her with a place to live and trying to make things easier for her. But even if what Branson said were true, you men can't take matters into your own hands, and attempt to burn down Mr. Cordell's shop!"

Mack looked up at the marshal. "Yer right sir; we should have thought this thing all through before coming here tonight!" He paused for a moment and then blurted out. "Can . . . can we make this deal with Mr. Cordell? Is that okay by you? I'd sure hate to go to jail over this!"

The marshal looked at the two men for a long moment and then walked forward and untied their hands. They stood up, rubbing their wrists, as the marshal spoke. "I'm with Mr. Cordell a hundred percent. You boys keep your noses clean, along the lines that Cordell has suggested, and no charges will be pressed against either of you. But it's very important that you keep up your end of the bargain!"

Mack spoke up. "We'll do it Marshall! Ya can bet on it! Can . . . can we go now?"

The marshal waved toward the door. "You can be on your way but drive carefully; it a bad night out!"

The two men paused at the office door and Mack spoke. "Thank you, Mr. Cordell. We . . . we'll see ya in church next week."

Randell smiled. "I'll look forward to it, and I want the two of you to meet Stella, and . . . and a little orphan girl."

174

When the two men left the shop, Marshall Jackson turned to Randell and held out his hand. "Mr. Cordell, I believe that was a mighty fine gesture on your part to make such a deal with those two young men, to keep them out of prison. I hope they never forget what you just did for them! You've given those men a second chance!"

The marshal stepped to the door of the office and looked across the shop toward the shattered window. "You've got a broken window. Can I help you board it up?"

Randell chuckled. "I'd appreciate your help. Then we can both get back to a warm bed!"

CHAPTER 21

The Sleigh Ride

C harles Adams guided the team of horses, and the large sleigh, to a halt in front of Nettie Herriot's rooming house. The temperature had risen to a pleasant twenty degrees and golden sunlight flooded the streets and windows of the small town. The songs of birds echoed along the streets as they fluttered from tree to tree in the midday sunshine.

Many of the residents of the rooming house, including Randell, Stella, little Susan, Mrs. Herriot, and Mr. Kincaid, had observed the arrival of the sled through the living room window. They immediately began spilling out the front door and tramping across the, snow covered, yard to the sleigh. Their shouts of greetings echoed along the street. "Good afternoon, Mr. Adams. What a large sleigh! Good looking horses! This will be fun!" With cries of happiness, and delight, they scrambled aboard the big sleigh and found seats on the bales of straw Charles had scattered about the bed of the sleigh.

Charles owned two sleighs. A small sleigh, which accommodated his family of six, and this big sleigh, he had built a few years ago from a hayrack. The big sleigh would accommodate a large group of people. Three years past he had removed the wheels from one

176

of his hayracks and had built large runners to replace the wheels, turning the hayrack into a large sleigh.

The streets of Blackberry lay under a heavy layer of snow, and more would accumulate as the winter wore on. In years past, travel by sleigh during the long winters had been very common in Northern Minnesota, however, over the past few years, sleighs had fallen out of use, in favor of the family auto.

Charles' sleigh-ride outing was an annual affair, and anyone in the village could join in the fun. The ride always included a stop at his home, where Beth treated everyone to hot chocolate, apple juice, and fresh, homemade cookies. Charles was, by nature, a friendly and outgoing man, who enjoyed doing things for people. He never charged a fee for these sleigh rides. Many of the people of the little community of Blackberry looked forward to the annual ride in his sleigh. It was always a fun filled outing across the winter landscape of northern Minnesota.

Little Susan's eyes were aglow as Randell lifted her up onto the hayrack and then assisted Stella onto the sleigh. Within moments they were seated on two bales of straw. Susan looked about the sleigh at everyone and her eyes were large and shiny as she exclaimed. "Oh, this is fun!"

Charles' four children sat beside him in the big seat at the front of the sleigh. He had picked up Helen Bedford when he had passed her little cabin shortly after leaving his dairy. Everyone was bundled up against the winter cold, however, the sunny day, and the absence of any wind augured for a pleasant winter outing.

As everyone found a seat on a bale of straw, Charles passed out heavy blankets for the passengers to tuck in about their legs: this would assure that everyone was warm and comfortable during the outing. When his passengers were all seated he climbed up into the driver's seat, took up the reins, and clucked to the team of horses; a black and a grey, named Joe and Pete. Instantly the big sleigh began moving along the snow-covered street, amid renewed shouts of approval. He made a couple of additional stops to pick up more passengers, and then headed the team of horses toward the home of his parents, Carlisle and Captolia Adams, who lived near the edge of town.

Michael Kincaid sat next to Mrs. Herriot on a shared bale of straw. He laughed as he tucked a blanket around her to make sure she didn't get cold. "Well, this is a first for me! I've never been on a sleigh ride before!" He surveyed the load of passengers and chuckled again. "All we need now is for someone to lead us in singing *Jingle Bells!*"

Nettie Harriot looked sideways at her boarder and returned his laugh. "Not a bad idea; perhaps you should stand and lead us in this little song?"

"Not likely," he snorted. "That's a little out of my line of work! As you know, I'm only a lowly writer, not a singer or musician! I'm a city man and I'd never even heard of a hayrack, or a hayrack converted into a sleigh, before last week! This business of writing my novels from the location where the story takes place has opened up a whole new world to me." He let out a hearty laugh: "Both as to the character of the people in small towns, and what they do with, and for, each other."

Nettie Herriot laughed back at him. (Laughing was an activity she had rarely indulged in for many years, but the reconciliation with Randell and Mr. Kincaid, and the coming of little Susan to her boarding house, had brought happiness and laughter into her previously stern life) "It just goes to show you that city folk need to get out and broaden their lives!" she said.

"Interesting! Most city dwellers would see it the other way around!"

She laughed again. He enjoyed hearing her laugh. It was a sharp contrast to her dour disposition of a few months ago. "But they're wrong!" she exclaimed. "Our lives aren't nearly as dull as those city folks think!" She looked at him and winked. He was surprised, as he had never seen her indulge in jesting or kidding. "It can actually get pretty exciting around this little town from time to time!" She lowered her voice as she leaned close and whispered. "Sometimes it's even a little too exciting, since everyone in the community knows everyone else, and what they're up to!"

Kincaid leaned back against the side of the sleigh and observed some of the people of the small town of Blackberry, Minnesota. *What an interesting cross-section of humanity! And they sure made for interesting writing material!*

Randell covered Susan and Stella's legs with a blanket. "Are you both warm and comfortable?"

Stella's face carried a broad smile as she looked up and exclaimed. "Randell were as snug as a bug in a rug!"

Little Susan, who was snuggled close to Stella, giggled and mimicked Stella as she looked at Randell. "Yes, Daddy, we're like a bug in a rug!" She looked at Stella and giggled again.

Randell seated himself on an adjacent bale of straw and watched the snow-covered streets of Blackberry glide slowly past the sleigh. His heart was full of exhilaration. It had been a long time since he had been this contented and happy. In fact, it had been well over twenty years! The events of the past days and months, since his return to Blackberry, filled him with wonder, and a little awe. He had his old cabinet shop back. Most of the people of the community had accepted him, and many were his friends. A little orphan girl was now calling him "Daddy." And most astonishing of all, Stella Cunningham had re-entered his life. A year ago, he could not have envisioned any of this happening to him, especially the return of Stella Cunningham. Where would these unexpected events lead?

Within a few minutes Charles pulled the sleigh to a halt in front of his parents' home, and Captolia and Carlisle Adams soon found a bale of straw to use as a seat. Captolia had hugged her son as he helped her up onto the hayrack. "It looks as if you've got a large group today Charles, and, as usual, it appears that everyone is having a great time!"

Charles smiled at his mother. "Yes Mom, it's an especially interesting group of people this year. I think they're all enjoying themselves." He gazed up at the blue sky. "It's a beautiful winter day for a ride in the sleigh."

Within moments the sleigh was gliding along the road leading out of town. Charles held the horses back and they moved past the snow-covered fields and trees at a leisurely pace. Charles smiled to himself as the light-hearted chatter of his passengers drifted forward to the driver's seat.

The early afternoon sun danced across the snow-covered fields and pastures. The snow frocked pines and spruce, which lined the road, sparkled like diamonds in the brilliant sunshine. The heavy snow seemed to muffle all sound except the clip-clop of the horse's hooves, the soft whisper of the sleigh runners, and the talk and laughter of the happy passengers.

Charles guided the horses and sleigh around a bend in the road and startled two, buck deer. The deer lifted their heads, snorted, and quickly bound away into the safety of the woods. Little Susan squealed as she pointed at the deer. "Oh, Mommy, see the deer!" Stella glanced at Randell, smiled, and pulled the little girl closer to her.

As the sleigh glided silently along the road, Stella looked toward the front of the hayrack and watched Charles as he drove the horses. He sat ramrod straight. and she could see that he was a comfortable and confident teamster. His four children sat next to him and were all engaged in happy, animated, conversation as they laughed, and pointed at horses, cattle, and birds. She could see that Charles was the contented father of four happy children. As she watched Charles she remembered what he had said to her about taking little Susan. "Stella, it will all work out!" She hoped he was right.

The big sleigh continued to glide silently over the snow packed road. Stella's heart was a kaleidoscope of wonder, and amazement, at what had happened to her since she had returned to Blackberry, a dejected, sick, and dying woman. Her past had been so unhappy, and painful, that anything was an improvement. Her life *had* improved immeasurably since her return to Blackberry! Would this happiness continue for her, or would it revert to the pain and sorrow, which had filled her life over the past twenty years? Or would it come to a sudden end with her death?

She remembered something the Pastor of the little church had said during their Bible study last week. "God has a character of love toward all that he has created, and kindness is a product of love. When we love someone, we will be kind to them!"

Kindness and love! Perhaps they were the key to her future happiness. And, she had hope now! Something that had not been present when she had taken the bus back to Blackberry. The Blackberry doctor had said she might not die! She would cling to that hope. She would cling to it for the little girl who sat at her side.

Her thoughts were interrupted as the sleigh glided along the edge of an ice-covered lake. Some teenagers had cleared the snow away from its frozen surface and were playing a game of hockey. Their game came to a temporary halt, and they shouted and waved, as the big sleigh slipped past.

An hour later Charles pulled the sleigh to a halt in his farmyard. With much laughter, giggling, and many smiles, his passengers alighted and were welcomed into the house by Beth. "There's hot chocolate and apple juice, as well as donuts and rolls on the kitchen table. Just help yourself. I hope everyone enjoyed the sleigh ride?"

Kincaid spoke first. "It was the most fun I've had in ages; didn't even get cold!" Everyone nodded their heads and gave verbal expressions of their agreement.

The twins, Morton, and Marie, with shy smiles, made their way across the room to where Susan sat between Stella and Randell. Marie looked up at Stella. "Can the little girl come and play with us? We've got some toys and picture books in our bedroom."

Susan slid quickly from her chair and looked at Stella. "Can I go play with them Mommy? Please!"

Stella patted her on the head. "Of course; you run along and have a good time playing with your new friends!"

"Oh goodie," she exclaimed, as she skipped across the room.

The hot chocolate warmed her frail body and the roll was sweet and delicious. Stella looked about the living room and turned to Randell. "It's a lovely home, and so neat and comfortable!"

"Yes, it's a very nice home. I've been here before when I came to visit Beth, shortly after I first returned to Blackberry, and when I remodeled the kitchen last summer."

Stella looked up to see a middle-aged lady making her way across the living room toward her. The lady was short, hardly exceeding five feet. Her hair was streaked with grey and was pulled back in a tight bun. Her face was pleasant, and smiling, as she spoke. "Hello, I'm Captolia Adams; Charles Adam's mother. I don't believe we've had the pleasure of meeting before."

Stella and Randell rose quickly to their feet. "It's very nice to meet you Mrs. Adams. I'm Stella Cunningham and this is Randell Cordell."

Captolia's eyes were kind. "We haven't met, but I know who you both are. My son and daughter-in-law have told me some about your return, after a long absence." She smiled. "Please relax; I'm not here to censor either of you!"

"I was just remarking to Randell that this is such a lovely and cozy home," said Stella.

'Yes, isn't it! Come, I'll give you both a quick tour of the house."

Randell looked at the two women. "You two go ahead, as I've seen the house. I'll stay here in case Susan needs something."

He watched as Captolia Adams led Stella across the living room, her voice full of animated exclamation's dealing with the

182

furnishings and decorations of the room. He returned to his chair. He could hear Susan's giggle coming from the bedroom.

Charles' mother walked Stella through every room in the house and then into a small library and office. Mrs. Adams waved her hand across the room. "This is Beth's office and writing room." She looked at Stella. "You know, of course, that Beth is quite an accomplished writer? She is first and foremost a wife and mother, but she can also write great short stories. I believe she makes a good deal of money from her writings. And this room is where she writes her stories." She pointed to a typewriter setting on the desk. "That's her new typewriter. I understand it's the latest model. It looks so nice and sleek compared to her old typewriter. You saw her old typewriter on the chest in the living room." Captolia looked at Stella. "Beth found the old typewriter in the attic of the abandoned cabin they lived in when they came here five years ago. It belonged to Louise Cordell, Randell's deceased wife! I . . . I think she keeps the old typewriter in memory of Louise!"

Stella wasn't sure just where this conversation was leading, and she was startled and apprehensive. She glanced at Mrs. Adams. "Yes, I . . . I know about the old typewriter. Beth came to visit me, shortly after I returned to Blackberry. She told me about finding the old typewriter, and the story she wrote about a sick woman dying all alone in a little cabin."

Mrs. Adams smiled at Stella, as if to quiet her concerns about the topic of the conversation. She motioned Stella to a chair. "Stella, if you don't mind I'd like to visit with you for a few minutes, and perhaps give you some encouragement. Beth has told me about your return to Blackberry and your serious illness. And, of course, I know all about your running off with Randell, twenty years ago. In fact, nearly everybody hereabouts knows what happened those many years ago."

Captolia motioned Stella to take a chair, as she seated herself at an adjacent chair. "Stella, I'm not interested in rehashing what you and Randell did years ago. That's all in the past and is best forgotten;

put out of mind!" She reached forward and took Stella's hand in hers. The touch of Captolia's hand reassured Stella. She sensed that Captolia was a woman full of kindness, love, and tenderness. There was no harsh judgement in her face, or voice.

"Stella, I would like to tell you about some women who lived a long time ago, during Bible times. I believe the experiences of these women will give you some encouragement, and hope, as you work to rebuild your own life."

Stella sat in the chair, her face pale, and her lips trembling a little. Mrs. Adams comments forced painful memories to the forefront of her mind. "I . . . I don't know much about the Bible," she stammered. She looked up at Mrs. Adams and a trace of a smile came to her eyes. "But Randell and I are meeting with the pastor of the church twice a week, and he's studying the Bible with us, and I . . . I'm learning a lot and enjoy the studies very much."

Captolia's face was filled with reassurance as she said. "Stella, I think the Bible studies are great! It tells me you're headed in the right direction. In addition to your Bible studies, I would like to tell you about several women who made some serious mistakes in their lives. In fact, their mistakes were very similar to your mistakes! However, these women were able to overcome their tragic errors and go on to live productive and happy lives. Stella, I believe the example of these woman can help you do the same!"

Captolia pulled her chair a little closer to Stella. She began by telling Stella the story of Rahab, a Canaanite woman, a harlot, who lived in the walled town of Jericho. When the Hebrew spies had come to her home Rahab had not attempted to take advantage of the men. Instead, she had given them aid when they were about to be discovered. Mrs. Adams told Stella how Rehab had, by giving her heart to the Lord, ceased being a harlot. Captolia then told Stella about the woman who was taken in adultery. "Taken in the very act!" She told Stella how Christ had compassion for the woman and had told her that her accusers had all fled. Christ had then told the woman that she should go and sin no more. In short, she needed to make a fresh start, and change the way she lived. Christ told her, that if she had faith, she could change her life from a sinful woman, to a loving and kind woman. And then, Mrs. Adams told Stella about the Samaritan woman Christ had met at the well. The woman had had affairs with several men. Captolia related how Christ had invited her to drink from the pure waters He offered her, and how those "waters" of truth, compassion, and forgiveness, would change her life. She told Stella how, much to the surprise of almost everyone, the woman had become a witness for Christ to the villagers where she lived.

Mrs. Adams voice was full of compassion, and understanding, as she continued. "Stella, the Bible is not a book about perfect, sinless, people. Quite the contrary! The Bible is filled with stories of the lives, the mistakes, the sins, and the triumphs, of ordinary people. These people were all sinners, and many had made quite a mess of their lives! But because they put their faith in God they were able to change their lives and became productive citizens. It's really quite amazing!"

Stella sat quietly, thinking of what Mrs. Adams had just told her. "I . . . I didn't know about these women. Thank you for telling me of them!"

Mrs. Adams continued. "Stella, when these women changed they began a new life of giving, instead of taking. That was the key; that was the difference! Stella, you should 'make friends with giving!' Make giving, and love for others, a guiding principle in your life! If you do this, I have no doubt that much good will come to you!'

"Yes . . . yes, I see what you mean. We should each give to make the world a better place instead of taking all that we can for yourself! I think that has been the cause of many of my problems and heartaches over the past years!"

Captolia continued. "Stella, one of the greatest tragedies in life is to be all alone and not to be loved. From what I can see, this little girl you have taken in, I believe her name is Susan, has learned to love you a great deal. Stella, she's giving you her love without any conditions! She doesn't care a whit about your past! Oh Stella, don't be afraid to return her love! I . . . I believe this little girl will be a great blessing to you, and you will be a wonderful blessing to her!"

The two women stood, and Mrs. Adams pulled Stella's frail body to hers and hugged her tight. "Stella, I have no interest in your past and I don't know much about your present illness, but I encourage you not to lose faith. I want you to know that both my husband and I will be praying for your recovery from your illness, and, perhaps as important, we will also pray that you may find peace, love, and happiness, in the years to come."

Stella's eyes were full of tears as she whispered. "Thank you, Mrs. Adams. Thank you so much for telling me about the women from Bible times, and . . . and for praying for me." In a spontaneous action Stella's arms encircled Captolia as she exclaimed. "And I . . . I do want to change, just . . . just like the women you told me about!

CHAPTER 22

University Hospital

The early morning sun cast long, grotesque, shadows through the bare limbs of the oak trees and onto the hospital lawn. The grass was showing a strong hint of green and the bare branches of the trees were beginning to swell with fat buds, heralding the advent of the long-awaited spring. Randell Cordell stood at the second story window of the University Hospital and watched as a squirrel scampered about the lawn and then dug with frantic efforts about the base of a tree, as it searched for buried acorns. Two blue jays flew from tree to tree and then flapped away over the trees and were gone from his view. A small lake, of perhaps half an acre, occupied the far edge of the hospital grounds, providing a pleasant view for the patients fortunate enough to have rooms on this side of the hospital.

He turned from the window and glanced to his right. Susan was seated on a cushioned chair turning the pages of a children's picture book he had carried along to the hospital. Her face was filled with a smile and he knew she was very happy to be here with him in the waiting room. The three of them had arrived shortly after seven. The paperwork had been completed shortly before eight and the nurse had taken Stella away to prepare her for surgery.

When the nurse had led Stella away she had spoken to Randell. "When Miss Cunningham has changed into a hospital gown and is fully prepared for surgery I'll return for you and . . . and the little girl.

You'll be able to come into the prep room and visit with the patient for a few minutes before she's taken to the operating room." The nurse's brow had been furrowed as she cast a quick, side-ways, glance at Susan. Children were not usually allowed into patient's rooms, except during visiting hours, and certainly not into the surgical prep area.

Randell had spoken with Dr. Blackstone and Dr. Hadley, the surgeon, about bringing Susan to the hospital and into the prep room. "The little girl is an orphan, who lost both of her parents in a car accident, and she has become very attached to Miss Cunningham." He had paused, and his face had been filled with concern as he had continued. "We had planned on leaving her with friends during Miss Cunningham's stay in the hospital, but the child is deathly afraid she will be permanently separated from Miss Cunningham. Is it possible for you to make an exception and allow the little girl to be with me, and under my careful supervision, whenever we are here at the hospital?"

Dr. Blackstone had sat in silence for a moment. "I think we can bend the rules a bit." He had glanced at Dr. Hadley. "In fact, I believe the presence of the little girl may actually benefit the patient in her recovery from surgery. Do you agree?"

"Yes, I concur. I see no harm in the presence of the child unless some unforeseen complications should arise."

A few days before leaving for the hospital, Randell had approached Charles and Beth Adams and asked if they would be willing to look after Susan, at their home, during the approximately three-week period they would be at the University Hospital for Stella's surgery and recovery.

"Of course!" replied Beth. "We'll be very happy to keep little Susan during Stella's surgery, and for as long as she's in the hospital."

Stella and Randall had sat Susan on the edge of her little bed and Stella had said to her. "Mommy still has a tummy ache and both Mr. Cordell and I will need to go away for several weeks while the doctors fix Mommy's tummy ache. Would you like to stay with the twins, Morton and Marie, while Mommy and Mr. Cordell are away?"

But Susan had become frantic with fear. She had flung herself onto Stella's lap as she had sobbed. "You don't want me anymore and are going away and will never come back, just like my other Mommy did!" She had looked up into Stella's face through tear filled eyes. "Oh, please can I go with you? I'll be really good; I promise!"

The child's sobs, and anguish, had been too much for Randell. He had swept the little girl up into his arms. "Of course, you can come with us. I . . . I think you'll be a big help to Mommy while she's in the hospital!"

Stella had looked at Randell. "Do you think the hospital will let a little girl into the prep room and then into my hospital room? Hospitals are pretty strict about such things!"

Randell had put on a confident face. "I'll speak to the doctors. I'll work it out one way or another!" He had spoken with conviction and had hoped he could pull it off for the sake of both the little girl, and Stella. He felt sure that Susan's presence would comfort and cheer Stella while she was in the hospital. Perhaps even hasten her recovery from the surgery.

He had left the shop in the care of his three men, Robert, Todd, and Julian. They were all capable men, and he felt comfortable leaving them in charge of his business. However, he did telephone and talk to Robert every morning to review the days orders and work schedule.

He turned from the child and looked out through the window and across the grass and trees toward the lake. He watched two robins prance about the lawn as they hunted for early spring worms. The long northern winter had fought a bitter battle, but spring had finally won the struggle. The little lake was free of ice, and within a few weeks the mowers would be at work cutting grass, the trees would be filed with leaves, and flowers would cover the meadows.

As he gazed out the window he felt a tension, a pain in his heart and body, and he was restless and uneasy. The time for Stella's long-awaited surgery had finally arrived. Today, or very soon, the truth about the tumor would become known. Was the tumor a cancer, or not? Would Stella live or die? He could not remember such stress and tension, even in the cold foxholes of Belgium, with bullets screaming past, and shells bursting all about. It seemed to Randell that the tension and stress was even present here on the surgical floor of the hospital. Everyone seemed to be focused on preparing one patient, Stella Cunningham, for surgery! He knew this was just his imagination at work, a product of his tension. The day for the surgery had now arrived, and he was focused on only one patient. He could not squelch the fear and concern which filled his heart.

Over the past few days his neck, shoulders, and back had taken on a dull pain and ache again, and he had not been able to sleep well. His thoughts were ever with Stella, her wellbeing, and today's surgery. He could not recall when he had been so bound-up in the wellbeing of another person. His life, and plans, such as they had been before her unexpected return, had been upended. Nothing was ever going to be the same for him again. Stella's return, and a little orphan girl, had changed everything in his life.

Would the surgery be successful, or would it be a death sentence? The doctors had hedged; they were not sure. Following his examination and completion of additional tests, Dr. Blackstone had said to Stella and Randell. "I concur with Dr. Jensen's diagnosis. You have a very large tumor, which must be removed." The doctor had seated himself directly in front of Stella and his voice had been full of compassion as he had continued. "Miss Cunningham, this will be a delicate and difficult operation of three to four hours. However, I have every confidence in Dr. Hadley, the surgeon who will conduct the operation."

His voice had been full of compassion as he continued. "I'm aware you've been told the tumor is most likely cancerous. We will not know for sure until the tissue samples are returned from the laboratory, however, I believe the odds are against such an outcome. It has been my experience that these types of large tumors are seldom cancerous. They are usually just large growths. I understand it will not be easy for you but try not to worry about the possibility of cancer." He had smiled at her. "Worrying won't make one wit of difference to the outcome!"

The voice of the nurse interrupted Randell's thoughts. "Mr. Cordell!"

At the sound of her voice Randell turned from the window and Susan looked up from the picture book. "Yes Ma'am."

"You, and the little girl, may come into the prep room and visit with Miss Cunningham for a few minutes before she's taken into surgery. Please come with me."

Randell had spoken with Susan before they had arrived at the hospital. "Susan, we are going to take Mommy to a place for sick people who have a tummy ache. It's called a hospital and it's very important that you be very quiet while we are there. You mustn't run and make any noise."

Susan had nodded her head up and down. "I'll . . . I'll be quiet Daddy. I promise to be really good!"

The nurse pulled back the curtain to allow Randell and Susan entry into the little room. Stella lay in the hospital bed, clad in a light blue hospital gown. A light cover was pulled up well past her waist. The head of the bed had been raised and her head was resting on a pillow. Her eyes darted from Randell to Susan. Her face was pale and filled with anxiety and fear.

Randell lifted Susan and sat her on the edge of the bed. Susan looked at Stella and it seemed to Randell the little girl immediately sensed the gravity of the situation. Susan sat in silence for a moment and then she slowly reached and stroked Stella's face with a tender touch. "I . . . I love you Mommy." Stella pulled the little girl into her arms and held her close as she whispered. "Oh . . . oh Susan, I . . . I love you so much!"

Susan snuggled close beside Stella and patted her on the shoulder. Randell pulled a chair close. "How are you doing Stella?"

Her face was full of distress. "I . . . I know the doctor told me not to worry! But I can't help it!" She looked into Randell's eyes. "I'm scared Randell! I'm afraid the tumor will either be cancerous, or I'll never wake up from the surgery!"

She dabbed at her eyes with a tissue and Susan continued to pat her shoulder. She looked directly at Randell as she spoke. "Randell, when I came back to Blackberry, a few months ago, I had lost all hope for any kind of a future, happy or otherwise. I just wanted some help until I died." She lifted her head from the pillow and her voice was filled with pathos as she said. "But . . . but now, so much has changed, and I have this little girl, and I have you, and I have new friends. Oh Randell, I . . . I don't want to die! I want to live!" She glanced down at the little girl snuggled at her breast. "I love this little girl and I want to be her mother! I want to care for her! I want to live for her!" Her head slumped back onto the pillow as a barely audible sigh escaped here lips.

Randell rose from the chair and stood at the edge of the bed. He took her hand in his. "I understand, Stella. I . . . I know this is all very difficult for you. Few of us ever face the surgery you are undergoing in a few minutes. I wish I knew how to take the fear and uncertainty away, but Stella, I want you to know that I do care, and I also love this little girl, and . . . and if anything should happen to you, I promise I'll look after her, and love her!"

Stella slowly raised her head from the pillow and fixed her eyes on Randell. "Randell, it's more than little Susan." She pulled her hand from his grasp and reached up and touched his cheek. "Randell, I . . . I must tell you, before they take me a way! Oh Randell, I've fallen in love with *you*. I love Susan, *and* you! I love you both!" Her head fell back onto the pillow and she was silent for a moment as she gazed into his startled face. Her voice was filled with wonder, and questions, as she whispered. "Is . . . is it alright for me to fall in love with you?"

Her anguished and poignant words were interrupted by the nurse as she drew back the curtain. "Mr. Cordell, you and the little girl will have to leave now. It's time to take Miss Cunningham to the operating room."

As he turned to the nurse Stella's last words were pounding through his head like the rumble of a fast-moving freight train. "I'm sorry, Ma'am, but may I have prayer with Miss Cunningham before you take her to surgery? It'll only take a minute!"

"Yes, I'll return in a couple of minutes, but don't dawdle!"

Randell turned back to Stella. He leaned forward and lightly stroked her cheek, and his voice was soft with care and compassion as he spoke. "No Stella I don't think it's bad for you to fall in love with me. Love is never bad!" He paused and then continued. "Stella, I . . . I want to have prayer with you before they take you to surgery."

"Yes, Randell, please pray for me! I'd . . . I'd like that very much!"

Randell took her hand in his, and then reached and took the hand of Susan. As he bowed his head he saw the little girl bow her head and close her eyes tight. He tried to keep his voice calm as he prayed. "Dear Lord, this little girl and I are asking you to be present in the operating room today and guide the hands of the surgeons. And we especially pray there will be no cancer; and that Stella can return very soon to her home and continue to be a mother to this little girl. Thank you, Lord; Amen."

As Randell opened his eyes, Susan spoke. "I want to pray for Mommy too! Can I pray for Mommy? I learned how to pray in church!" Stella voice was full of tenderness as she said. "Yes, Susan, you can pray for Mommy! I would like that very much."

The little girl immediately clasped both of her hands together and bowed her head. "Dear Jesus, please take my Mommy's tummy ache away. Amen."

When Randell looked up, the nurse stood at the entrance to the little room. "That's a right nice prayer, little girl!" The nurse advanced into the room and stood in silence as Randell lifted Susan from the bed, and then she spoke to Susan. "It's time to take your Mommy to the operating room!"

Susan waved her little hands at Stella as she was wheeled from the room. "Goodbye Mommy; Daddy and I will be waiting for you when you come back!"

The heartache and pain that had gripped her only a few minutes ago slipped away, and her heart was now full of love and hope, as she was wheeled away from the prep room and down the hallway toward the surgery. The voice of the little girl echoed through her now peaceful and happy mind. *"Daddy and I will be waiting for you!"* How wonderful that someone cared for her and were even looking forward to seeing her again! People who loved her were waiting for her return! Her fear was gone, and she closed her eyes in peace, as the nurse pushed her toward the operating room.

Randell struggled to maintain his composure as he watched Stella, and the two nurses, recede along the corridor. The events of the past few minutes had left him badly shaken. She had told him that she *loved him!*

Slowly he turned and took the little girl's hand in his. He tried to keep his voice calm as he said. "We haven't had any breakfast. Shall we find someplace to eat?"

Susan looked up at him with a smile. "I think Mommy's tummy ache will be gone when she comes back."

Randell knelt and drew the little girl close. Her faith was boundless, and unafraid. He hoped it was not in vain. He knew he loved this little girl. "Yes . . . yes," he whispered. "I'm sure Mommy's tummy ache will be gone very soon!"

They walked to a nearby diner he had seen. Randell dawdled over his breakfast of hotcakes and eggs. Stella's words continued to reverberate through his head and heart. *"I love both of you"* She had never told him before, even twenty years ago, when they had run off together, that she loved him. Their relationship had been built on opportunity, and passion! There had been no foundation of true love. Did she really mean what she had said, or had it just come out under the stress of the imminent surgery? If she really meant what she had said it changed everything for Stella, for him, and for the little orphan girl! He had a strong suspicion the three of them had started walking along a new pathway today!

When they had finished eating their breakfast he took the little girl's hand and they walked back toward the hospital. Susan hopped, skipped, and giggled, as they walked along the sidewalk. Randell looked down at her. *What a delightful little girl!* She had brought so much joy, love, and happiness to him and Stella! She had been a catalyst for change in their lives!

He chose a route which would take them along the little lake. They still had at least two hours before the surgery would be completed, and the doctor reported to him. The spring sun was warm and pleasant, and he found a small bench to set on. Three ducks waddled along the shore of the little lake, only a few feet away from where they sat. He had stuffed a piece of toast into his pocket and now he retrieved it, broke it into small pieces and handed them to Susan. He motioned toward the ducks. "You can feed the bread to the ducks. Just throw the pieces of bread in front of them and watch them gobble them up."

She laughed at the silly antics of the ducks as they fought over the pieces of bread. "Oh, the ducks are funny," she exclaimed.

His thoughts drifted back to Stella. She would have enjoyed watching little Susan feed the ducks! Now that she had been taken away to surgery, and her life hung on what the surgeons found, he was aware he missed her terribly, and he wished she were here with him and Susan. Just the three of them, setting on the park bench as a family. The word "family" startled him, and he gazed across the lake, his brow knit in wonder at what this all meant for the three of them. He and Stella would need to marry if the three of them were to become a real family! His mind was full of turmoil as he continued to watch Susan throw bread to the eager ducks. Stella's words: "I have fallen in love with you," continued to echo through the chambers of his mind.

He wondered how the surgery was progressing. The tensions had not abated. His shoulders and leg hurt, and he was full of anxiety and fear. What if the tumor were cancerous? The doctor had said. "Don't worry about it. You can't change anything by worrying!" Well, that was easier said than done!

He reached out his hand to the little girl. "Come, it's time we started back to the hospital."

She looked up at him with big eyes. "Carry me Daddy, carry me on your shoulders!"

"Carry You!" His face carried a broad grin as he looked down at her. "I can't carry you," he teased! "You're such a big girl; you're too heavy for me to carry!"

She giggled, as she shook her head of golden curls. "No, I'm not too big for you to carry. I want to ride piggyback on your shoulders. Please, Daddy!"

He laughed as he grabbed her about the waist and swung her up onto his shoulders. "How's that!" he exclaimed. "Is that fun?"

Her arms encircled his forehead as she laughed and giggled. "Giddyap, horsey, go! Giddyap Daddy!"

He laughed and set off along the walk leading to the hospital. Susan sat, laughing and giggling, on his shoulders. She giggled again, "Giddyap horsey!" His heart was full of love for the little girl, and hope for Stella.

196

Within a few minutes they were back in the surgical waiting room. Susan looked at the picture book for several minutes and then she put the book aside and laid her head in his lap. Within a few minutes she was sound asleep. The little girl wasn't worrying about the outcome of the surgery! He wished he had her faith. The untroubled faith of a child!

Randell had closed his eyes and nodded off when he heard the surgeon's voice. "Mr. Cordell, sorry to interrupt your nap, but I know you'll want to hear my report."

Randell shook the drowsiness from his head and looked up at the doctor. "Oh yes, Dr. Hadley! I'm sorry I nodded off."

"That's quite all right Mr. Cordell. Setting in a waiting room can be quite boring." Doctor Hadley pulled up a nearby chair. Susan had not stirred and continued to sleep; her golden curls scattered across Randell's lap. The doctor glanced at the little girl. "She sure is a sweet little girl, isn't she? I'm happy we let her come to the hospital. I believe her presence will be beneficial for the patient during her recovery."

Randell's heart was pounding. "Yes, she is a wonderful little girl. Stella loves her very much, and . . . and I love her a great deal also."

The doctor looked at Randell. "Mr. Cordell, based on the outcome of the surgery, which I can tell you went quite well, I believe Stella and this little girl, (he paused and smiled) and perhaps you, as well, will spend many happy years together. The surgery was a complete success and I am quite confident the lab reports will come back negative. There will be no cancer. Barring unforeseen complications, I believe we will discharge her in about ten days." The doctor placed his hand on Randell's shoulder. 'The only negative news I have is that she will never be able to bear any children."

Randell's heart was about to burst, and he could hardly speak. "Thank . . . thank you doctor! Thank you so very much. That . . . that is wonderful news!"

The doctor placed his hand on Randell's shoulder. "I know you're happy with this good report, and I'm very pleased to be able to give it to you." The doctor shook his hand and left the waiting room.

Randell sat in numb silence, his mind a cauldron of emotions. He looked down at Susan. She was sleeping, but he couldn't restrain himself. In one swift motion he swept the little girl up into his arms and held her close. Her eyes popped open with a start. He was laughing, and crying, as he looked into her questioning eyes, and exclaimed in a loud voice. "Susan, the doctor was just here, and he said that Mommy's tummy ache is all gone. Isn't that wonderful!"

The little girl's arms entwined about his neck and there was a childish lilt in her voice as she exclaimed. "Oh yes, I knew the doctor would fix Mommy's tummy ache!"

CHAPTER 23

Healed, Body and Soul

S tella paused at the crest of the small mountain. Here, high above the village, there was no sound except the soft rustle of the afternoon breeze through the pine, birch, and aspen trees, and the calls of birds, as they flew from tree to tree. Even though it was well past noon the air was cool and refreshing and carried the scent of pine. The walk up the steep path had tired her, and her breathing was heavy from the effort. She looked about for a place to rest. The nearby flat stump of a tree, which had been logged off many years ago, provided her with a place to set, and with a sigh of relief she slumped down onto the old stump.

Slowly her breathing returned to normal as she took in the loveliness of the valley, spread, like jeweled tapestry, below her. At the bottom of the vale the pastel-colored houses of Blackberry, with grey shingled roofs, lay clustered along the tree lined streets. In the midst of the town the white church spire rose up into the sky. Beyond the town the road ran curving off into the distance. The valley itself stretched northward, broad, and sunlit, bounded by fields, meadows, forests, hills, and small mountains. Above it all was the pale blue sky with fat, white clouds, floating; suspended, in time and space.

Near the edge of the town the placid waters of the lake sparkled in the afternoon sunshine. A few homes lay scattered, like doll houses, along the shore of the lake. Stretching out beyond the lake lay fields of corn, oats, and bright green meadows full of cattle, which looked like toys, and over it all hung an almost imperceptible opal-tinted haze that softened the brightness of the colors. Her eyes swept across the small town and then across the fields, meadows, and tree-covered hillsides, and she sensed a quiet and peaceful oasis of serenity, calm, and beauty.

The hush of the mountain top was in sharp contrast to the hustle, bustle, and noise, of the cities where she had lived for much of her past. The stillness of the forest, and promontory, where she sat, seemed to speak to her with soft voices of comfort and peace. She continued to gaze across the valley as her thoughts traveled back. Back, over the whole of her forty years.

She remembered her childhood. At first, happy and carefree, as with most children, and then her growing anger and rebellion against the strict constraints of her parents, especially her mother. Why had those rules been such an agitation to her when they hadn't had the same impact on her younger brother?

As she pondered the question she remembered something the pastor had read from the Bible during one of their Bible Studies. She couldn't remember the exact words, but she remembered the scripture said that wise people lived by the law of God, and that God's law was a fountain of life, and a shield against the evils of the world.

She had rebelled against the rules of her mother and the church they had attended. She understood now that those rules (laws) were there for her wellbeing and protection, and in rebelling against her parents rules she had sown the seeds of her unhappiness and degradation.

Her reflections moved forward to her deception of Randell into aiding her, and her friends, in tunneling into the bank vault. Her heart was filled with remorse, and pain. She had seduced him into this deception, and her seduction had led to the lonely death of his wife, Louise, in the little cabin.

She gave a heavy sigh as she remembered the years of back-breaking labor in the hot and sultry prison laundry. Each twelve-hour day had left her tired, worn-out, and exhausted. When she had been released from prison she had secured employment in the munition's factory, with a steady paycheck and reasonable hours. The war had come to an end, and so had her job. All attempts to find work had failed. Her prison record, and reputation, sealed her doom! Hopelessness, desperation, and loneliness followed. And then she had begun to experience an actual want for food and a place to sleep. She had wandered the streets and alleys, all alone, afraid, and without real friends.

And then, with a shudder, that slashed through her body like a sharp knife, she remembered the humiliation of submitting to the vile and dirty men. Most of all she remembered their hands. Their dirty and rough hands! Their touching, groping, pushing, moving, squeezing, shoving hands! Hands everywhere on her body! With an audible cry she remembered their grunts and their smell!

Her head was now bowed forward, and a few tears flowed along her cheek as she sat on the tree stump. Time seemed to stand still as the memories of those terrible months filled her mind with anguish and pain.

Slowly she lifted her head and gazed across the green vale, which lay below her, and her eyes fixed on the church spire. The church and hamlet lay peaceful and serene, amidst the green valley, in sharp contrast to her tumultuous past. As she focused her mind on the pastoral scene, those dreadful memories began to fade into the far recesses of her mind.

Those turbulent scenes, of her sordid past, were gently replaced by the memory of Randell Cordell taking her to Mrs. Harriet's rooming house, where she was given a nice room, a warm bath, a hot bowl of soup, and a comfortable robe. Her heart welled full of happiness as she remembered the visit of Beth Adams, offering comfort, forgiveness, and help. And then a vision of a golden-haired little girl, setting at a small table, head bowed, coloring in her color book rose up, sharp and clear, in her mind. She recalled a sleigh ride through a winter wonderland, and stories by Mrs. Adams, of women from Bible times. Fallen woman who had overcome their sins and started new lives. Lives of service to others.

And then the lilting, and sweet voice of the little girl welled up in her heart. *"Daddy and I will be waiting for you!"* And the little girl and Randell *had* been there when she had awakened from the surgery! It had been wonderful to open her eyes and see their smiling faces!

She sat in silent contemplation for many minutes as her heart filled with all that had taken place since her return to Blackberry, a broken and dying woman. And then, with wonder and thankfulness, she whispered into the stillness of the mountain top. *"It's over, it's past! I've been healed, I've been saved, changed, and I'm now cleansed, made whole again, and . . . and loved! Oh, thank you Lord!*

Her gaze swept across the peaceful valley again. The incongruity of what had happened to her left her stunned and breathless. Oh, wonder of wonders! She had been rescued by Randell Cordell, the very man she had wronged those many years ago! And she had been introduced to true love by a little golden-haired orphan girl, who had given her unconditional love. How very mysterious! How very improbable! Love and giving had triumphed!

There, in the silence of the mountain top, she knew the loneliness, humiliation, and disgrace, would never come again. She had been healed of her cancer, and her sins had been forgiven, and a new, and untarnished, future lay open before her. She was determined, from this day forward, to live by God's law; she would no longer rebel against that wonderful, blessed, decalogue, that spread happiness and contentment in its wake.

A cloud moved slowly across the sun, casting long shadows along the mountain top, and then floated along the valley and across

202

the lake. Stella Cunningham continued to think of many things as she sat on the tree stump, looking down on the little village. Her tears were now gone and there was a radiant smile on her shining face.

She held her gaze on the peaceful valley below, as she remembered the admonition *of Captolia: "Make friends with giving. Make giving of your time, and means, a guiding principle in your life."* As the weeks had slipped by, she had begun to understand a great deal more of what Mrs. Adams had meant. She should not shut herself up in her past grief and pain. She should let go of the mistakes of the past, and embrace a life of giving, as opposed to selfishness, and taking from others. Yes, she wanted to become a giving and loving woman. She must give to Randell, to Susan, and to all the people of the little village nestled in the valley below her! She was determined to think of new ways to help others.

She remained there on the mountain top for a long time, contemplating and thinking. Thinking mostly of Susan and Randell. Those two were the focus of her thoughts. The man and the orphan girl had now become the center, the fulcrum, of her life. She must think only of their happiness and wellbeing, not her own. She now had a clear understanding that her own happiness was intertwined with the happiness of these two people. Everything else was secondary!

Once again, her gaze traveled out across the sun-light valley, over the rolling meadows and up toward the far hills. Her heart was singing with love and joy. It was bursting with feelings and sensations she had never experienced before. She had fallen deeply in love with this little orphan girl, and with this wonderful man! She wasn't in love with the same man she had ran off with twenty years ago. No, he was a different man now, as she was a different woman! True love had come into her life and had replaced the selfishness, which had controlled so much of her past.

The shadows were now long, and the sun hung low above the haze filled western sky, as she moved, with brisk steps, along the trail that led down the mountain, into the valley, and to the little village.

Randell and little Susan would return soon from their excursion to Grand Rapids. Randell had come to her shortly after lunch. "I have some errands to run in Grand Rapids and I think I'll take Susan along with me. She loves to ride in the pickup and look for cows and horses. She won't be a bother, and when I'm finished with my errands we'll stop at the soda fountain and share a dish of ice-cream, with chocolate spread across the ice cream, and a cherry on top. We'll have a wonderful time!"

Stella's face carried a radiant smile, and her heart was singing, as she walked along the trail leading down the mountainside.

CHAPTER 24

Forgiveness

On this pleasant summer day Stella Cunningham and the orphan girl, Susan, stood under the arch at the entrance to the Blackberry Cemetery. Stella looked to her left and then to her right, scanning the numerous tombstones marking the resting places of many of the past residents of the little community. The little girl tugged at her hand. "Mommy, where are we taking the flowers?"

She looked down at the little girl. "Honey, we're going to place them on a lady's grave, but we need to find her grave. It's somewhere here in the cemetery, but I don't know where."

"Who is the lady Mommy? Did I ever see her?"

She looked down again at the little girl. "No Susan, you never met this lady. She died many years ago; long before you were born."

Little Susan was full of questions. "Did you know her a long time ago, Mommy?"

Stella stood in silence, gazing across the cemetery for a long, lingering, moment, as she contemplated a replying to the child's inquiry. It was irrational, but her heart was beating faster than normal, and she felt uncertain and unsure of herself.

The little girl tugged at her hand again. "Did you know her Mommy; was she a pretty lady?"

Stella knelt beside the little girl. "No Susan, I never knew this lady." She fell silent for a moment. "But I . . . I did know her, in a strange way, a very long time ago. I . . . I wish I had gotten to know her better!" She stood to her feet and looked around the cemetery again. There were many headstones, in both directions from the entrance. Where was the stone marker for the grave of Louise Cordell? She looked down again at the little girl. "I want to put these flowers on her grave. I . . . I think she would like the flowers; don't you think so?"

The little girl glanced up at the vase of flowers, and her face was filled with a smile. "Oh yes, Mommy, I'm sure she'll like the flowers! They're very pretty!" The little girl glanced out across the cemetery. "Let's go and find the lady!"

They moved forward a few halting steps into the cemetery, and then stopped again. Stella's heart continued to beat fast, and she felt strange, awkward, and out of place as if she shouldn't be here. Her knees felt a little rubbery and weak.

Her decision to leave the rooming house and walk to the cemetery, to find the grave of Louise, had been made somewhat on the spur of the moment, although the idea had lain dormant in the back of her mind for some time. She had resisted going to the cemetery because she knew it would be very painful. But she must "speak" with Louise Cordell about the future of Randell, herself, and the little girl.

The seeds for the visit to the cemetery, had, in fact, been sown on the day of her surgery. Those seeds had been planted when she had told Randell—blurted it out---that she not only loved the little girl, but she loved *him* as well. It had been a bold and desperate statement, made under the stress of being taken away to life-or-death surgery. Perhaps she would never see him again! She had felt compelled to tell him she loved him!

In the ensuing weeks the subject had not been broached. Perhaps he had not believed her, or he didn't love her, and hoped she would eventually leave Blackberry. But her heart, and his actions, told her otherwise. In fact, she was sure he also loved her, and would soon tell her of his love. His daily care for her, and Susan, demonstrated his affection for her and the little girl! She knew he was bargaining with the owner to purchase a house on the little lake at the edge of town. She believed he was buying the lake property to provide a permanent home for the three of them.

And then her heart gave a start and her knees grew weak again. Marriage to Randell Cordell seemed preposterous to even consider. This was the town where she had seduced him twenty years ago into abandoning his wife, the woman who lay here in the cemetery, and whose gravesite she was now looking for. Would the people of this community ever accept such a thing? Her eyes roamed across the headstones as she contemplated on such a possibility. Could she and Randell really marry now, after these many years, and make a home for this little orphan girl?

Slowly she relaxed, and her breathing became easier. Yes, she believed the people would accept her marriage to Randell. They would do it because they had seen their lives change over the past months, and because she and Randell would be providing a home for the orphan girl. She was sure she was right, but perhaps they should speak to Beth Adams. Beth would know if their marriage would be accepted.

She had spoken to only one person about her love for Randell. She had been setting on the rooming house porch two weeks ago, reading a book, as Susan had played in the yard with two neighborhood children. Michael Kincaid, the writer, had come out onto the porch, stood for a while, looking along the tree lined street, and then had taken the chair next to hers. They had sat in silence and then he had turned to her, and without preliminaries, had said, "You and Randell should get married and provide a home for Susan!" His face had been serious as he had continued. "Don't put it off; you should do it soon!"

She had been taken by surprise at his boldness. "I'm sure you know of our past. I . . . I do love him, but do you believe the people of this town will accept it if we marry?"

He had sat in silence, as he watched the children play, and then replied. "They'll accept it! It all happened many years ago and the two of you have returned and made new and better lives for yourselves, and especially for the little girl." He had looked directly at her. "I'm not blind; I can see you have fallen in love with him and I'm quite sure he loves you. I think he's wrestling with the problem of marriage, just as you are. His past haunts him from time to time, but I suspect he's about to come to grips with it. If I don't miss my guess he'll ask you to marry him within a few days, or weeks. Don't turn him down Miss Cunningham. Say yes when he asks you!"

She had looked along the porch at Kincaid. "I do love him now. I didn't twenty years ago, but I do now. I . . . I'll say yes when he asks me."

"Good!" He had smiled at her along the porch. "Stella, love between two people is an interesting phenomenon. Oh, I know all the books, including mine, romanticize love and put a lot of emotion, and such stuff, into it. But real love is a decision which you make. You decide to care for, and cherish another person, regardless of the cost, and inconvenience. Through 'sickness and health,' as the vows say. If you think on it, that's what you have done with little Susan, and you can do the same with Randell, and he can do the same with you. That decision to love wasn't there twenty years ago, as it was all built on deceit, taking, and passion. A very poor foundation upon which to build a lifetime of love, devotion, mutual assistance, and care.

"It's different, and better, now between you and Randell. It's much better because Randell made the difficult, and painful, *decision* to help you when you came here last winter, and because you made the *decision* to give love and comfort to a little orphan girl when she

208

was in desperate need." He had paused and looked directly at her as he continued. "I didn't know you twenty years ago, but I suspect you have now learned to help others, instead of attempting to take what you can get from others. Taking from others is the cause of many of the problems in people's lives!"

Stella and the little girl continued to stand just inside the entrance to the cemetery. Her breathing had returned to near normal and her knees had regained some of their strength. A small truck coasted slowly to a stop in front of her and the man leaned out of the open window. "Ya look a little lost ma'am. Can I help ya find the grave of someone? I work here, taking care of the place."

She stepped forward to the door of the pickup. "Please sir, I'm . . . I'm looking for the grave of a Louise Cordell. She died a little over twenty years ago. Do you know where her grave is located?"

He smiled at her through the open window. "Sure, it's not far from here." He opened the door, slid from the pickup, and pointed. "It's over there. Three rows over and about ten headstones down. Ya can't miss it!"

"Thank you," she said. She turned to the little girl. "Come, we can find the lady's grave now!"

Within a few minutes Stella and Susan stood looking down at the grave of Louise Cordell. She carefully placed the vase of flowers on the grave, just in front of the headstone. Except for the plaintive call of a few birds, and the low moan of the whistle of a faraway freight train, a hushed silence filled the little cemetery. She stood in silence, glancing from time to time at Susan, who stood at her side. The little girl seemed to understand the solemnity, the gravity, of the moment, and she stood in silence.

Slowly Stella sank to her knees at the edge of the grave. The little girl glanced at Stella and then knelt beside her. And then she began to speak in a soft and halting voice. "I'm very sorry Louise for taking your husband from you! It was an awful thing to do! Will you please forgive me!"

She looked up for a long moment and then back down at the grave. "And Louise, I've fallen in love with *him*. I'm in love with him, and this little orphan girl! I . . . I would like to marry him, and the two of us will be the parents of this little girl. Can . . . can I marry him? Is it all right for me to marry him?"

She fell silent, as there was nothing more for her to say, and once again she heard the call of the birds and the faint moan of the train whistle. Slowly she rose to her feet and looked about the cemetery, and then down at the little girl. "Shall we go and find Daddy? I would like to see your Daddy."

Little Susan looked up at her. "Can we go to Daddy's shop and see him?"

"Yes, we'll go to his shop and surprise him. Do you think he will like that?"

The little girl tugged at her hand. "Come on Mommy, let's go and surprise Daddy!"

* * * *

The deed lay on his desk. He leaned forward in his chair, picked it up and scanned through it again. It was a simple, straight-forward document; a deed to two acres of lakefront property with a large house and work shed. The terms were all clearly set forth in the document. All he had to do was to sign it, in front of a notary, and delivery the deed and down payment to the lawyer, and the property would be his. The terms had been agreed upon yesterday and the paperwork delivered to him only an hour ago.

He sat, staring at the deed. Sign and deliver it and he would have a home for himself, Stella, and little Susan. But there was one problem: they would have a home only if he were to marry Stella. He had to ask Stella to marry him before signing the deed! He needed to do it soon! In fact, he should do it today! He should take Stella to dinner tonight and ask her to marry him. He should have asked her before now, but he had been afraid. He wasn't afraid she would refuse.

Quite the contrary, he was sure she would say "yes." Then why had he hesitated to ask her?

He laid the deed on his desk and leaned back in his chair. His office was quiet, except for the hum of a saw from the shop floor. Silently he stared at the walls of the little office, his face a mask of uncertainty, and the pain and heartache of the past tugged strongly at his heart. His terrible actions of twenty years ago reared their ugly head up before him and seemed to fill the little office; jeering at him, condemning him! The face of Louise seemed to stare out at him from the walls of his office. Her face seemed to be etched into the wall, but he couldn't clearly see her. Was she frowning at him, or was she smiling at him?

He blinked his eyes and rubbed his forehead. He needed to get a grip on himself. There was no face staring out at him from the walls! What he had done twenty years ago was past, and what he did today, and tomorrow, would not impact Louise. She would remain dead, and unknowing, there in the grave on the north side of Blackberry, regardless of what he did today or tomorrow.

He sighed, he couldn't undo the past, all he could do was live the present, and plan for the future. He could live to give comfort, security, and *love,* to Stella, and the little girl, Susan! He could give of his time, means, and love, to help these two people. One, a healed woman, with a tragic past, and the other an innocent orphan child.

He would face the matter head on. Tonight, he would take Stella out to dinner and ask her to marry him. He felt quite sure she would say yes; hadn't she told him she loved him just before she was taken away to her surgery. Yes, he was sure she would say yes to his proposal.

It was settled in his mind and he started to rise, to return to the shop, when suddenly the door to his office burst open and little Susan came bounding across the room, around his desk, and into his arms. "Daddy, Daddy did we surprise you! We've been to the cemetery and we decided to come and surprise you!"

211

He held the little girl close for a moment as his eyes went to the door of his office. Stella stood looking at him. Her face filled with a warm smile. He released the little girl and she climbed onto his lap and snuggled close to him. He looked down at her. "Yes, you did surprise me." He looked again at Stella. "You've been to the cemetery?"

"Yes, we walked from the rooming house. It's a very nice day, and I . . . I felt I needed to visit the grave of Louise. I've never been to her grave."

"Did you find her grave?"

"Yes, one of the attendants pointed out the location. I . . . I took some flowers and placed them on her grave." She paused and advanced a step inside his office. "I . . . I went because I wanted to visit her grave, and . . . and tell her I'm very sorry for what happened twenty years ago! Was it all right for me to go to her grave?"

She looked very nice in the new summer dress he had purchased for her a few weeks ago. And since the operation, to remove the tumor, radiant health had returned to her and she was now a beautiful woman. He was in love with both Stella and the little girl, and he enjoyed taking care of them and buying things for the two of them. It was a wonderful responsibility! "Yes, I'm glad you went to the grave of Louise! In fact, I think it was a splendid idea."

He motioned to a chair. "Please set down Stella! Now that you're here, I . . . I need to ask you something. Something very important!" He leaned forward, picked up the deed, and handed it across the desk to her. "It's the deed to the lake property just outside of town. The house and property are mine if I sign and deliver it to the lawyer."

Stella looked at the deed for a long moment and then smiled across the desk at him. "Yes Randell, we do need to talk about providing a home for the little girl you're holding in your lap."

Susan smiled and giggled. She understood that they were talking about her. She liked the loving tone in their voices.

212

He stood to his feet, lifting Susan into his arms, as he walked around the desk. Instinctively the little girl's arm snaked around his neck. Stella rose to her feet as he came around the desk, the deed still clutched in her hand.

Slowly he began to speak. "Yes, we do need to talk! Stella, so much has happened since you returned. Many things have changed for both of us. We now have this little girl, we've both grown to love, and who needs a mother and father to love and care for her. And . . . and Stella, as crazy as it sounds, I believe you and I have made the decision to love and care for each other. The ghosts of our past have haunted both of us. Stella, I believe those long shadows of the past are now gone and will never return. We're both changed and cleansed of those awful shadows!"

He encircled her with his free arm and looked down into her face. "Stella, I believe we should marry and provide a home for this little girl. Oh Stella, will you marry me? If you'll agree to marry me, I'll sign this deed and the three of us can move into our very own home!"

Stella glanced at Susan's smiling face, and her voice was soft, but firm, as she looked up into his eyes. "Yes Randell, let's marry and provide a home for this little girl!"

She moved back a step. "Kincaid says the people of the town will accept our marriage, and I . . . I think he's right, but I think we should go and speak with Beth Adams and make sure she agrees.

Randell was smiling as he said, "I agree. Let's go and pay a visit to Beth Adams in the morning.

Susan interrupted their conversation. "What's *married* mean?"

Stella and Randell both burst out laughing.

CHAPTER 25

Shadows of the Past

Beth Adams sat at the desk in her study and stared at her typewriter. It was a new and handsome machine, but sad to say, it wasn't capable of writing by itself. She had returned a half hour ago from a brisk morning walk and had gone directly to her study. With considerable resolve, she had loaded a sheet of paper into the typewriter. She was determined to begin writing the book-length novel her agent had urged her to write. She stared at the machine. Writer's block, that's what they called it! Was she experiencing that dreaded affliction, which seemed to come, sooner or later, to all writers? Had her mind gone dead, refusing to organize words into sentences and paragraphs? Words were not the problem. The story was the problem! What was the story? What was the plot?

Her agent had written to her. "Beth, it's time for you to write a book. You need to expand your horizon from writing short stories. You have established an enviable reputation with your human-interest short stories, and its time now for you to write a full-length novel! I'm confident I can sell any book you write to a national publisher."

She sighed and leaned back in the swivel chair. All four of her children were at their grandparents for a few hours. She was all alone and the house was quiet. Perfect conditions for contemplation, and writing.

She gazed out the window at the shimmering aspen growing along the edge of the back yard, and her thoughts drifted to the improbable events of the past several months. The most startling had been the return to Blackberry of Randell Cordell and Stella Cunningham.

After spending many years in prison and a stint in the army, Randell had returned to Blackberry, in an apparent attempt to rebuild his troubled life. He had immediately purchased his old cabinet shop and it was apparently doing quite well. He had done an excellent job remodeled her kitchen. In addition, he had rescued her two youngest children when they had become lost in the forest. She saw him each week at the little community church. She believed he had changed. He was no longer the wayward man who had deserted his wife for a loose woman.

Most shocking of all, the loose woman, Stella Cunningham had returned to Blackberry on a bitterly cold winter day. She had returned a broken, soiled, and very sick woman! Her sudden appearance, and sad condition, had shocked the people of the community. But the unexpected had happened! Stella, at the suggestion of Beth, she had become the guardian, a new mother, to a little orphan girl, who desperately needed someone to love and care for her. The little girl had been the medium of transformation of Stella, from a selfish and taking woman, into a loving and giving woman. Beth visited with both Stella and the little girl frequently, and their love and devotion to each other was obvious to her.

Stella's surgery had been successful, and she had fully recovered from her illness. The church pastor was studying the Bible with her and she also attended church each week. It was apparent to Beth that Stella had changed from the rebellious and immoral woman of twenty years ago to a loving and giving woman.

Beth's musings on the return of Randell and Stella were interrupted by the slam of a car door. It couldn't be Charles, as he had left only an hour ago to help a neighbor repair his binder and wouldn't return for several hours. Beth left her study and walked to the living room window. Little Susan was bouncing up the sidewalk toward the house, her golden locks flying in the breeze. Randell Cordell and Stella Cunningham were walking behind her. Beth noted they were holding hands.

When Beth opened the door, Susan looked up at her with beaming eyes. "Good morning Mrs. Adams!"

Beth knelt and gave Susan a warm hug. "How are you Susan? You look so nice today, and your dress is so pretty."

Susan's face was filled with a huge smile as she exclaimed, "Daddy gave me the dress!"

Beth stood to her feet and welcomed Randell and Stella. "Come in! I'm pleased that you have come to visit me."

Beth ushered the visitors into her living room and motioned them to chairs. She noticed that Stella's face carried something between a smile and a vague look of concern. "Beth, we hope we aren't interrupting you, but we need to visit with you. We . . . we need your advice about something!"

"Well, I'm not sure how qualified I am to dispense advice, but I'll be happy to visit with you concerning anything you wish to discuss." She turned to Susan. "Susan the twins, Marie and Morton, aren't here, as they're visiting their grandparents today, but would you like to go into their room and look at some of their picture books?"

Susan looked at Stella, and Stella smiled back at her. "It's all right, you can go with Mrs. Adams and she'll show you the picture books. Mommy will come get you when we are ready to leave!"

When Beth returned to the living room she seated herself near her two guests. "Stella, you look very nice. You've filled out some and look so much better since your surgery. I'm so delighted the operation was a complete success!"

Stella's face was full of happiness as she said, "Oh, Beth, I'm feeling so much better since the surgery, and I've so many things to be thankful for! These months since my return to Blackberry have been so very good for me. Despite my past, nearly everyone has been so kind and helpful!" She glanced toward the twin's room, where Beth had taken Susan, and then back at Beth. "Beth, we want to talk to you about making a real home for little Susan." We . . . we want your advice!"

Beth leaned forward in her chair. "Like I said, I'm not sure I'm very good at giving advice, but what are you thinking of for the future of the little girl?"

Stella fell silent for a long moment as she glanced at Randell, a look of wonder, and hope, on her face. "Beth, this may come as a surprise to you, but Randell and I want to marry, and adopt Susan!"

Randell leaned forward in his chair. "Beth, you know all about the two of us, and . . . and the terrible mistakes we both made years ago. What . . . what will everyone think if we marry now? Will the people of this community accept our marriage and adoption of Susan?"

This announcement didn't come as a shock to Beth. As hard as it would have been for her to have imagined such an outcome five years ago, when she had written the short story of the wickedness of these two individuals, the love of a little girl, church attendance, and Bible Studies, had changed the lives of these two people; in ways no one would have thought possible.

She smiled at the anxious faces of Randell and Stella. "I believe it's a wonderful idea and I think most folks in the community will agree with me. In fact, I believe the sooner you get married, and provide a home for Susan, the better!"

Randell's face was all smiles as he spoke. "Oh, thank you, Mrs. Adams, we were hoping you would agree that it was all right for us to marry. We promise we won't let you down!" There was a huge smile on his face as he continued. "When we return to town I'm going to sign the deed for a house and acreage near the lake at the edge of town. It will be our new home for the three of us!"

Excitement and happiness ingulfed Stella as she jumped to her feet and threw her arms around Beth. "Thank you, Beth," she cried, "for all you have done for Randell and me, and for your confidence in both of us!"

Within a few moments Randell returned from the twin's bedroom with Susan. He knelt, and his voice was choked, as he said, "Susan, your Mommy and I are going to be married and then the three of us will move into a house near the lake. It will be our new home. You'll have your very own bedroom! Would you like that?"

The little girl looked up at Stella, whose face was full of excitement and happiness. "Can I take my bed and table and chair, and my coloring books to the new house?"

Stella was beaming as she said, "Yes, you can take all of your things with you to our new home."

"Oh, goodie!" she exclaimed." Then she looked up at Randell. "Daddy, what does it mean that you and Mommy are going to get married?"

His face was filled with a broad smile. "Susan, it . . . it means that we will be your new Mommy and Daddy forever!"

Susan flung her arms around Randell's neck. "I . . . I like that!" she exclaimed! "I want you to be my Daddy and Miss Cunningham to be my Mommy, for . . . forever!"

* * * *

Within a few minutes Stella, Randell, and Susan had left Beth's home. Stella had said to Beth as they arrived at Randell's pickup. "It'll be a small private wedding and we'll appreciate it if you will help us plan the ceremony and determine who we should invite."

She had again enveloped Beth in her grasp. "Oh, Beth, thank you for your love and friendship. I . . . I'll never forget you, as long as I live!"

Beth walked slowly back to her study. Her mind full of what had just taken place. She sat down in her chair again. What had just happened in her living room was amazing, and certainly very improbable. After reading the diary of Louise Cordell she could never have envisioned that fifteen years later Randell Cordell, and the women he had ran off with, would come into her life, marry, and adopt an orphan girl.

Her thoughts were drawn to a Bible text. She reached and retrieved her Bible from the shelf near her desk and thumbed through the concordance until she found the text she was looking for in the book of Isaiah. Her face was filled with a knowing smile as she read.

> *Come now, and let us reason together, saith the Lord: though your sins be as scarlet, they shall be as white as snow; though they be red like crimson, they shall be as wool.*

The Lord had forgiven the scarlet sins of Randell and Stella, and He would no longer remember those indiscretions. This man and woman, and a little orphan girl, were embarking on a new, and happier chapter in their lives. How wonderful were the fruits of love and forgiveness!

She could hardly wait to tell Charles the news. She knew he wouldn't be surprised. He had told her. "Don't worry about encouraging Stella to take the child. It'll all work out!" He had been right; it was all going to work out!

Beth returned to her desk and looked down at her typewriter. What she needed to do now was to concentrate on writing a book. She needed a plot for the book. She must have a powerful and compelling human-interest story for her first novel!

The smiling and happy face of little Susan, walking hand in hand, with Randell and Stella along the sidewalk and to the car, a few minutes ago, returned to her mind. What a wonderful little girl, and

219

she would soon have a loving mother and father, and the three of them would have their own home on the edge of the lake!

She looked up from her desk, a startled look on her face. Here was the plot for a novel! She could write a book about the rescue of two fallen and troubled adults by the love and devotion of a little orphan girl. She would build on the short story she had written five years ago about an abandoned woman dying alone in a little cabin. The book would begin with her marriage, and the couple's first home in the cabin. She would write of the husband's infidelity and abandonment of his wife. The prison terms for both the husband, and the woman he had ran off with, would be in the book. The man's stint in the army and the woman's eventual degradation of selling her body for money, to buy food, would be woven into the tragic tale. She would write of their improbable return to the scene of their disgrace. And then, the story would be centered on the needs, and love, of a little, golden haired, orphan girl and how this little girl, and Bible studies, and making friends with giving, had changed the lives of these two flawed people.

She was sure it would be a compelling story. It would be a book the readers would love. It would be a "page turner!" In an instant the title for the book came to her. The typewriter held a sheet of paper. She quickly sat down and typed: *SHADOWS OF THE PAST*.

CHAPTER 26

A New Beginning

S usan knelt in the seat between Randell and Stella as Randell drove the pickup from the Adams home, out onto the county road, and past the little cabin where Helen Bedford now lived. A happy smile was spread across the little girl's face. She didn't understand the conversation about marriage, but she had understood enough to discern that Randell and Stella were now her new parents and she no longer needed to be anxious about being sent back to live with the old couple. Randell and Stella were her new Mommy and Daddy, and her little heart was filled with joy and contentment.

As the car slipped past the cabin, Randell and Stella were each silent, held by their own painful memories of what had happened in the cabin twenty years ago. A few minutes later Randell glanced along the car seat at Stella and smiled at her. "Would you like to go by the house on the lake and see it before I sign the contract? I have the contract in my pocket."

"Yes, please. I'd like to see the house." She glanced at him, with what appeared to be something between a sly, and happy, smile. "After I've seen the house, I . . . I have something I want to discuss with you. I think it's very important!"

He smiled to himself. He was tempted to ask her what she wanted to talk to him about, but demurred. She would tell him in due time. She had stirred his curiosity.

Within minutes he brought the car to a halt at the front of the house. They sat in silence, their eyes wandering over the house and grounds. A white picket fence enclosed a large, grass covered, yard. Colorful marigolds, chrysanthemums, and purple asters filled the flower beds, planted along the front and sides of the house. The home and yard seemed to glow with charm and serenity in the shimmering light reflected from the lake.

Little Susan stood in the seat between them. "Is this our new house?"

Randell encircled the little girl with his arm. "Yes, this is our new home. Do you like it?"

"Oh yes!" she exclaimed. "It's so big!"

He pointed toward the side of the yard. "I'll get you some playground things. Perhaps a slide and swing set for you and your little friends to play on."

"Oh, goodie!" Her arms encircled his neck. "Thank you, Daddy!"

Randell looked along the seat at Stella. "Now that we've talked it over with Beth Adams, and she has given her approval for us to marry, it's all settled! Unless you change your mind, this will be our new home?"

She laughed. "No Randell, I'm not going to back out! As I told you there in the hospital, I've fallen in love with a kind, considerate, and wonderful man; a much different man than the one I knew years ago. And Randell, I hope you have fallen in love with an entirely different, and much better woman, than the one you knew twenty years ago."

He reached past the little girl and took Stella's hand. "Stella, I have also fallen in love with you! It's very strange! I would never have thought it possible. In fact, when I was discharged from the army, I had no desire to ever see you again. You had brought me so much pain and heartache! But Stella, we've both changed since then!"

She squeezed his hand. "Randell, it's not passion, self-centeredness, and taking from others, as it was before. I believe it's a pure and true love now! A love that is centered around our mutual love for each other, and our devotion to this little girl standing between us. Let's plan on getting married within a few weeks. Just as soon as Beth and I can come up with a simple wedding plan. We don't need anything fancy!"

Susan smiled and snuggled closer to Stella. She liked to hear them talk to each other. Somehow it was comforting to her, and she always liked to hear the word *love*. She was sure it was a nice word. Whenever she heard it she always felt good.

Randell turned and looked toward the house. "We're here, so let's go in and I'll show you the home we're about to buy."

"Yes, I want to see every room in the house, especially the bedrooms, and then I want to talk to you about something." As she got out of the car, she said, "The house is so nice with the white fence, the green grass, the flowers, and the lake. I love it already!" She looked across the hood of the pickup at Randell. "Randell. I . . . I never thought I would live in a home this big, and nice!"

He looked across the hood of the car at her. "The Lord has blessed us Stella! When I returned here, I never dreamed of owning such a home."

Randell led Stella and Susan through every room of the house. "As you can see, it's a large home. The previous owner has left a few pieces of furniture, but we'll need to purchase quite a bit of additional furniture, and I plan on building some furniture and installing new cabinets in the kitchen and bath. Once I sign the contract I'll get right to work on the cabinets."

They paused in a small bedroom and he knelt and spoke to the little girl. "Susan, when we move here, after your Mommy and I are married, I think this room will probably be your bedroom. Do you think you will like this room for your bedroom? It has a nice window, and you can see out across the lake!"

Susan threw her arms around Randell's neck as she exclaimed. "Oh Daddy, I like my bedroom! When will we move here?"

"Very soon; within a few weeks. We'll move in just as soon as your Mommy and I are married." There was that word, "married," again. She wished she knew what it really meant, but she was sure it was a nice word.

When they had finished touring the house they stood on the back porch, looking out across the lake. Several wooden chairs were scattered about the porch. Susan climbed up onto a chair and pointed toward the lake. "Mommy, Daddy," she exclaimed, "see the ducks; aren't they funny!" She turned to Randell and her face was aglow. "When we move here to our new house I'll feed the ducks, like I did at the lake at the hospital. That will be fun!"

Randell and Stella found chairs and sat in quiet contemplation as they gazed out across the small lake and toward the lofty pine and spruce trees, which bordered the lake. The afternoon sun danced across the sparkling surface of the waters of the lake and reflected onto the porch as dazzling gold and silver beams. A small gaggle of geese swam slowly across the lake, a fish splashed the surface, sending small ripples toward the shore. Four ducks waddled along the shore near the house.

Randell had been taken with the pristine setting of the home, amidst the inviting beauty of the pure and unspoiled lake and the lofty pines. This home by the lake would be a wonderful place for Susan to grow up. But a tinge of sadness filled a corner of his heart. He wished there could be more children. A child for each bedroom! He would like a house-full of children.

As Randell gazed across the lake, his mind was full of wonder at the events of the past months. He knew the die had now been cast and he would soon marry the woman he had ran off with twenty years ago, and the two of them would adopt the little girl who stood on the chair, looking across the lake. All of this was most improbable, and a few months ago he would have dismissed it as fantasy. Much had happened during those eventful months! Stella's tumor had been removed and it had not been cancerous. Church attendance, and the Bible studies with the church pastor, had brought both he, and Stella, close to the Lord, who now guided their lives. Business was very good at his cabinet shop, and the people of this community were now his friends and companions.

He was sure the most important, and significant, event of the past months had been the entrance of a little orphan girl into their lives. The responsibilities of caring for this child, and her responsive, and uninhibited love, had been the catalyst, which had brought about profound changes to two troubled, and fallen, adults. Love for the little girl, and her love in return, had been a solid foundation upon which to build new lives and make a new beginning. During their Bible studies, the pastor had read 1 John 4:16 to them. *And we have known and believed the love that God hath to us. God is Love; and he that dwelleth in love dwelleth in God, and God in him.* True and honest love had changed everything for him, for Stella, and for the little girl.

Even Susan ceased her chatter and fell silent at the beauty of the lake, the trees, and the flowers. Stella broke the reverie as she turned to face him. "Randell, I told you, as we drove here, that I wanted to speak to you about something, however, I wanted to see the house before talking to you." She smiled at him, and he thought there was a twinkle in her eyes, as she said, "You'll remember that during our last Bible study the pastor reviewed the story of Mary, who came to the feast at Simon's home, and broke the Alabaster Box of costly perfume and washed Jesus' feet and head with the perfume. You remember the pastor explained to us that she did this because she was so very thankful for the forgiveness she had received for her past sins, and the new life Christ had helped her find.

"Yes, I remember the story. It's a very touching and sobering story."

Stella rose from her chair and leaned against the porch rail, her face full of radiance and happiness as she looked at him. Her smiling face was a sharp contrast to the haggard, and lined, face of the woman who had stumbled into his office on that cold winter day. "Randell, I've been a great sinner, but I've been forgiven by Christ for those multitude of sins. And I believe I've also been forgiven, and accepted, by the people of this community!"

She paused and fell silent as she looked along the shore of the lake for a moment, and then she turned back to him. "Randell, I can't purchase costly perfume and wipe Christ's feet, but I feel that I must do something to express my thanks to Him for forgiving me. He has set me free from the sin and shame of my past, and I know it will never return, unless I forget His forgiveness and his law! And Randell, I also need to express my thanks for this wonderful little girl and the happiness she has brought to me. And last of all, I need to express my thanks to you for your kindness and love in helping me. Randell, without your loving assistance it's doubtful if any of these good things would have come to me!"

She looked directly at him from across the little porch. "Suppose you had refused to help me and had turned me away on that bitter winter day! I doubt I would have survived for more than a day or two. Oh, Randell, my cup is full to running over! I must find a way to give tangible thanks to God for these many blessings."

Randell broke into her comments. "What you say goes for me as well. I was unfaithful to my wife and then deserted her to a lonely death. And I have also been forgiven by the people of this community. What . . . what do you think we could do to express our thanks for the forgiveness which has been extended to us?

Stella's eyes turned from Randell to look at Susan, who stood gazing at the antics of the ducks as they waddled along the shore of the lake. When she looked back at Randell her voice was a little choked, as she said, "Randell, I believe I've found something we can both do to express our gratitude to the people of this community, and to Christ, for their forgiveness!"

Randell interrupted her again. "I've . . . I've recently started paying a tithe, a tenth, of all my profits from the shop, but that's something I should do as part of being a Christian. We should do something else, but what?"

She stepped forward, grabbed a chair, and pulled it close to him. Randell detected a mixture of fun and seriousness on her voice, as she spoke. "I thought you would agree. I want to tell you about a little baby boy!"

There was a startled look on his face. "A baby boy?"

She smiled, almost laughed, back at him. "Yes, a baby boy! A boy who needs someone to love and care for him! The elderly lady who used to care for Susan visited me the other day and told me she and her husband have taken in a three-week-old baby boy who was been abandoned by his unwed mother."

Her eyes were sparkling now. "Randell, I believe we should take this little boy and give him a loving home. He can be a little brother to Susan, and they can both grow up here in this house by the lake. The two of them can play in the yard and swing in the swings you're going to install. Oh Randell, it can be our way of showing our gratitude for the forgiveness we have both received, from God, and the people of this community. Taking this little boy can be our 'Alabaster Box' gift!"

Randell was on his feet now. "Yes! Oh Stella, it's a wonderful idea! Let's adopt the little boy! I can hardly wait to see him!"

Stella stood, and came close to him, and there was a twinkle in her eye. "Randell, I've got an even bigger, and better, idea." She chuckled as she said, "I've seen today that this is a large house with several bedrooms. As you know, I can't have any children, and . . . and Randell, I want a house full of children to care for, and love! I believe we should plan to adopt several more children over the next few years! Children who need love and affection, and someone to care for them. I . . . I would like that very much! Would you like to do that with me? Let's do it together!"

"Wow, you do have some big ideas!" And then, in an action born of love, compassion, and thankfulness, he swept her into his arms and kissed her, and they clung together for a long moment. Little Susan watched her new Daddy and Mother kiss and her face carried a broad smile. She understood the significance of a kiss. It meant love and she liked love.

He had not kissed her for over twenty years, but the church attendance, the Bible studies, the approval of Beth Adams to their marriage, the beaming presence of the little girl, Stella's heartfelt expression of a desire to adopt a baby boy, and to bring joy and love to a house full of children, had all combined to bring about a transformation of mind, and character. A change from selfishness, to love and giving. The kiss signified, a new commitment, a new beginning for two flawed people.

A new, and pure, love had been born out of the ashes of the old passion and deceit! They had both been forgiven and were now cleansed and made whole. Together they would build new lives as a husband and wife, and as parents to Susan, a baby boy, and to other children. Their new lives would be based on service to helpless little children. Their lives would be built on giving, instead of taking!

He could hardly contain his excitement as he whispered. "Stella, Stella, I love you!" He held her out at arms-length and his voice was full of happiness and love. "Oh Stella, I like your idea to adopt the baby boy and other children. The boy can grow up to help me in the shop. Oh, it's a wonderful idea. Let's turn this large house into a home for children. It will be a token of our gratitude to God for his forgiveness, just like Mary, expressing her thanks to Jesus, with the costly perfume."

The little girl drew close and looked up at Randell and Stella. She tugged at Randell's jacket. "Pick me up Daddy!" Randell reached and swept her up into his arms.

The man and woman stood on the porch of their, soon to be home, and looked out across the shimmering waters of the lake. Randell's arm encircled Stella and held her very close. Susan snuggled close to his chest, her head resting on his shoulder. The little orphan girl's heart was filled with contentment and happiness. She didn't understand this talk of forgiveness, and gratitude, and adopting a baby boy, but she knew in her little heart that she was loved by this man and woman, who had become her new Mother and Father. She had found love again, after the loss of her first parents. Love had come back to her, and she was very happy as she continued to watch the antics of the ducks.

The End

We hope you enjoyed reading Shadows of the Past! Help other readers find books they'll enjoy by going online to Amazon and writing a review, or telling a friend about this book.

About the Author

O. L. Brown is retired and lives with his wife, JoAnn, in Mesa, Arizona. His books are gentle, straight forward tales, which take the reader through a clear plot about mostly ordinary, likeable people, and their disappointments, tragedies, loves, and triumphs, to an interesting ending, which will leave the reader pondering the vagaries of life and feeling happy and satisfied. His books are not about dysfunctional people, and there is no gore, sadism, or heavy language in his books.

Go to https://www.amazon.com/author/amazon.com.olbrown for information on all of his books.

Mr. Brown welcomes your comments and inquiries at obrown281@aol.com

Made in the USA
Middletown, DE
10 October 2022